HENRIETTA CLANDON
THIS DELICATE MURDER

VERNON LODER was a pseudonym for John George Haslette Vahey (1881-1938), an Anglo-Irish writer who also wrote as Henrietta Clandon, John Haslette, Anthony Lang, John Mowbray, Walter Proudfoot and George Varney. He was born in Belfast and educated at Ulster, Foyle College, and Hanover. Four years after he graduated college he was apprenticed to an architect and later tried his hand at accounting before turning to fiction writing full time.

According to the copy of Loder's *Two Dead* (1934): "He once wrote a novel in twenty days on a boarding-house table, and had it serialised in U.S.A. and England under another name . . . He works very quickly and thinks two hours a day in the morning quite enough for any one. He composes direct on a machine and does not re-write." While perhaps this is an exaggeration, Vahey was highly prolific, author of at least forty-four novels between 1926 and 1938.

Vahey's series characters were Inspector Brews, Chief Inspector R.J. "Terry" Chace, Donald Cairn (as Loder) and William Power, Penny & Vincent Mercer (as Henrietta Clandon).

With a solid reputation for witty characterisation and "the effortless telling of a good story" (*Observer*), Vahey's popularity was later summed up in the *Sunday Mercury*: "We have no better writer of thrill mystery in England."

HENRIETTA CLANDON

THIS DELICATE MURDER

With an introduction by Curtis Evans

DEAN STREET PRESS

Published by Dean Street Press 2020

Copyright © 1936 Henrietta Clandon

Introduction Copyright © 2020 Curtis Evans

All Rights Reserved

First published in 1936 by Geoffrey Bles

Cover by DSP

ISBN 978 1 913054 93 9

www.deanstreetpress.co.uk

STRING PUZZLES BY THE COZY FIRESIDE

The Mysteries of Henrietta Clandon

Who is "Henrietta Clandon"? We don't know—we wish we did!" Anyhow, "she" has written one of the best murder novels we have read in a long time.

--newspaper advertisement by Geoffrey Bles,
publisher of the Henrietta Clandon detective novels

TODAY we know, as the coy "she" above hinted, that Golden Age mystery writer Henrietta Clandon, author of seven detective novels between 1933 and 1938, was in fact a man: John George Haslette Vahey (1881-1938). Women mystery writers adopting the guise of masculine or sexually ambiguous pseudonyms was a common enough practice during the Golden Age of detective fiction, as it had been with their Victorian and Edwardian sisters. Margery Allingham wrote a trio of mysteries as Maxwell March, Americans Dorothy Blair and Evelyn Page five as Roger Scarlett and Lucy Beatrice Malleson over three score as Anthony Gilbert, while the names Ngaio Marsh, Moray Dalton, E.C.R. Lorac and E.X. Ferrars--the latter three respectively pseudonyms of Katherine Mary Dalton Renoir, Edith Caroline Rivett and Morna Doris MacTaggart, aka Elizabeth Ferrars--left readers in doubt as to the authors' actual genders and male book reviewers often referring, in their early years, to the excellent books by Messrs. Marsh, Dalton, Lorac and Ferrars. When in doubt, assume it is male, so the thinking then seemed to go. (More recently the late scholar and mystery fan Jacques Barzun referred to Moray Dalton as a "neglected man" while another, Jared Lobdell, speculated that "Moray Dalton" might have been yet another pseudonym of prolific British Golden Age mystery writer Cecil John Charles Street.)

It was commonly believed, in those days, that men were more credible to readers as writers of detective fiction. It also was presumed that readers of detective fiction were predominantly male as well. "[T]he detective story . . . is primarily a man's novel," emphatically declared a woman, American Marjorie Nicolson, then serving as dean of the English department at Smith College, in "The Professor and the Detective," an essay originally published in the *Atlantic Monthly* in 1929. "Many women dislike it heartily, or at best accept it as a device to while away hours on the train. And while we do all honor to the three or four women who have written surpassingly good detective stories of the purest type, we must grant candidly that the great bulk of our detective stories today are being written by men."

This was an attitude which began decidedly to change, however, with the rise of Britain's so-called four Queens of Crime in the 1930s: Agatha Christie (first mystery novel published in 1920), Dorothy L. Sayers (1923), Margery Allingham (1928) and Ngaio Marsh (1934), not to mention a slew of additional talented British women detective writers, such as the aforementioned Anthony Gilbert and others like Patricia Wentworth, Moray Dalton, Gladys Mitchell, Annie Haynes, E.C.R. Lorac, Joan Cowdroy, Molly Thynne, Helen Simpson, Ianthe Jerrold, Elizabeth Gill, Josephine Bell, Mary Fitt, Dorothy Bowers, Harriet Rutland and, coming along a bit later in the 1940s, Christianna Brand and Elizabeth Ferrars. (In the United States there were, aside from Roger Scarlett, an admittedly minor player in the world of Golden Age detective fiction, the hugely popular Mary Roberts Rinehart and Mignon Eberhart and their many followers.) By the late Thirties and early Forties readers and reviewers alike had concluded that classic detective fiction was a form of fiction at which women excelled as much as, if not more then, the male of the species. It was, indeed, the men who might have been well advised to watch their backs, for fear of fatal feminine thrusts from wicked-bladed letter openers or jewel-encrusted hatpins.

It is this altered environment which led to the appearance, with the novel *Inquest* in 1933, of another purported woman crime writer, one who was emphatically a lady in tone, if not in fact: Henrietta Clandon. In the hands of Dorothy L. Sayers and, I would argue, Agatha Christie, with such novels as *Strong Poison, Have His Carcase, The Murder of Roger of Ackroyd* and *The Murder at the Vicarage*, there had arisen so-called "manners mystery" murder fiction, filled not just with corpses, crimes and clues, but witty and sardonic observation of people and social mores. (Male authors Anthony Berkeley/Francis Iles and C.H.B. Kitchin were also signal contributors in this regard.) Margery Allingham would follow suit in 1934 with the marvelous *Death of a Ghost*, accompanied by Ngaio Marsh's debut novel *A Man Lay Dead*, but Henrietta Clandon actually had already anticipated the two younger Crime Queens with a fully developed manners mystery in 1933.

When he created Henrietta Clandon, John Haslette Vahey was no new hand at mystery mongering. Born on March 5, 1881 in Strandtown, a district of Belfast, Northern Ireland, Vahey was the middle son of Herbert Vahey, a superintendent of Inland Revenue (i.e., tax collector), and his wife Jane Lowry Vahey, a daughter of a wealthy Belfast watchmaker and jeweler. Like his contemporary, author and crime writer E.R. Punshon, "Jack" Vahey, as he was known, after walking away from careers in business around the turn of the century (in Vahey's case insurance and accountancy), had started writing fiction professionally. Vahey published his first novel in 1909, while residing at a Bournemouth boarding house with his elder brother, who also wrote fiction, and he began turning out mysteries in the classic mold by the late 1920s, primarily under the pen name Vernon Loder, whose work recently has been highly praised by vintage mystery authorities Nigel Moss and John Norris. (Moss calls Vernon Loder "a paradigm of the English Golden Age mystery writer.") Jack Vahey's other known pen names—those besides his two most notable ones, Vernon Loder and Henrietta Clandon--are John Haslette, Anthony Lang, John Mowbray and the hobbit-ish Walter Proudfoot; under the entire tribe, whose output included mysteries, mainstream, adventure and espionage novels, and school tales, he ultimately produced sixty-five books, making him a prolific author indeed. Vahey boasted that he once composed a novel over a span of twenty days at a table at the boarding house, afterward serializing it in both the United Kingdom and the United States under different pseudonyms.

By 1933, when Jack Vahey at the age of fifty-two created Henrietta Clandon, he had as Vernon Loder already published eight detective novels in five years, and no fewer than three additional Loder novels would appear in print in 1933. Many of the Vernon Loder titles were published in both the UK (with the prestigious Collins Crime Club) and the US (with Morrow, publisher of Christopher Bush and, shortly in the future, Erle Stanley Gardner and Carter Dickson.) Why, then, one might ask, did Vahey start publishing under yet another pseudonym?

When one reads the Clandons, the "why" becomes readily apparent, for Vahey with this new line clearly was attempting to do something different, and more ambitious, with his crime fiction than he had with Vernon Loder, et al., as pleasing as some of the Loder novels are. The Henrietta Clandon novels are the most carefully crafted mysteries that Vahey ever wrote, models of manners mystery which present to the reader wittily epigrammatic and cuttingly sardonic murder in its most deceptively cozy British guises of country houses and villages—quintessential malice domestic, as it were. Critics responded favorably to the Clandons, sensing an enticing new spice of mystery in the air, one which seemed exquisitely feminine.

Dorothy L. Sayers herself welcomed Henrietta Clandon's *Inquest* in the pages of the *Sunday Times*, where Sayers was the crime fiction reviewer from 1933 to 1935, as "an attractive and promising piece of puzzle making." She added that the "book is very well written, the dialogue being quite exceptionally fresh and well-managed, and the characterization good," before adding encouragingly: "This appears to be Miss Henrietta Clandon's first detective story; I hope we shall hear more from her again." Score one for the ladies!

Of a later Clandon novel, *Rope by Arrangement*, Sayers keenly pronounced, employing a most apt image, that the novel's merit lay "in a kind of quiet tortuousness; to read it is rather like working out an intricate little string puzzle by the fireside. . . . the tale makes very agreeable reading." Nor was Sayers alone in her praise of Clandon. Concerning *This Delicate Murder*, Torquemada (noted crossword puzzle designer Edward Powys Mathers) in the *London Observer* praised its "wit" and the "nearly watertight impeccability" of its puzzle. For his part crime writer Milward Kennedy, Sayers' successor at the *Sunday Times*, in reviewing the superb inverted poison pen mystery *Good by Stealth*, which recalls not only works by Francis Iles but ones by Anthony Rolls and Richard Hull, lauded the author's "gift for irony in the depiction of the criminal's mind." An able literary limner like Henrietta Clandon, observed Kennedy admiringly, "can suit style to subject, and even enable us to see character in its true colour though revealed by colour-blind eyes." Perhaps Anthony Berkeley, reviewing crime fiction as Francis Iles, summed up best when he declared that "Henrietta Clandon's novels are always welcome. She has developed a style of her own in crime fiction."

Sadly, the steady series of Clandon mysteries was abruptly halted after the appearance of the seventh Clandon novel, *Fog off Weymouth* ("quite charming narration," pronounced Torquemada), which was published in March 1938, just three months before Jack Vahey's death at age fifty-seven on June 15. I do not know what killed the author, but only three years before his death he had flippantly boasted, in a letter to the *London Observer* signed "Vernon Loder," that "I have not spent a day in bed in thirty-two years," despite the fact that "I add great quantities of salt to my food, and vast quantities of sugar to tea, coffee and lemonade." As a remedy against the chronic throat inflammation he had suffered between the ages of fourteen and twenty-one, he had taken up smoking eucalyptus cigarettes (forerunners of menthols, recently banned in the state of Massachusetts). Salt, sugar and cigarettes—perhaps Jack's death should not have come as a surprise. It will be recalled that thriller writer Edgar Wallace, who died from a diabetic coma and double pneumonia in 1932, consumed copious amounts of sugary tea.

At the time of his untimely demise Vahey resided with his wife, Gertrude Crowe Barendt, formerly a music teacher from Liverpool, at a flat in affluent Branksome Park in Bournemouth (today Poole). A final Vernon Loder, *Kill in the Ring*, a boxing murder tale far removed from the milieu of Henrietta Clandon, was published in October and, after that, Vahey, who left no children, was largely forgotten. His elder brother, Herbert Lowry Vahey, a more peripatetic author than Jack, survived him by two decades, but though he wed as well, he left no children. Jack's younger brother, Samuel Lowry Vahey, an insurance executive who migrated to Canada and later Houston, Texas, predeceased Jack by a decade.

Where did Jack Vahey get his mind for "delicate murder," his ability to compose a quietly tortuous mystery resembling "an intricate little string puzzle"? He was educated at Foyle College, Londonderry, Northern Ireland and in the city of Hanover in the state of Saxony, Germany (which perhaps helps explain his later marriage to an Anglo-German wife), and his favored hobbies were shooting and fishing, but perhaps he carried within himself something of his canny Scots-Irish maternal grandfather, John Lowry, who died in Belfast in 1886, when Vahey was five years old. Old John Lowry was a highly respected maker and retailer of watches and chronometers (a time measuring instrument used in marine navigation to determine longitude), who owned a big shop in the High Street and did regular business as well in London. Pieces which Lowry designed are highly sought collector's items today. (For example, the website of David Penney's Antique Watch Store offers an exquisite "top quality" nineteenth-century chronometer by Lowry with gold hands and a "very rare sapphire roller.") At the old man's death, he left an estate that was valued at, in modern worth, some 470,000 pounds (over 600,000 dollars), indicating that he was a top person in his field.

A well-plotted Golden Age mystery, after all, resembles not only a string puzzle or Rubik's Cube, but a clock--whether or not unbreakable alibis and railway timetables are involved. Vahey's grandfather John Lowry possessed more than the consummate skill to construct intricate mechanical devices, however; he had, as well, personal experience with criminals. In 1867 Lowry, sounding like detective writer R. Austin's Freeman famed medical jurist sleuth Dr. John Thorndyke, testified at the criminal prosecution of one Bernard O'Kane for allegedly passing counterfeit coins around Belfast. At the trial, it was reported, Lowry established that the coins at issue were fake, being made of "base metal." Eleven years earlier, burglars had daringly invaded Lowry's shop at 66 High Street. The watchmaker had spent the evening and early morning hours on the roof of his house, where he had been engaged in "comparing his time by transit observations of the stars" until one o'clock in the morning. During this time he heard noises on the roof, but took this to be merely the nocturnal perambulations of a cat. Later that morning, when the entire household had gone to bed, a felonious party took a pane of glass out of a skylight and with a rope descended into the house. Fortunately, "the shop being well secured, the goods locked in a large safe, a party well-armed sleeping in a room connected with the shop, and doors properly barred inside, the robber or robbers could get no farther than the kitchen and back room, from which they took several articles of dress and even some eatables," departing without detection. It is the sort of setting that with embellishment might have inspired Edgar Wallace's famous mystery *The Clue of the New Pin* (1923), in which a shady businessman who keeps all his spoils hidden away at his home in a massive basement vault, securely locked up at night to make it impregnable, is found shot to death, inside his own locked vault. There is no gun anywhere to be found, merely a single pin. . . .

Great outré stuff for a classic Golden Age mystery (though in violation of the rules of Father Ronald Knox and the Detection Club, a mysterious "Chinaman" lurks), which might have been just the thing for that earnest fellow Vernon Loder. In Jack Vahey's more up-to-date and sophisticated Henrietta Clandon tales, however, finical readers should rest assured that murder is something altogether more refined, a delicacy which can be served to polite society in the drawing room, along with buttered scones and tea. Just keep an eye out for arsenic and acid bon mots.

This Delicate Murder

IN ROBERT Altman's *Gosford Park* (2001), a film inspired by British country house mysteries from the 1930s, odious million-aire industrialist Sir William McCordle hosts a weekend shooting party at his rural estate, Gosford Park. During a pheasant hunt conducted in the woods, a bullet grazes Sir William's ear. Later that day, the millionaire is found murdered in the library, having been, seemingly redundantly, both poisoned and stabbed. Was the shooting incident from earlier in the day a murder attempt as well?

Tycoons' bodies in libraries are familiar to readers of vintage British crime fiction, but murders during shooting parties are rather less common. It would seem that the landmark shooting party mystery in written form is famed Russian author Anton Chekhov's only full-length novel, appropriately titled *The Shooting Party*. Chekhov published the novel serially in Russia in 1884 and 1885, a few years before the first appearance of Sherlock Holmes in the short novel *A Study in Scarlet*; but an English translation of Chekhov's novel was not published until over four decades later, in 1926, the same year that saw the publication of Agatha Christie's landmark detective novel, *The Murder of Roger Ackroyd*. Henrietta Clandon's *This Delicate Murder* (1936) was one of the more notable shooting party mysteries that followed the English translation of Chekhov's novel into print, three other significant examples being J.J. Connngton's *The Ha-Ha Case* (1934), John Ferguson's *The Grouse Moor Mystery* (1934), and Henry Wade's *The High Sheriff* (1937).

During the Victorian era the formalized group hunting of game birds--such as pheasants, pigeons, grouse and prized woodcocks--became common on large British country estates, with great improvements having been made in the efficiency and safety of shotguns. Yet these shooting parties still provided ample scope for both fatal accidents and murderous shenanigans, what with all those guns going off and bullets whizzing about. In the United Kingdom in 1893 there were a couple of particularly infamous hunting fatalities: that of twenty-year-old Windsor Dudley Cecil Hambrough and twenty-five year old William Dillwyn Llewellyn, at, respectively, the Ardlamont estate in Argyll, Scotland and the Penllergare estate in Swansea, Wales.

On August 25, 1893, Willie Llewellyn, a celebrated cricketer at Eton and Oxford and a grandson of botanist and pioneer photographer John Dillwyn Llewellyn, was found dead in the woods at Penllergare on the evening of the announcement of his engagement to Gladys Rice, a daughter of the sixth Baron Dynevor. Willie not having returned from a day out with a shooting party, a search for him was commenced, whereupon the gamekeeper discovered his lifeless body on the grounds, with a fatal gunshot wound over his heart and his waistcoat singed. An inquest recorded a verdict of accidental death, although at the time of this writing Willie Llewellyn's Wikipedia page claims that the young man committed suicide.

Just fifteen days earlier, Cecil Hambrough had died in similar mysterious circumstances, from an ostensibly accidentally self-inflicted gunshot wound, administered during shooting on the grounds of Ardlamont Hall in Scotland, which had been rented for the season by Cecil's tutor, Alfred John Monson. When authorities learned that only six days before Cecil's untimely demise, Monson had taken out life insurance policies on his young charge's life worth a total of £20,000 (over two million pounds today), made out in favor of his, Monson's, wife, the tutor was arrested and charged with Cecil's murder. Although no less a personage than Edinburgh surgeon Joseph Bell, Arthur Conan Doyle's real life model for Sherlock Holmes, testified on behalf of the prosecution, arguing that murder had been done, a verdict of "not proven" was returned by the Scottish jury. The next year Monson sued Madame Tussauds, which had placed a wax replica of him at the entrance to its Chamber of Horrors, for libel. Monson won his case, thereby establishing in the UK the legal principle of "libel by innuendo," and was awarded for his pains all of one farthing in damages. What was dubbed the Ardlamont Mystery later inspired Scottish chemistry professor and mystery author J.J. Connington's 1934 detective novel *The Ha-Ha Case*, which preceded Henrietta Clandon's fifth detective novel, *This Delicate Murder*, into print by two years. (For more on the Ardlamont affair, see Daniel Smith's *The Ardlamont Mystery*, 2018.)

This Delicate Murder is the first of the Henrietta Clandon detective novels that is narrated by Henrietta Penelope ("Penny") Mercer, wife of novelist Vincent "Vincie" Mercer and herself an author of mysteries written under the pen name "Henrietta Clandon." (It is all highly meta.) The two immediately previous Henrietta Clandon novels, *Rope by Arrangement* (1935) and *Good by Stealth* (1936), include forewords written by Henrietta Clandon, in which she explains that under her pen name she has sponsored these first person novelizations by other hands of real life criminal imbroglios (respectively Mr. Montgomery Brace and Miss Edna Alice). Presumably we are meant to understand that the first two Henrietta Clandon detective novels, *Inquest* (1933) and *The Ghost Party* (1934), are accounts of murders written by Penny Mercer herself, although it is left unclear whether these accounts are entirely fictional or are, rather, putatively based on real life events, like those in *Rope by Arrangement* and *Good by Stealth*.

In any event, it is in *This Delicate Murder* that Penny Mercer finally steps out from behind the concealing curtain and herself narrates a murder case, one in which, like in *Rope by Arrangement*, she and Vincent themselves recently figured. The two Henrietta Clandon novels which follow *This Delicate Murder*, *Power on the Scent* (1937) and *Fog off Weymouth* (1938), follow this same pattern and are narrated by Penny as well.

In *This Delicate Murder*, Penny and Vincent become embroiled in a vexing murder case when they fatefully accept an invitation from bestselling novelist Lionel Fonders to be his guests at a shooting party at his charming Queen Anne country estate, Chustable Manor. The other guests at the party are all, with one exception, writers, like the Mercers. These guests are: Benjy Doe, who makes "a moderate living" from "moderately well written" novels, and his sister, Vanity, "a reviewer for a highish-brow weekly"; Addie Stole, author of desert romances in the arid tradition of E.M. Hull; Gerald Whick, a sour-tempered satirist; Bob Varek, "born Robert Fuggle, but not proud of it"; and, finally, the unfamiliar Keble Musson, who turns out to be Lionel Fonders' American agent. (In real life Musson was a Canadian company who published English thriller authors Edgar Wallace and Sapper.) Also on hand at Chustable is a classic butler with "the manner of a dean, white hair, a pink, smooth face, an intelligent but deferential eye, and soft hands," memorably named Gormer (as in gormless, perhaps); and a woman-averse Scottish gamekeeper named MacPherson.

The Mercers do not like Lionel Fonders--no one does--and they simply abominate literary soirées, Penny declaring that "for downright boredom, mixed with unpleasantness, give me the society of six novelists with swollen heads and epigrammatic tendencies." Yet they accept their invitation anyway, thinking they will get some good "copy" at Chustable. Vincent bluntly pronounces the objectionable Lionel eminently "killworthy," which turns out prophetic indeed when the bestselling author is found fatally felled by a bullet during the shoot (through an eye socket, no less). When Vincie himself becomes the chief suspect in his host's unnatural death, the Mercers importune that clever attorney and amateur sleuth William Power (see *Rope by Arrangement* and *Good by Stealth*), to find the fiend who put paid to the noxious scribbler. With so many authors at hand, the field of suspicion is wide. Fortunately there is Vincent's "rough map" of Theby Wood, where the fatal shooting took place, to help the reader along. Can you keep pace with Power?

This Delicate Murder is a delightful murder story, with some amusing literary satire. (Writers should especially appreciate it.) To be sure, there are some then topical jokes which may bemuse the modern reader. When Penny complains that "It's the suspense [of the murder investigation] that is trying. Almost worse than waiting for Partridge's great detective novel to come out," for example, she is jabbing at long deceased Bloomsbury Group member Ralph Partridge (1894-1960), a reviewer of detective fiction who over his many years at the job seemed to dislike most of the detective fiction which he read. However, there is much in the novel that should please today's fans of vintage mystery, with its narrative that "goes fast because of its wit," as reviewer Torquemada observed, yet offers as well a very pretty problem in ballistics. So appealingly combining literary with scientific interest makes *This Delicate Murder* something of a *rara avis* in detective fiction.

Curtis Evans

ROUGH MAP OF
THEBY WOOD

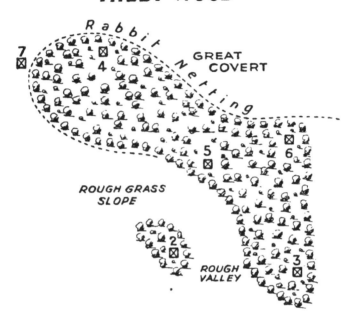

Rabbit Netting

GREAT COVERT

7
⊠

4

ROUGH GRASS SLOPE

5

6

2

ROUGH VALLEY

3

LITTLE COVERT

1

GRASS SLOPE

GRASS SLOPE

PIGEON "HIDES" ⊠

1	B. Doe.
2	G. Whick.
3	L. Fonders.
4	B. Varek.
5	A. Stole.
6	V. Mercer.
7	Musson.

DISTANCES BETWEEN "HIDES"

No. 1 to No. 3	150 yds.
No. 2 ,, ,,	90 yds.
No. 4 ,, ,,	210 yds.
No. 5 ,, ,,	100 yds.
No. 6 ,, ,,	102 yds.
No. 7 ,, ,,	250 yds.

CHAPTER I

I WAS just contemplating the slush which a failed frost leaves on our streets, and wondering when the next car would skid opposite our windows, when my husband came in.

He was wearing a queer sort of smile, one that I knew well. He wears it when he is asked to supply gratis contributions to charitable anthologies, also when he is about to tease me, or has thought of a comical twist to give one of his characters.

"Penny," he began, "would you like to go to a party of authors?"

This seemed to me an obviously rhetorical question. I had once heard Mr. W. B. Maxwell remark in a speech at a dinner that he favoured the Society of Authors, but authors' society was a different matter. It sounded supercilious, but made me laugh. Apart from that, it is my considered opinion that the nicest authors (and there are some, whatever people say), go sour on herding. Mix the rennet of a mob with the sweet milk of the most agreeable writer, and you have a junket that does not lie easy on the stomach.

"Don't be funny, Vincie," I replied.

"Well, I am going," he told me. "So comfort me with apples, or something. And change your mind if you can."

I looked at him. He was quite serious now. He was going to a party of authors, and would have to listen to them talking shop, and perhaps do a little shopping himself in self-protection. He would also make enemies, for it is beyond the wit of any author to do otherwise when he meets his own kind. If there are "four-and-twenty ways of constructing tribal lays," there are at least as many ways of quarrelling with your fellow craftsmen in the scribbling business.

"Then they must be hand-picked," I said, "and not more than four."

"There are eight," he replied, as he supplied me with a cigarette, and drew me back from the window to a seat; "and they are hand-picked by that sweep Lionel Fonders."

"What's he paying you, and where is it?" I asked.

"It is," said Vincie, "in his country home. It is a shooting-party. He has a butler now, pheasants, a keeper, manorial rights, bought with the property. Scorpion as he is, I admit that he had to give a party to show them off. As for payment, we shall also get publicity. There will, I am sure, be photographers from town, and we shall be smiling down at some dead birds at the famous novelist's, Mr. Lionel Fonders, shoot."

"Then it is lasting longer than one evening!" I said. "Worse and worse."

"It lasts four to six days," he said. "And there will be five guns. I am at present inquiring if there are any steel waistcoats on the market."

"Are you one of the guns?" I asked.

"I am, my dear," he replied, "but I am not going without protection."

"Have you ever fired a gun in your life?" I asked severely.

"I have," he said. "When I was a boy I shot at least two rooks. And mine host is lending me a gun. It appears that he has two pairs."

"He would," I agreed. "Just as he has two secretaries, where half a one would do, with his output."

"What about changing your mind, Penny?" he asked.

"I have," I said. "Apart from going there to save you from murdering Lionel, when you are in danger I must be at your side."

"Good," he remarked gratefully. "I am now on my way to a shooting-school, where I shall practise on clay disks known as pigeons, thrown into the air by a spring, falling gracefully to earth before my charge catches them bending. The invitation is from Tuesday to Monday. The manor is at Chustable. We shall be met at the station by cars."

With that he kissed me, being still an affectionate creature, even after five years of husbandship, and went out.

Having agreed to go, I admit that my feelings were mixed. Of all the arrant snobs, boosters, pompous, pretentious, and ill-deserving asses I have known, Lionel is the star and crown. Handsome enough to be run after by women who don't know him, lucky enough to make about seven thousand a year, with two books a year, greedy enough to want more, conceited enough to think he deserves it, always grousing in high places because there are too many of other people's novels published, for ever complaining that he has to pay supertax, Lionel is what Vincent sometimes calls "kill worthy."

He began with nice harmless books that did not sell; he went on to nasty ones which did sell. He has never had a good review, or a bad market.

Books in the United States, serial, film, dramatic rights, foreign rights, add to his income. Why? Well, this is a great mystery, even greater, if you look at it rightly, than any that took place the following week at Chustable Manor. As Vincie says, death is natural, even if it comes unnaturally, but Lionel's sales come under the heading of latter-day miracles.

Jealousy, you say? But who grudges Henry Welsh Old his sales, or best-sellerdom? Not a soul with any decency in him. But enough of that. Lionel was to be my host, and I was to eat his salt, and share the publicity he could not get alone. Even I, in gross ignorance of these affairs, know that you cannot show yourself looking at a bird and calling yourself a shooting-party. That would undoubtedly be Lionel's ideal, if it were possible. Even "Mr. Fonders and a Bird" might be misinterpreted if shown in the *Weekly Rattler*.

But why me? Why Vincie? We are both novelists, and when I was a publishers' reader, and Lionel was starting his career, I might have *seemed* useful. And who were to be our fellow guests?

I tried to guess. In the first place, Lionel would wish to impress. Would he ask a party of authors who would be impressed; or a party of authors of note who would not, or would see that they did not show it? I rather hoped that he would pick them on the former principle. Little people in the literary world can be fussy, catty, petty, and prickly, but for downright boredom, mixed with unpleasantness, give me the society of six novelists with swollen heads and epigrammatic tendencies. Hell, Vincie says, will be peopled with them.

Still, Lionel had a press-agent, and it was up to me to have a look at the social column in the newspaper. I rarely look at it, but now I fetched the paper, and there it was, sure enough.

Benjy Doe, and his sister. Benjy made a moderate living from novels which were moderately well written; his sister, Vanity, was a reviewer for a highish-brow weekly. Then there was Addie Stole, who pranced on the desert still, even when sheikhs had passed their first freshness. Fourth came Mr. Gerald Whick, a satirist; fifth Bob Varek, born Robert Fuggle, but not proud of it, an unknown man called Keble Musson, and "Mr. and Mrs. V. Mercer." I felt happier when I read the names. Those I knew were not bad creatures, though what a week in company with each other under Lionel's roof would do to them, I could not say. Literary parties are like children's parties all too often: they begin in smiles, and end with all-in wrestling to the accompaniment of screams and tears.

I couldn't even look forward to a feast of reason and a flow of soul. For those who are fluent on paper are often dreadfully tongue-tied in company. The uninitiated sometimes sit next to authors, and hope for entertainment. If the food is good, they don't hear much; and if it isn't, they don't hear much either. I once dined next to an eminent man who had the greatest difficulty in imparting to me the fact that he wasn't fond of artichokes. I listened attentively, thinking there must be some subtleties embedded in his halting dialogue, but there weren't any—merely artichokes.

Lionel, of course, knew that. I don't mean the artichokes, but the inarticulateness of ordinary authors when not talking of their own work. He himself is fluent; not clever but fluent. And even if we did not listen to him all the time, we would see his house, his butler, birds, keeper, and estate. Lionel is not the only one of his kind. I remember another man, who had a butler, and never asked anyone to see him on the man's day out. But that is perhaps too sweeping. He asked Vince once, by accident, and that was the occasion when Vincie learned that the butler *was* out.

Well, that was all I could do about the matter for the moment, and I decided to kill my second villain, and put it on the hero. I had a cup of tea at my typewriter, and at six Vince came back.

"Slain him?" he said to me.

"An hour ago," I said. "And you?"

He shrugged, then winced. "I hit two clay pigeons, and have a sore shoulder," he said.

"How spiteful they must have been!" I suggested.

"It was the gun that turned nasty on me," he said, sitting down. "Every other time I pulled the trigger it showed resentment. 'Give him the butt!' it said—bad as a gillie when you're salmon-fishing. I pulled both triggers once for luck, and it hit me most spitefully on the chin. The man with me kept on saying 'Bird on the right,' or 'left,' and I kept on plastering the air in search of those clay plates. Between the sixtieth and sixty-fifth shots I saw that one had come apart. The man said it was defective, but that was sheer envy. The eighty-fourth shot shattered the second clay. The ninety-first shot punched me on the same spot on the chin, and I returned the pop-gun, and came away."

"I hope," I said, "to see Lionel upset the feelings of his gun. Or shall we women not be allowed out?"

"My dear girl, you sit on a shooting-seat behind the gun, and admit his skill—if he has any. If not, I believe you swear you saw the birds fall behind the stand. I shouldn't be surprised if Lionel wants you all to sit round him."

"And from that a question arises," I said. "What do we wear, apart, of course, from our regulation evening kit?"

I had noticed that Vincie brought a small parcel in with him, but had not inquired as to its contents. He was wearing his plus-fours, not having changed since his visit to the shooting-school, and now opened the parcel, and produced a pair of what looked like cloth dog-collars.

"'Nothing to wear? Why, go just as you are, and I'll warrant you'll prove the most bright and particular star of the stuck-up horizon.'" He quoted the old recitation. "Now these are anklets to protect me from the damp bracken. I remain otherwise as I am. I had an idea of a deer-stalker cap, but hear they are not so fashionable now as once."

He went over to get a couple of the smart weeklies, and discovered a sporting photograph. "Here we are. And here is a live peer no better dressed than myself. As for you, Penny darling, this girl on the left strikes me as having pinched that tweed suit you had last winter. I don't recommend the hat, though. A good rule, they tell me, is to wear in the country the shabbiest thing you have. All the best people do it. An apparent scarecrow in a field is just as likely to be a marquess. I hope you know what I mean?"

"Are you sure plus-fours and golf stockings are right?" I asked.

"When I went rook-shooting I wore flannel bags, tennis shoes and a blazer," he said, adjusting his anklets and looking at them admiringly. "But I was younger then, and it was later in the year. Look at these. If I were a Frenchman, they would be called '*très snob*'!"

They did subtly change the aspect of his lower limbs, taking the four out of plus-four, so to speak. "I think they give you a doggish air, Vincie. And you are right about this girl. I shall take my last year's tweed suit, and that sporty swagger-coat I bought last week. It will be just right. I have a shooting-stick, so that is all I shall want."

"Strong brogues," he said. "Indispensable."

"Three guineas, or about," I said inexorably. He fished three notes from his pocket. "Make it pounds, my dear, and it's a go."

"Having settled that," I said, "let us return to motives. What does Lionel want of us, when he might have had a party of best-sellers?"

"That would mean bloodshed," he replied gravely. "There are, as you know, two kinds, or species, of best-sellers; the first loves being it, but hates to be called it. He wants the money for spending, and the credit for conceit. The second class is best-seller pure and simple, though often merely simple. Both species are only tolerable in the presence of their inferiors."

"Very nice, but doesn't answer my question," I said. "What's the catch?"

"We may hear when we get there. I haven't a notion at present. By the way, I said we would be met at the station with cars. We shall. Two."

"How do you know?"

"I met Spooner to-day. He's been there, and he described to me very graphically the struggle Lionel had over choosing a car. It appears that he could have had a Rolls, but that only seats seven, and seven look frugal even in a Rolls. So he compromised by buying a Sunbeam and a large Austin. He saved even then, and can still bring up his guests in style."

"What about the extra chauffeur?" I asked.

"The question occurred to me, and Spooner answered it. It seems that there is a man to do odd jobs, and clean the cars. He also drives, and the only other expense is a uniform."

"I don't know how Lionel does it?"

Vincie smiled. "You're like some of your fellow novelists, darling—short on economics. You can put up a damn' fine show on seven thousand a year, even allowing for income-tax. It's only in novels that the man with one thousand a year can just afford a daily girl to help his wife."

"I have a faint idea," I remarked, scorning the suggestion that I knew nothing about money. "You know old Tishy?"

Tishy is the name of a well-known editor in circles which bear for him affection and respect, and has an origin in racing, I believe. Vincie nodded. "Tishy? He loathes Lionel."

"Quite," I agreed. "Lionel may want me for a bridge."

"There is that," he said. "But now I must go to change. Also to put away my cartridges. It seems that you bring those. I'm taking two hundred."

"Two hundred!" I gasped. "What shall we do with the birds?"

He grinned. "First, we don't get them. Secondly, my sponsor this afternoon said if I was anxious to get a brace I should need a lot. The cracks fire off thousands every year. A winning old fellow that—told me if pheasants only flew backwards, there'd be more carrying their tails behind them, like the sheep in the rhyme."

"Too cryptic," I complained. "If they flew forwards, the tails would be behind them, surely; and if backwards, before them?"

Vincie laughed as he got up. "My informant referred to what he said was a common, but not praiseworthy practice, darling; which consists in cutting off the birds' tails in mid-air, which leaves them rudderless, but otherwise intact. As soon as pheasants learn to go in reverse, they will save their tails at the expense of their heads."

"I think you had better go and change," I said.

CHAPTER II

WE SET off on the Tuesday with a markedly sporty appearance. I wore my oldest tweeds, heavy brogues, and carried a shooting-stick. Vince wore a tweed cap and plus-fours, with stout shoes and anklets. I thought the latter was rather ostentatious, since we were not likely to meet with wet bracken in the train, but he said he wanted to get used to them. At first they gave him the feeling that his garters had come down. The cartridges were packed with our luggage.

At Waterloo we were in good time, and found Benjy and Vanity Doe on the platform. Benjy was carrying a gun-case, which he would not entrust to the porter. Addie wore a tailor-made in heather mixture, and obviously envied my swagger-coat. She had also a shooting-stick, but it was a very elaborate one, while mine was plain but good.

Benjy is very tall and thin, and he wore a Donegal tweed suit, which looked too new for the country, a hard collar, his school tie, and a pair of brown boots with lumpy soles. After we met he was uneasy about himself for some time, till I showed him a copy of the *Sketch*. Here was a marquess at a shoot, wearing obvious reach-me-downs, with trousers so baggy and ill-fitting that it reminded me of that oddly phrased advertisement one sees: "Misfits from Savile Row." I often wonder what Savile Row thinks of it. I used to think that you were fitted there, whether you were or not. I know my own swaggerest dressmaker insists that all her creations fit perfectly, even if I can't get them on, or off. They have a cachet, she says. "They stick in your throat, that's what that means!" Vincent assures me.

Vanity is a very clever, but plain, young woman. Like most high-brows, she is fond of her food, and very scornful about those who are indifferent to the claims of gastronomy. But I like her because she considers me too low to converse with, and only talks to me. And she is very conscientious. She won't review her brother's novels, when most of her colleagues will even review a pal's.

"Do I look right for a shooting-party, Penny?" she asked me, as we idled on the platform.

"Perfect," I assured her. "As long as you take care to fly in the normal position, you're safe."

"Who's going to fly?" said Benjy, who was rather literal.

"It's one of Penny's jokes," said Vanity.

"Merely a question of keeping your tail behind you," said Vincie, with great gravity.

Vanity stared at him, and then down the platform. "Who's the gun-woman?" she asked.

Of course, it was Addie Stole. Her sheikhs were always firing off guns, as they careered over the desert on pedigree dromedaries, with a girl across the saddle-bow, and she had a natty leather gun-case in her hand. Otherwise, she was suitably clad, in workmanlike tweed, and strong stockings, with brogues. Incidentally, I got mine at a sale at Hepeter's, for one-pound-twelve, so was twenty-eight bob up on Vincie.

Addie is pretty, after a fashion, and very quiet really. She is shy with men, and a bit dumb, if you know what I mean.

"Are you all going down to Mr. Fonders's?" she asked me, when we had exchanged greetings.

"To Lionel's? Yes."

"I have never met him," said Addie. "Is he nice?"

"All a matter of taste, my dear," Vincie assured her. "What's this coming up?"

"Mr. Whick," said Benjy, who did not like Mr. Whick. "He's got a gun, too."

Mr. Whick writes long satirical poems, in which he scarifies all the people he doesn't like. I figure in one of them as "Penny Pumpernickel," but I like the man, because I know he pays for publication, and can't help disliking the folk like ourselves who do not.

"The gun is mightier than the pen this time, Gerald," I said, as he came up; "but perhaps you're less dangerous with it."

"I brought it to shoot Lionel," he said. "I can't miss that head of his, can I?"

"They're decreasing the size of the target at Bisley," Vince said, "but Lionel exposes himself more and more each year. Shall we get into our compartment before the train actually starts?"

We got in; the guard walked back down the train fingering his whistle, and then I saw a man dragging a recalcitrant dog after him at top speed.

"Great Scott! it's Bob Varek," said Benjy. "Never knew he had a hound."

"It's a Labrador," said Vincie, as we waved to Bob to come to us.

"I have a friend who breeds them," Vanity said gravely. "That isn't one."

"It's a Springer," Whick told us; "kind of spaniel."

Bob crowded in, dog and all, and when we had seated ourselves again, he agreed that it was a sort of spaniel, not exactly a Golden, or a Springer, or Clumber—just a sort of.

"Springer blood, for all that," Vince told him. "Get down, you ruffian! What did you bring him for?"

"Useful at the pick-up," he said.

"What's that?" asked Benjy, looking at the dog suspiciously.

"Collecting the game," said Bob.

"What actually are we going to shoot, Mr. Doe?" Addie asked.

"Ah, there you have me. Pheasants, isn't it, Vincent?"

"There will be pheasants, Benjy. That is the only truthful way in which I can answer your question. What's your form, by the way? My own life-bag to date is two rooks, young at that, like myself at the time, but I expect you're a hardened gun-man."

"Well, no," said Benjy. "I have taken lessons."

"Not at the school where the old man works off the jape about the pheasants' tails," I said.

"Oh, is that what you meant a while back?" said Benjy. "No, it can't be the same. My teacher wasn't very jocular, and the only remark he made was something I couldn't understand."

"Give our brains a chance, then," said Whick sneeringly.

"He simply said that the attendant must have speeded up the clays under the impression that I was Lord Walsingham."

That beat us all. Whick turned to Addie Stole.

"As a devotee of the wild, I expect you carry a gun, Miss Stole?"

She blushed. "I have a sixteen-bore in the rack."

"That the best kind?" Benjy inquired. "If so, they choused me with a twelve."

"It's smaller, that's all," said Addie. "Smaller charge."

"Are you not afraid to fire it," said Vanity. "I am gun-shy, I know."

"I have shot a little," Addie admitted. "Mostly rabbits."

Whick turned on Vincent. "Now, my dear fellow, you must be a spectator."

"I am a gun, though without one," my husband smiled. "I am going to use one of our host's expensive weapons. I need something like that to do myself justice."

"Same here," said Bob. "I thought I might as well bring the pup in reciprocation—sort of."

"Meantime," I said, looking hard at Gerald, "you come here and put us all through our paces. What about you? Do the pheasants blanch and wilt when you get the drop on them?"

"I was at Henry's shoot the other day," he said vexedly, for all satirists are very thin-skinned.

"Well?" said Benjy. "And—"

"I was there," said Whick.

"Any deaths in the air while you were there?" Vincent asked.

"Or among the beaters on earth?" I asked, having read a book on shooting over the weekend.

"Oh, go to blazes!" he said.

Try stinging a satirist! It's great fun.

"Very short notice, wasn't it?" said Vanity, who loathes even the mildest brawls. "Benjy was asked by telephone."

"So was I," said Varek, with a puzzled expression, "but what about that?"

Vincent had been rung up by Lionel at his club, and Addie had been asked by someone who knew Lionel who proposed her. Whick was the only one who had had a note—a short one.

"I know," I cried, when we heard this. "We're the Highways and Hedges!"

"Any relation to the Board of Agriculture and Fisheries?" Whick asked.

"No; that's quite respectable, I believe," I replied.

"I think you are right, Penny," Vanity said, her lips compressed. "He asked other guests, and they refused."

"So we're the sweepings," said Benjy bitterly. "How like Lionel."

"Sweeps to the sweep," Whick murmured, as if he had exceeded his normal allowance of wit. "Dirty dog!"

Vanity wrinkled her nose. "I wish everyone would forget these abominable scraps of American slang," she said. "Destroying our language!"

"Enriching it, that phrase," Vincent suggested. "And I deny that it is American, my dear girl. Good English, all of it."

"That review of yours is a poem in itself," Whick snapped. "A bad poem in worse prose."

"Then I suggest that you use it for your next effort," said Vanity. "It will be at least intelligible."

How I love these dog-fights. So does Vincie. But they both shut up after that, and the conversation went back to sporting matters.

The guns would be: Lionel, Vincie, Addie, Verek, Whick, Benjy.

The applauding throng would consist of: Myself, Vanity.

"That gives us three men each," I remarked, when I had enumerated the sporting classes. "I suppose we sit behind one, and watch the other two through glasses?"

"Wrong again in your count," Vincie said. "There's a bloke called Musson, if he shoots. Then there will be several drives."

"Avenues?" said Vanity.

"No," Benjy said. "We don't explore those. Drives. The beaters drive the birds. They beat them out of the bushes, don't they, Vince?"

"So I hear."

Vanity looked worried. "What pleasure there can be in shooting crippled birds—" she began, to be interrupted by a howl from Whick.

"First they beat the birds, and then the birds beat the guns. How lovely!"

"The beaters merely drive the birds over the guns," I said, "and I suppose Vincie means that they will do it several times. If so, we spectators—you and me, Vanity—can take it in turns to sit with the various performers."

"I don't want Vanity behind me, putting me off with her yammer about the S.P.C.A.," Whick remarked violently.

"There won't be any cruelty at *your* stand," Benjy said stoutly. "I can bet my top-hat on that."

It was a mercy, in a sense, that the train soon reached our station. A company of best-sellers would have been worse, of course. But we loved each other quite well enough to go on with.

"Does Mr. Fonders really wear an eyeglass?" Addie asked, as we slowed for Chustable.

"He wears an eyeglass because he has a glass eye," Whick said.

All Addie's heroes do—the eyeglass alone, of course—and she looked wounded, under the impression that Whick was making fun of her.

But that was not the fact. Nowadays, when people tell you all about their most intimate innards, even when you are at the meat course, it is nothing to mention dentures or artificial eyes. But I did not like to be too personal in my description of Lionel at first, since it is obvious that I do not like him.

He says he lost his eye in the war. I did not know him then, but there is a scurrilous story to the effect that he hit it on a peg in a cupboard under the stairs when some maroons went off unexpectedly.

"True," said Vincie. "A relic of the war."

"A what?" said Whick.

Vincie scowled at him. "Here we are. Look out for a title for your new satire, Gerald. What about 'Bloomsbury at the Battue'?"

The train stopped, and we got our effects, and streamed out on to the bare platform, to get a decided kick out of the station-master's greeting.

"Mr. Fonders's party, sir?"

"We are," Benjy said importantly.

"This way, sir."

An author may be no hero to his rivals, but country station-masters are in another category. The stout man in uniform led us, beaming, to the station yard, where two cars awaited us.

Two chauffeurs touched their caps, and a porter with our united luggage piled high on a truck sweated behind.

Whick jumped into the Sunbeam, after helping Addie in. He was followed by Bob Varek. The two Does, Vincie and I, got thankfully into the Austin.

"Satire has sunk low since the days of Pope," Vanity murmured.

"Literature has gone to the devil altogether," Vincie agreed. "Bar our four noble selves, I see no hope for it."

Chustable is set in very charming country, well wooded, with river valleys, and hills of small elevation, but picturesque irregularity. The manor lies two miles from the station, is surrounded by a large park, and has two entrances. I could just see a glimpse of its mellow brick, set on top of a slope among woods, as our cars turned in at the South Lodge.

I know Lionel rented it cheaply, and the house was not really large. He had a thousand acres with it. I heard later that the trouble was drains. But, as Vincie says, Lionel's books must have put him beyond troubling about a small thing like that.

It is a fair question to ask why we went if we disliked the man so much. It is, I think, equally fair to reply that if you never accepted invitations to the houses of people you disliked, you would be shorn of much entertaining—and Lionel would have had no guests at all.

But to return to the house. It was Queen Anne, had a suite of five reception-rooms, and nine bedrooms. I think there was accommodation for five servants as well.

As we drew up on the gravel sweep, we saw Lionel and another man on the steps of the porch.

He looked almost distinguished, as he came forward to welcome us, in his knicker-breeches with brown leggings, loose grey tweed shooting-jacket with chamois-leather gun-pad, and his eyeglass glinting in the bright winter sun.

When I had spoken to him, I had leisure to inspect the last guest. He was a bulky man, about six feet high, with a thatch of unruly dark hair tending to curl, and a very surly, disagreeable face. He saw my glance, and came to me.

"More devotees of *le Sport*, I suppose?" he said mockingly. "My name's Musson. Who are the other merchants?"

"Suppose you go and ask them, Mr. Musson?" I said. "But be careful! Most of us are armed."

He guffawed as he glanced round at the butler picking up two gun-cases. "That's why I'm not shooting to-morrow."

"That, or a natural desire to appear at your best?" I said. "Well, you can number the tribes if you wish. Come along, Vanity."

"Why Vanity, I wonder?" we heard him murmur as we walked into the house. "And what about?"

CHAPTER III

WE COULD, of course, trust Lionel to choose the right butler. Gormer had the suavity of an archbishop, the manner of a dean, white hair, a pink, smooth face, an intelligent but deferential eye, and soft hands. I believe he was a poor hand at cleaning plate, and no great judge of wine, but as a figurehead he was superb. Lionel would have loved a footman, too, but it was either that or giving up one keeper. I believe he did mean to give him up later, but at the moment he was a patron of sport.

At dinner, he had me on his right hand, being the only married woman present; and Addie Stole on the left, being the only other woman who had a presentable face. Vanity, poor dear, is not a show-piece, in that sense. But within, if not without, she is more than presentable.

As dinner progressed, Lionel did some jugglery with the cutlery, and various salt-cellars and other things, to show us the lie of the different coverts, and explain how he meant to shoot them. Addie, as our gun-woman, was interested. I had a chance to get on with my dinner.

Vanity sat next Mr. Musson, and seemed to get on quite well with him. Lionel said he was a literary agent, his new one. I had never heard of the man, and was surprised to find that he treated Lionel as a butt for his wit. If you know what real best-sellers are to an agent, especially a new one, you will wonder as I did.

The food was good and well cooked. Lionel was less self-assertive than usual, so the party went very well. When he had explained his shooting plans, he turned to me, and said he wanted to know Bootle.

"Tishy?" I said.

"Well, yes. I have never met him, but I believe he is an agreeable fellow. Musson thinks well of him."

"He must be a *rara avis*."

"Musson will have his joke."

I shrugged my shoulders. "What was the matter with your last agent?"

He pursed his lips. "Nothing in particular here. I used to do my own work in the States."

"When is your next book coming out?" I asked.

"In the spring. I am gathering materials for it."

"Forward the muck-rake!" I thought, and added aloud: "Got your title yet?"

"I thought of 'Sun-bathers in Gehenna,'" he murmured.

"That'd teach them to take their lotions with them," I said. "I can see that, in your hands, it has possibilities."

"What is the plot?" Addie asked.

I turned to Benjy on my right. "The man Musson is a literary agent," I said. "I thought he was Lionel's head keeper."

Benjy stole a glance at the great bear. "So did I. Hairy about the hoofs, if you ask me. Unless he has something on our friend."

We all retired to the drawing-room for coffee, men and women together. Lionel was obviously drawn to Addie.

"I say, Musson," he remarked suddenly, when cigars and cigarettes were well alight, "as we have to start sharp in the morning, what about telling them exactly what we propose to do?"

We all looked at Musson, wondering what he had to do with it, and he seemed to realise the general feeling, for he rose with an odious smile. "Well," he said, "as I hear some of you have been to shooting-schools, I take it that you know the muzzle of the gun from the breech. But I don't think, going strictly from what I hear, that you know anything about the art of not shooting those about you."

"I do," said Vincie. "Not in my nature to abuse hospitality."

Musson grinned. "The thing is this. You will each have to stand at a point just outside the woods, barring one, who will go with the beaters. You will have to notice that there is a man on your right, and one on your left—unless you're a flank gun."

"That anything to do with the breech?" Benjy asked.

"Only 'the imminent deadly,'" said Musson. "When you know where you are, you will be careful not to fire, or point your gun, in the direction of the people next door. When the beaters have almost finished the drive, you will be careful not to fire at a low angle forward, for fear of depriving some mother or wife of her best beloved."

"Will you be with the beaters?" asked Whick, who was looking very sullen since dinner.

"I shall not be out driving," Musson said.

"Then I shall be careful not to fire at a low angle," Whick muttered.

"But surely," I said gently, "we are not to lose so much wisdom and ballistic genius tomorrow? Do come and join us."

He bowed to me ironically. "I am a coward, Mrs. Mercer, and not afraid to own it."

"I think it would be self-sacrificing on the part of the guns," Vanity said acidly, "if they retired to-morrow, and let Mr. Musson enjoy the shooting all to himself. That would be quite safe, I take it, unless he mistook the muzzle of his own gun for the breech, or whatever he calls it."

"Too cruel," said Musson, with an exasperating grin at her. "The fact is that I shall grace the gathering later in the day. The first drive is over the Home beat, the second at Theby Wood, the third will take place in the afternoon at the Dingle. After that, as a change from shooting high pheasants—"

"Excuse me," Benjy remarked. "You may know a lot about shooting, but you can't get away with that jape. We have all eaten high pheasants, and when they're high, they're dead."

Musson laughed heartily. "When they're high, they are least likely to die," he said. "High pheasants are those which fly high."

"Er," said Lionel, "I think, in view of the lack of experience of most of the party, Musson, we shall not have any high birds. Macpherson must see to that."

Vanity pointed her long cigarette-holder at Lionel. "Suppose the birds refuse to obey the keeper's orders?"

"That can be arranged," Musson said; "but you are all interrupting me. I was going on to say that, after the driving is over, we shall all shoot pigeons coming into the woods."

Vincie did not like Mr. Musson. "Then, if you are coming, I presume you brought your armoured car?"

"No, I forgot it. But every gun will sit in a hide put up by the keepers, in a clearing in the wood, or on the edge of the woods. The pigeons will come in overhead, so that, unless there are some high-flyers among you, no one is likely to get hurt."

"Thank you, Musson," Lionel said, with an air of relief. "Now they all know what to do. Shall we draw for stands now, or wait till the morning."

"May as well get it over now," Musson said, drawing a gadget from his pocket. "This, ladies and gentlemen, is the mechanical equivalent of the packet of long and short straws. Will Miss Stole, our sole Diana, come and try her luck?"

Addie got up, and it turned out that she drew Stand No. 3. The other guns got up in turn.

Vinnie was No. 1, Whick No. 2, Lionel No. 4, Benjy No. 5, Bob Varek No. 6. He and Vincie were on the flanks, said Musson, then suddenly recollected that one must go with the beaters.

"Any of you volunteer?" he asked.

Whick got up. I think he was afraid of Addie, who would be on his right. "I will, if you like."

"Your job will be more snap-shooting," said Musson. "Are you pretty quick, Whick?"

I am sure he did not intend to make fun of Gerald's name, but Gerald scowled.

"You Musson let your wit run away with you," he retorted.

"I vote they are both fined," Vincie said. "I have never heard more wretched semi-puns."

"Well, here we are," said the detestable man, grinning. "Mr. Whick can't hurt any of you. He goes with the beaters. Now, Lionel, is there any improving and not too competitive game we can play? I know authors have very short tempers."

Lionel nodded. "What about life-pool?"

Everyone but Vanity could play some form of billiards, so we all trooped into the billiards-room, Vanity accompanied by a book on the neo-Georgians which she had brought down with her.

At half-past eleven the butler brought in drinks, and Lionel shooed us off to bed.

"We want to be fresh and alert in the morning," he remarked. "I think you owe me four-and-three, Doe?"

"By the way," said Vincie. "What about my wife, to-morrow? Does she stand behind me and laugh?"

"If Henrietta," said Lionel, "will accompany me, I shall be very pleased."

My full names are Henrietta Penelope (hence Penny), so I said I would be charmed, "but what about Vanity?"

Vanity had proclaimed herself gun-shy, but her monkey was up, and I think she was anxious to see someone make a fool of himself. "I shall go with Mr. Varek," she said.

"So glad," said Bob mendaciously. "That settles the lot."

When we had retired, Vincie asked me what was the matter with Whick.

"I wonder what is the matter with Lionel—so subdued?" I said. "And what is that man Musson doing, careering over everyone?"

"Benjy has an idea that Musson is an English agent who has an office in America," he said.

"Well, Gerald has added to his usual foul temper. Did you notice that Lionel took very little notice of him?"

"That was obvious. Still, he was the only one of us who received a formal invitation, or said he did. I wonder why we all hate each other so, Penny?" he added. "Barring Benjy and Vanity, of course."

"Well, to-morrow's a new day, and I expect it will be great fun," I said consolingly. "I'm the guest at the show-off. Lionel must be pretty good, or he wouldn't ask me to his stand."

"Or pretty bad, which would account for his asking the present lot of duds," Vincie remarked. "In the Kingdom of the Blind, the one-eyed—"

He paused, catching himself up. "No, I didn't really mean to be personal; just rambled into it."

The following morning was cold and bright and sunny. It was really one of those winter days when even fuggy people feel the blood running more sparklingly in their veins, and authors begin to wonder if their next failure will be someone's book of the month.

We had a heavy breakfast at half-past eight, and then we adjourned to the gun-room, where cartridges were loaded into bags and guns put together. Vincie and Bob were given a gun each out of a case, while Lionel explained how good they were, and added that he had paid three hundred guineas for the pair. Musson said inconsiderately that it was lucky Lionel had only lost his *left* eye on the Somme.

"If it had been the other, you blokes would have had to use crooked stocks," he added. "Just too bad."

"Will you kindly go away, and polish your own gun, Mr. Musson!" Vincie remarked, opening his, and squinting knowingly down the barrels. "You like a choke, Bob?"

Vanity, who was wandering round, intervened. "Please don't quarrel so early in the day," she said.

"A choke is a narrowing of the barrel," Vince told her, "not a constriction of the temper. But I see our army is trooping out."

On the drive outside the house, there was a tall man with a grim face, carrying a gun-case, a short man with a rather foolish face, and a group of fourteen men of assorted sizes, faces, clothes, and sticks.

"We are going to do the Home beat first, Macpherson," Lionel told the keeper. "Here is a list of the stands, and the guests."

We, too, had involuntarily drawn up in line, and Macpherson had a good look at us.

"Ou, aye," he said.

Just that. "Ou aye." But I could see that he regarded us with suspicion, especially Addie, who had her gun up in close proximity to Musson's ear.

"No, I can't really hear anything," that irritating man remarked suddenly, "so you can put your trumpet down, Miss Stole!"

A faint grin came over the features of the grim Macpherson. He nodded, gave an order to the beaters, and as they marched off in charge of the under-keeper with the foolish face, he spoke once more.

"There'll be nae high burrds the morn. Wha's gaeing wi' the beaters?"

"I am," said Gerald, with a stare.

"Then ye'd best be aff!" said Macpherson. "Ye ken they're a' awa' the noo."

He turned about like a sergeant-major on parade, and stalked off. The others followed. Lionel and I, smoking cigarettes, brought up the rear.

"Perhaps you'll write a note to Bootle this evening?" he said, as we crossed the park land.

"Very likely," I replied. "By the way, what an odd man your agent is."

"A good fellow at heart," he replied, unconvincingly.

"Oh, these hidden hearts!" I complained. "Why are the best hearts so carefully concealed?"

He grunted and changed the subject. He was not at his best that morning, and I was quite content to savour the sunshine and enjoy the feel of the short, frosty turf under my feet.

We arrived at last at the edge of a crescent-shaped wood, and found some sticks planted at intervals along its face, with numbers on bits of paper.

"This is ours," Lionel said, indicating one, and planting his shooting-stick ferrule in the ground. "You will sit slightly behind me on my right"—he pushed my stick in. "As I wish to give fair play to all the guns, I am not using my second gun, and I shall load for myself."

"How British!" I murmured. "I'll look out for birds for you."

"We must wait for some time," he said. "You see, the beaters are starting half a mile away. We must give them time."

So we sat and smoked cigarettes, and he told me why he wanted to meet Tishy. The explanation seemed unsatisfactory, but I had to accept it, and agreed to write that evening. I could trust Jishy to deal faithfully, but politely, with this aspirant for his favours.

I became suddenly aware of a confused medley of sounds coming from the wood in front. Lionel sat up, fixed his eyeglass firmly over his counterfeit, loaded his gun, which was, I believe, called an ejector, and looked back at me.

"Please mark the birds!"

I had marked many things in my day, a great deal of typing paper, and even Vincie's collars, but this beat me. I had, of course, seen dead pheasants with labels on them, and I wanted to be helpful.

"Put tabs on them?" I said.

"Yes, keep tab on them, if you like to put it that way," he said.

He had hardly spoken before I witnessed the first miracle of that astounding day. Two large birds with long tails soared out of the wood and came towards us high up. They had had the temerity to disobey Mr. Macpherson, a thing I should have never dared to do.

Lionel stood up, aimed at one, fired, aimed at the other, fired. The foremost bird waggled his tail in an odd fashion and went on; the second bird kept his tail up and went on. Lionel opened his gun, and something flew back out of it and just missed my face. I moved my seat more to the left, and looked down. Now I knew why they called the gun an ejector. Empty cartridges.

Then I apologised. In the shock of discovering that the gun fired a missile at both ends, I had forgotten to mark the birds. So, apparently, had Lionel.

CHAPTER IV

WITH an icy but determined expression, Lionel loaded again. Now I heard two shots from the wood, and more yelling. I hoped no one was hurt up there, for Gerald Whick had seemed in a spiteful mood that morning.

Something made me look to one side. An obedient bird was making straight for Addie. It swerved, I think, and she shot it off Benjy's eyebrows, as the cricketers say. I was so busy looking that Lionel fired, and asked me why I hadn't marked his bird, before I gave my attention to him. He said it had fallen behind us. I know it was never picked up, but it may have been what they call a "runner." It must have got a long way before the pick-up, as they call the collection by dog.

I could now see that Benjy had left his place, and was arguing with Addie, who was waving her gun about to explain where she had actually aimed. At that moment a lot of birds came over them, but they were too busy to see them, though Lionel yelled: "Mark over!" Indeed, he turned sideways, and fired at some of the nearer ones. But they went on, and Benjy ran back to his stand just in time to miss a wood-pigeon.

There were more shots in the wood. Then two pheasants came over Vincie. He was merciful.

I wondered how Bob Varek was getting on. I saw a large animal come from the edge of the wood, obviously a hare. It ran a little, then sat down and looked at Bob. At least, that is what I think it did. I know he did not fire at once, and, meantime, two more pheasants had come over us, and Lionel had fired, and asked me to mark them. But I am sure I heard their wings overhead, and couldn't. Still, I said I had. I could always call them runners if they were not there.

Your "runner" is the bridge-player's psychic bid. If it doesn't come off it's all right, and vice versa. So I kept my eye on Lionel again. A pheasant came along at a nice height. He fired both barrels. It did not shake its tail, but seemed to waggle its head.

"Mark that bird," said Lionel. "I took it well forward."

"Yes," I said, and did my best to mark it, only it flew a long way, and I heard another rush of wings.

Shots from my right, from my left. Vincie shot a pigeon; Addie nearly shot Benjy again; Bob hit something. It may have been his hare, which decided to move on, and startled him into firing.

"More like my form," Lionel said suddenly, and a falling body thumped almost on my head.

I was beginning to warm up. "Make it a brace," I said.

More birds came over. Lionel was busy. He kept on changing position and opening his gun, so that I had to dodge from time to time as the spent cartridges volleyed by. Now I did see one runner. It was a fast cock and went like a greyhound. Another bird lay behind us. Nearer shots from the wood. Something whistled overhead, and Lionel yelled: "Steady there, you in the wood!" There was also louder yelling and tapping of sticks. I realised that the beaters were closing in, and no one must fire low. It was Gerald who must have forgotten that we were there outside.

Then came what I think they call a bouquet of rabbits. I admit that I was alarmed. They ran low, of course, and some got mixed up with us. I danced round Lionel as he twisted here and there. Addie was apparently not at all a bad shot, but very dangerous. She got two, and Benjy left his stand and came nearer us, for she was searching the terrain with traversing fire, Vince says, all round him. Vince got a rabbit, but he said it sat up, and he hardened his heart and slew it. They are pests, anyway.

Then came the beaters, the keepers, the dogs, and the pick-up. I mentioned Lionel's runners. But I was right. They were too quick on their feet and were never found. Lionel said he had seven down. I am sure he did say that to me. But the men and dogs didn't find any. I had the one that almost fell on me in safe keeping. Bob had shot his hare. In all there were six dead pheasants, one pigeon to Addie, and one to Vincie, and five rabbits. Lionel looked disappointed. He said he must have lent Vince or Bob his favourite gun. So Vincie exchanged for the next beat at Theby Wood. Vanity wanted Addie sent home. She said the girl had almost got Benjy. Benjy looked gloomy till he heard that we would have different stands next time.

The beaters at once went off at the double. I walked with Lionel, who was anxious to let me see what he could do with his favourite gun. Gerald Whick was now to come with us. Addie was to walk with the beaters. They hadn't seen her firing, and would not be afraid. In any case, as Lionel said, ten bob would make it all right with any casualty, if not serious, in that lot.

Theby Wood has a sort of dog's leg in it. Gerald was next to us on one side now, and Vincie on the other. Benjy and Bob were on the flanks. Again we sat and smoked cigarettes, and waited, till the noise arose, and the birds with it.

I must say that Lionel was persevering and quick. He let off about twenty shots in ten minutes, and at the next lot he got off eleven. Then his turn came to show the pests where they got off. A rabbit ambled out of the undergrowth, paused when it saw us, and collapsed.

"Ah!" said Lionel, as he ejected a cartridge into my tweed coat.

There were a lot of runners that time, but I had collected the rabbit and a pigeon. Vincie was glorying in a very fat cock pheasant he had shot. Whick had one, Bob had a rabbit, and Benjy, who had carefully got two pheasants crowding one another, had killed a brace with the same shot. That was the way it was done in the best circles, he told us at lunch, which was taken in the open air. The dogs were fed and looked more satisfied. They had worked hard, and only found four birds. Macpherson looked grimmer than ever, and pointed out Addie to Lionel.

"Yon wumman'll hae us all kilt!"

"I shall speak to her," said Lionel. "We'll put her on the flank next time. Next Mr. Whick, I think."

It was after lunch that the photographer came along. He was a nice young man, in one of those horrid green American hats. We rather crowded together to be taken. Vince said that was because if we formed a long line the game before us would look thin. He insisted on standing behind his own large cock pheasant, so there should be no mistake. Afterwards Lionel wrangled with Addie, and when that was done Gerald went up to him and said that he wanted to be on the far flank.

"Of two, which is the far one?" Lionel asked sarcastically.

"Whichever one is farthest from that girl," said Gerald.

"Of two, 'farther,' not 'farthest,'" Vanity corrected him.

"As the host, Whick," Lionel replied, "I must arrange the guns to my own satisfaction."

"You would!" said Gerald bitterly. "But I tell you that I am not going to be shot to make a joy day for her."

"Very well," Lionel said, "I shall have the stand next to Miss Stole. She, at least, can shoot something."

"She will before she's done," Gerald muttered, glancing over at Addie, who was having a lesson in Safety First from Macpherson.

"Well, that's settled," said Lionel, and turned to me. "There's the trouble of having a pair of guns. It must have been Varek who had my favourite this time. I'll ask him to change."

But the last drive of the day found me as unwilling as Bob to be next to Addie. I sat behind Vincie, and felt much happier.

"On his day," said my husband, grinning at me, "Lionel's a damn' fine shot. It may be Sunday or Monday, but not to-day."

"He had a good many runners," I remarked.

"Well, well," Vincie commented. "Lot of little Mercurys they must have been then, with wings on their feet. I distinctly saw them sliding across the sky northwards after he had greeted them. Not that I blame him. This has been a day of disillusion. I thought that large fowl like pheasants were dead easy. I see that they die hard."

Now came the last of the pheasants. I watched Vincie aim, and fire, and load again. I distinctly saw feathers fly twice, and the second lot were not tail feathers either. Still, the birds went on, and I hoped they were not much hurt, only perhaps affronted.

"Either a clean miss, or a clean kill," I said to Vincie. "That, they say, is the ideal. But look out! here's the nicest slow-mover I have seen to-day."

A brown bird, which I was sure was not a pheasant, came sailing towards us.

"In memoriam," my husband murmured, as he took aim at it.

"Too true," I said, as the bird checked, and then descended near my feet.

I ran out to collect it, and smiled back at Vincie. "It's Mr. Nosey Parker," I cried.

He stared at the long bill. "A woodcock!"

"No use?" I asked.

"Small enough," he replied, "but it will help out the bag."

But it was more than that, it seemed; it was a prize. After the drive, and before we had tea early, preparatory to larning the pigeons to be birds, the keeper congratulated Vince, and spent some time pulling out tiny feathers to put in our hats. Lionel looked surly. He said Addie should not come again. Twice she had fired across him, and once she had taken a pheasant at which he was aiming with special care. He did not say if the other gun really was his favourite. Personally, if the two pairs were all made alike, I did not see how he could tell.

Mr. Musson came down to tea, his face set in a superior smile, went to Macpherson, and returned with a gun under his arm, which made Vincie whisper to me that the man could not even shoot without swanking.

"What do you mean?" I asked.

"He has a twenty-bore," Vincie returned. "A double twenty."

"Well, Addie has a sixteen, if that means anything," I replied. "What is the point?"

He gave forth some of the wisdom he had absorbed at the shooting-school. "The twelve is the usual bore for the usual shot. Addie has a sixteen because she is a woman, and it's lighter. The twenty is lighter and smaller still. That is to say, it fires a smaller charge, there are fewer pellets, and it hasn't the long range of a twelve."

"Oh, I see," I said softly. "You can't hit a bird so far off, and it is more difficult to hit any."

"Quite, my dear. A man who can shoot well with a twenty is a crack."

It appeared that someone else noticed it, for Gerald growled out: "I say, Mr. Musson, coming the expert over us again, with your pop-gun! Or is it just to impress us?"

A certain number of pigeons, disturbed by the previous drives, were flying distractedly overhead. The words were hardly out of Whick's mouth, when Musson threw his gun up, there was a sharp crack, and a pigeon almost fell on the improvised tea-table.

"A fluke, of course," said Musson, with that horribly superior grin of his. "Tea going, Lionel?"

Gerald glared at him. His temper was fouler than ever now, so the rest of us took no notice of him, but hurried on with our tea. Lionel hastily began to explain to us that the "hides" were concealed in Great and Little Coverts in Theby Wood. To keep the pigeons from deserting it altogether, the keepers and beaters were placed in woods farther away, to frighten the birds back if they settled there. The idea was to keep them on the move, but give everyone a chance of shooting.

Vincie has made a rough sketch of the lay-out since, but Lionel explained how we were to be situated.

In Great Covert, Nos. 3, 4, 5 and 6 hides were occupied by Lionel himself, Bob, Addie and Vincie (with me). The farthest hide, outside the rabbit netting on the left tip of Great Covert, was to hold Mr. Musson. A tiny wood on a conical elevation held No. 2, where Gerald was to go, and Benjy was to have Hide No. 1, in Little Covert.

We were all provided now with shooting-sticks, as the hides were not permanent erections, but built by the keepers with branches, such as sportsmen in the highlands call bothies, I think. They were placed in little open spaces among the trees, except Mr. Musson's, which was just outside the wood, on the northern boundary of the shoot.

As we all set off together after tea, the idea was to drop each gun at his hide as we went along, so that the party would gradually diminish.

We had had tea on the grassy slope to the southeast of Little Covert, so we dropped Benjy at his place, and then Gerald Whick in the tiny wood. Lionel, as our host, did not go straight to his hide, which was nearest, but came on with us. Bob Varek, having discovered that Addie was to be within about eighty yards of him, decided to reconnoitre her position before going to his hide, but was pleased to find that many stout tree-trunks stood between them.

"You are a funk," she said scornfully. "As if my sixteen could shoot as far as that. Anyway, pigeons aren't rabbits."

"Thank Heaven for that!" said Bob, as he went back, "but I am not taking any chances." We had followed to see the fun, and now Lionel sent Musson on to the last stand, and turned to us.

"You're No. 6, Vincent; the north-east horn of the wood. Come along. We can cut across diagonally."

It was a pretty thick wood, of oaks, ash, and beech, with a good deal of holly, and some clumps of rhododendron. When we came to our hide, we found that it faced, that is to say the camouflaged entrance faced, south. As Lionel's shoot ended to the north of the wood, the pigeons would come in from the south, or south-east or west, where the beaters were to make a noise.

At the back of our hide was one of those plantings of high rhododendrons, put there for game cover, not ornament, and running for about forty yards in the shape of a horn.

"That's the last of you," Lionel said, as I set up my shooting-stick. "You have a clear field of fire for ten yards in front, Vincent, and I may say that you can, if you wish, shoot a bird sitting."

Vincie laughed. "No. I must be British, too."

Lionel smiled in a superior way. "Pigeons are always exempt from the rule," he said. "I hope you will have good sport."

"Do you know what I think?" I said, when Lionel had gone. "I believe he made that rule himself. He can't shoot for toffee."

"You may be right," said Vincie, "but I haven't earned much toffee myself to-day. I'm not a bally Musson, who can sweep even the cobwebs out of the sky."

"He admitted it was a fluke," I remarked.

"Fluke my eye!" Vincie retorted. "The man's an expert. That he's so dashed conceited about it, is another matter."

"Isn't that his gun now?" I asked, as we heard two cracks from somewhere to the north.

Vincie shook his head. "No, too loud, my dear. He's right beyond Bob Varek. That was Addie, or I'll eat my hat."

As he spoke, a pigeon flew over us, and vanished. He loaded his gun and kept an eye on the strip of sky across which it had dashed.

CHAPTER V

I NEVER saw anything so energetic as the pigeons that day. They seemed to hate to linger anywhere, and there was what looked like a constant game of First Across over our bit of sky.

Poor Vincie nearly went mad, and I admit that I was greatly worked up by the way he aimed here and there, shot as quickly as he could, and ejected spent cartridges all over me.

In the lulls, I asked him what made them so hard to get. He said they jinked, or else swerved down, or up, and so few of them came right over. He also suggested that it would be fairer if we had a wider strip of sky to operate in.

"Still, they must fly into it sometime," he added. "I mean to say, on the theory of probabilities."

"Didn't old Hiram Maxim work out statistics about gambling at Monte Carlo to show that, even if—" I began.

Two shots from Vincie interrupted me, and "again the game went on," as he remarked with comical bitterness.

In this next pause, we did hear the tiny, sharp report of Mr. Musson's twenty. We heard five shots from beyond Bob Varek's hide, and visualised five unfortunate birds crumpling up, and coming down to salute their conqueror.

Addie was also at work. She may not have fired low enough to hit us, but twice we heard shot charges slash through the leaves overhead, and consoled ourselves with the reflection that the pellets must have spent most of their force before they came near our tree-tops.

Vincie was a true prophet. At the next onrush of birds, he aimed at a leading pigeon. It went on, but the second-in-command foolishly flew right into the charge, and came down.

Another solitary one, tired of the game, dropped on to a branch over our heads at the back.

"Shall I?" said Vincie.

"The sauce of him," I nodded. "Tell him where he gets off!"

So we had two pigeons, and though we got no more, and our strip of sky was unpopular after that, we did not feel too bad. Vincie, however, gathered up the cases which were strewn all over the hide, and buried nineteen in a hole he made in the ground.

"Dead but not forgotten," I murmured.

"Better forgotten," said Vincie. "If that pig Musson snoops round here, and sees forty-one cases, he'll have great fun over it."

"He's more likely to try to catch Gerald out, after their passage-at-arms," I said, as we lit cigarettes. "Gerald, by the way, has been odd this time. His clashes with Musson look to me a by-product of something he has against Lionel."

"The ways of literary vendettas are always strange," Vincie said. "I don't think Lionel has forgiven him for *Outsiders in Olympus*, where he was concealed as 'Vulcan the Smith.'"

"The dirty member of the hierarchy?" said my husband.

"Yes, but that would wring Lionel's withers, not Gerald's."

The sun had gone down in a glory of red and gold, and the branches of the trees in front of us were black and sharp, against a sky of darkening blue. Dusk was creeping in the wood, and for the last minute or two we had not heard a single shot.

"How do we know when to go 'lowing homeward o'er the lea'?" I asked.

"I suppose someone comes to tell us," he said doubtfully. "Anyway, we'll pick up those pigeons, and get ready to go."

Fortunately we heard some people coming through the wood towards us. It was Addie, Bob and Musson. When they entered our clearing, we saw that Musson had a string of pigeons, Addie a woodcock (that was the time she shot into the trees) and Bob a pigeon. Mr. Musson was grinning horribly, and waved his hefty shooting-stick at us when we emerged.

"Well, good people," he said. "I thought I heard machine-gun fire over here. Just two birds? Well, well!"

Addie and I went on, and she spoke to me in a low voice. "Bob and I went to pick him up at the other end. I am sorry we did. He was gloating over his catch, and said he had only fired twelve shots."

"Perhaps he buried the deaders," I said.

"He wouldn't bury them. He wants to show off," she said.

"The cartridge-cases," I remarked.

"Oh," said Addie, "I see."

I hoped she would not suspect that I had had recent experience of this method of improving a man's average. And afterwards I was sorry I had told her. Meantime, she was very full of her feat of shooting the only other woodcock, and would not admit that she had fired in our direction at all.

"The fact is, Addie," I told her, "you have got so used to your old sheikhs, dashing about firing off their rifles in the air at random when they feel joyful, that you have acquired the habit."

She grinned. "Well, I have shot something, and killed no one," she said.

"Perfect," I agreed. "Here is a day of novices without a single accident; not a cripple or a corpse. And that with a lot of authors who can hardly bear the sight of one another."

"Bar me," she remarked. "Well, no, I don't really like Mr. Fonders. He tried to be a bit skeikh-like not so long ago, and then Mr. Musson is a bit of a pig."

"That's two hates, Addie," I replied. "There are six of us; multiply by two, and we have twelve, and still no dirty work at the cross-roads."

We came out of the trees to the little clearing where Lionel's hide stood, and shouted to him to come out and show his bag. But he did not reply, and Musson from behind called out that he might have gone on to collect Benjy and Whick.

But Addie had gone ahead, and she pointed forward. "He's hiding."

"I spy!" Bob shouted. "Come out and show yourself!"

Lionel, as I now saw, was certainly in the hide. He seemed to be playing a childish game of hide-and-seek on the floor, which had led to Bob's half-ironical challenge.

Almost simultaneously I trod on a dead pigeon, and jumped. Here was one head of game to prove that Lionel had not been idle. As I bent to pick it up, Vincie went ahead of me, and into the hide. He came out quickly, and stared at us, his face white.

"Don't like the look of him," he said in a gulp. "Had a stroke or something."

Musson, always to the front in organising and taking control of affairs, passed Vincent and strode in. We gathered round the hide, and saw something of the body through the walls of loose branches, and bits of bracken used for camouflage.

I could see that Lionel's gun had fallen against the back of the hide and remained aslant there. He lay on his face, his hands stretched out to each side of him, his face slightly turned, so that it was not all in contact with the ground.

In the moment before Musson bent and lifted him up, I thought of several things. I was sorry I had joked about our corpseless day—though we did not know that Lionel was a corpse. I remembered that he was fond of his food, pretty full-blooded, and the type that one does, as a layman, associate with seizures. Finally, I wished we had not come. Then Musson held

Lionel up with one strong arm, and almost as promptly laid him down again.

"Damn it, he's been shot!"

The strong meat of Addie's novels had not habituated her to the sight of real blood. She went behind a tree and was sick. I am not usually queasy, but I stepped into the hide and put a handkerchief over the dead face.

"Shot? What nonsense!" Bob Varek exclaimed angrily.

"Unless he poked his eye out on a thorn," Musson said, "and I don't think there are any thorny branches here."

Vincie went down on his knees, and held his watch-glass before the lips that just showed under my little hanky. He felt the pulse and heart, and got up.

"The trouble is that it's damned nonsense, and true, too," Musson remarked. "Unless two or three pellets balled together, which does happen sometimes, we were all out of effective range of this. Not to speak of having trees and bushes between us and Fonders."

I thought I would go out to look after Addie, and meanwhile Bob dashed out to get a doctor on the telephone at the house.

I found Addie sitting on a fallen tree-trunk, looking better and more composed, after her bout of nausea.

"What did happen. Penny?" she asked me.

"It's his eye," I said, with a shiver of disgust. "The left eye too. Musson says he must have been shot, unless he left his place and hit it on a thorn."

"His—good eye?" she asked, rather curiously I thought.

"No," I told her, "the other eye."

"But wouldn't the glass—" She stopped and bit her lip.

"Well, I forgot that, Addie," I said. "Of course a thorn would be stopped or deflected by the glass eye."

"How could he have been shot?"

"Well, he was really out of range, my dear, but if one pellet did carry so far—"

Addie looked at me. "Penny, they take their eyes out."

She made me jump. "Don't get nervy and hysterical," I said.

"I mean that they do sometimes," she said. "I have a friend whose aunt, an old lady, has two. Do you think he can have done that?"

I saw what she meant. I wondered if there was any muscular fatigue involved in holding an artificial eye in its place all day. For either a thorn or a nearly spent pellet would be turned by the hard surface of the glass.

Vincie came up to us. "Penny, Bob has gone to get a doctor. If Addie here will run across to get Whick and Benjy, they can look for the beaters, or get them somehow, and we'll have Fonders carried to the house. And the sooner we do the better. It is just about to get dark."

Addie was quite ready to leave the scene, and went off towards Little Covert. Vincie turned to me.

"Look here, old girl, Musson is right. However it was done, it looks as if a shot had hit Lionel in the eye socket, and done him in. He had obviously fired his gun, but accident can be ruled out."

"You are sure of that?" I said.

"In the sense that he shot himself by accident, yes. The charge would have blown his face off."

I nodded. "If the poor devil was to die, it would have been better if it had," I said. "So I think."

Vincent looked at me curiously. "What do you mean, Penny?"

"I mean that Addie was the nearest," I said.

He started. "Addie? Why, she got on pretty well with him, I thought."

"She as good as told me that he tried to get what the Americans call 'fresh'," I replied, "but I merely meant that she was shooting rather at random to-day, and may wonder all her life if she hit him by chance."

He looked interested. "Yes, I see. She was as near as anyone to this hide. We were about as near, but, as you saw, I only fired upwards. Was anyone else near?"

"I'm not a good judge of distance, old thing," I said, "but Gerald on the little island wood didn't seem very far off."

"And there weren't woods all the way between them," he murmured. "Not like Addie and ourselves."

Musson came up at that moment. "Nasty job, this," he said. "Only one redeeming feature about it, and that's the accidental nature. Every year someone gets peppered at a drive, and the only difference here is that Fonders happened to get it in the eye. Worse than the eye, in the sense that it was easier penetrated. I should say it was about the spot at the back where the optic nerve emerges. What do you say, Mercer?"

"The eyeball would obviously have been some small protection," Vincent agreed. "You know you can get a pretty smart blow there without actual damage."

There is no use in taking two bites at a cherry, and the point would come up whether we liked it or not. "Mr. Musson," I said, "if we could find the glass eye, we might be able to decide if he did hit a thorn."

"Mrs. Mercer," he said gravely. "I picked it up under him—or where he had been lying. It wasn't smashed. Meanwhile someone ought to run to the house for torches. We can't get him out on a stretcher in this wood without some light."

It was true. Even the sky was darkening now, and in the wood we could hardly see each other's faces. Vincent at once set off, and Mr. Musson offered me his cigarette-case and began to speak.

As I lit a cigarette, I thought how characteristic it was of the man as we had seen him. Big, capable, egotistical, he had only to see a situation to begin analysing it, starting to organise everyone about him and setting every one to rights.

"I don't know what chances Fonders had after he got in here, Mrs. Mercer," he began, "but there are just two empty cartridge-cases in the hide, and we know he shot one pigeon. Now we were all really out of range, but we have to consider an unhappy fluke. There is sure to be an inquest, and they will want to know, for form's sake, how he was shot."

"They'd be duds if they didn't," I said.

"You and your husband were in No. 6 hide, weren't you?" he went on. "I imagine it's a hundred yards away from here, but you will know if your husband fired in this direction."

I nodded. "Yes, he must have done, or roughly. But I saw every shot, and they were all taken at pigeons overhead, or at a pretty high angle." I paused and added: "I suppose shot does travel in a parabola, Mr. Musson?"

"Roughly, yes. But I am quite sure, Mrs. Mercer, that a pellet simply falling, after having exhausted its impetus, would not penetrate the brain, as the shot seems to have done in this case. If you are quite sure that he did not fire at a low angle, that wipes your husband out."

"I am quite sure," I said.

I could see the end of his cigarette glow brightly in the darkness. He relieved my mind by nodding. I could see the bright spark bend downward and come up again.

"My own idea," he said in a serious voice, "is one I don't like to give voice to."

I knew what was coming. Addie, the reckless; poor dear! I decided not to mention the pellets we had heard thrashing the tree-tops in our direction.

"Yes?" I ventured.

"One or two of the guns were distinctly nervous about being placed next Miss Stole," he said. "Lionel said to me when I came down from the house that she had put the wind up Mr. Doe by firing across his face."

"Well, I'm afraid she did," I said, "but there are the trees here."

At that moment, we heard shouts and voices coming up to the wood, and it was not long before three beaters, led by the head keeper, Benjy and Vanity, and Gerald Whick, were with us in the dark clearing by the hide.

CHAPTER VI

I AM afraid that most of the party were more interested in their own reactions to, and possible indirect connection with (as a lawyer might put it) the tragedy, than in the tragedy itself. Some people had achieved a liking for the late Lionel Fonders, but they were few, and not guests at his shoot. In fact, as Vincie remorsefully put it, we were cads to go there at all, when we knew we couldn't stick the man.

In a sense that was true, but it was harsh. None of us expected that he would die; most, being writers to whom everything is grist, were anxious to join in a pheasant-shoot. One or two were conscious thereafter that their former accounts of life in country houses did not tally with the facts. Sport (and ballistics) is a frequent stumbling-block to the author.

The one who had most cause to grumble at the event was, I thought, Mr. Musson. He had lost a good job, and a paying client. Authors flock to the agent of best-sellers, thinking there must be some magic in his touch with publishers.

But, as I said, the party mostly discussed its own interests, and the dead man now in the house itself hardly attracted any personal attention.

Dinner that evening was not a quiet meal. The doctor had come and gone, the police had sent a sergeant over, who had heard what we all had to say, and philosophically decided that these things did happen when a lot of people shot in company, and occasionally at large. In fact, he was rich in experiences, from the year when old Sir Humphrey's hat was mistaken for a rabbit, to the former season when a guest at Chustable Hall lost his left eye, as a fellow guest failed to see that a woodcock was occupying a place midway between them.

"Eyes is not uncommon, gentlemen," he said, and we knew what he meant. "It just happens that this shot went through."

"There will—will be an inquest, sergeant?" Benjy inquired.

"I'm afraid so, sir; but formal, that's what it will be. Nowadays, with so many gentlemen doing themselves in, there has to be. But that won't take long."

"Shall we have to stay for it?" Gerald inquired sulkily.

"Or be down here for it, sir."

"Well, Mr. Musson," I asked at dinner, for we had all involuntarily come to look on the man as running the show, "you saw the doctor. What did he say?"

"He said the pellet had penetrated the brain, Mrs. Mercer."

"Does he know anything about shooting?" Bob Varek asked.

"I gather that he does. Country doctors get asked out a good deal, if they are at all presentable."

"Then he knew the ranges from the different hides," Vincie said.

Musson nodded. "He did. I told him. What he made here was only a rough examination. He was puzzled."

"Then the sooner he gets unpuzzled the better," Addie said suddenly. "I'm not going to have it said that I shot Mr. Fonders by accident."

"You were nearer than we were," Gerald said.

"Oh, was I?" she said bitterly. "I think you were as near as I, and Mr. Doe not much farther away."

Vanity stared at her disagreeably. "I was with my brother, and he did not fire a single shot in that direction. And you know very well that you almost shot him earlier in the day."

"I shall never hear the end of that," Addie retorted; "but he is still alive, and it's beside the point. I only say that he and Mr. Whick were not much farther away than I, and there was an open space between."

Musson looked at her ironically. "I had an idea that there would be a shemozzle over responsibility," he remarked, "but let me finish. The doctor was puzzled to find that the entrance of the pellet was so large. I presume that none of you was firing anything larger than number five, say?"

Vincie and Gerald Whick admitted that they were using five in the guns for the pigeons, and both explained that they had heard pigeons were hard to bring down. The rest used six, the most common of sizes for game.

"I was using five too," Musson said. "It hits harder. For pigeon you need it with a twenty."

"But what is the point, in any case?" I asked.

"Well, unless two or three pellets balled—that is, stuck together, something like swan-shot must have been used, or that is the doctor's opinion," he told us. "As you all want to have the thing thrashed out, I asked him if it would not be better to have a post-mortem, and he agreed."

"Why a post-mortem?" Gerald Whick snapped. "Dash it all, what good can that do?"

To our surprise, Addie was all for the idea. "I can tell you one thing it can do, Mr. Whick. I used number six, and the doctor can't get the pellet out unless he does a P.M."

"Why not?" Benjy asked.

"Well, I mean to say, he must have probed when he was here just now, and yet Mr. Musson seems doubtful still about the size of shot."

"You're quite the little detective!" Gerald sneered.

Musson laid down his knife and fork, and held up his hand. "That is the point. He couldn't find the pellet."

"When will he do the P.M.?" I asked.

"He will come to-morrow morning at ten, and the superintendent of police will come with him. But don't worry. Accidents will happen, as the sergeant told us."

"We ought to have a plan made of the wood," Vincie said.

"Splendid! Can you draw?"

"I can, a little."

"Right." Musson nodded. "You turn out early to-morrow, and make a sketch. I'll come along with Macpherson, and we'll measure the distances from Lionel's hide to all the others, so that we can plot it out. The police may do that, but it can't hurt."

"I don't like that man," Addie said.

"He didn't like you," Gerald said disagreeably. "I think keepers probably hate people who put the wind up them."

Disliking Gerald, and coming to the assistance of a member of her own profession and sex, Vanity Doe butted in.

"What is past is past," she said. "I do not intend, and I am sure I can speak for my brother, too, to mention Miss Stole's reckless shooting at the inquest."

"At your brother, you mean," Gerald said.

"I do not intend to mention at the inquest—" she began, flushing.

"Just a moment," Musson interrupted. "Mr. Whick means that Macpherson may mention it. He complained to Fonders."

Addie suddenly burst into tears, and left the table.

Vanity rose, and with a scorching glance at Gerald went after her.

Mr. Musson looked at us all in turn, and resumed his dinner.

"Well, I think that's that," Gerald said. "We'll have the P.M., and know where we are. Of course none of us can be detained, but we can stay on till the inquest if we wish, I suppose?"

Musson looked up. "I took the liberty of telephoning to Fonders's lawyer. He will be down to-morrow to go through his papers. I am sure he will have no objection to you all staying on till the inquest is over."

"I have to go to town," Gerald said. "I mean to say, if we're not going to shoot, I prefer London."

"Then you will leave your address," Musson said. "They will want to serve a subpoena, I expect."

"I'll do that," Whick replied.

"Incidentally, I suppose you will take charge of all Fonders's literary affairs?" Vincie asked.

"He had just appointed me his agent in New York," Musson said. "I am not his English agent, and even then, that was for future work."

"So this is a nasty smack for you?" Gerald remarked, with a trace of ill-natured triumph in his voice.

"It has that appearance," Musson replied gently, "but life's like that."

Vanity and Addie returned in time for coffee. They had made it up. Addie had dried her tears, and both began an animated discussion on the lost art of poetical satire, which presently drew an angry Whick into its audible orbit.

Musson grinned, shrugged, and we others drew together and discussed the late Lionel's marvellous sales.

"Sixty-two thousand of the English seven-and-sixpenny edition," Musson said. "And he got twenty per cent. That's four thousand six hundred pounds odd. Then there were the sales on our side, and later there would be film rights. I am speaking of his last book. I didn't come in on that."

"How was it done?" Benjy asked.

"Heaven knows! Just happened that he hit the taste of multitudes. He gave me the figures himself."

We shook our heads in respectful silence, and suddenly we heard Addie's voice.

"I must say that I don't call silly abuse *satire*, even if it does rhyme."

And then Gerald: "And I say that it's a pity old Hichens started half you women looking about for Gardens of Allah! Sheikhs? They're about as romantic as rag-pickers."

Vanity leaned forward to look at him. "Why only mention women-writers? Male envy again, I expect."

The butler had come in to remove the coffee-cups, and he looked so disapproving at the unseemly wrangle that Vincie mentioned it when the man had gone out.

"I expect he thinks we are a bit noisy, with his master lying overhead," he added.

"Quite right," said Musson. "Let's stop squabbling, and try to see how this affair can have happened." He turned to Addie. "Do you know, Miss Stole, what charge your sixteen-bore fires?"

She started. "I bought ordinary cartridges."

"I know, but nowadays they are often chambered to take what would be a light twelve-bore charge—longer cartridge-case, you know, and about an ounce of shot."

"I'll get you one," she said, rising.

Gerald stared at him in a hostile way. "Want to look at one of mine?"

"No, I don't. I have seen your gun."

Whick sneered. "Then what about yours, since you make such a point of it?"

Musson smiled exasperatingly. "I was going to tell you that my twenty is bored to take a larger charge than the normal. It fires seven-eighths of an ounce of shot in a two-and-three-quarter-inch case."

"How does that compare with a twelve-bore?" I asked.

"It has three-sixteenths of an ounce less shot," he replied.

Vincie nodded. "Let's take the twelve-bore as normal, since most of us had 'em. What would you say the range is?"

"I should say that you can kill a bird, if you shoot straight, up to sixty yards; at seventy there would be little chance, and in many cases the charge wouldn't carry a hundred yards."

Vanity began to smile. "I am not a very good judge of distances, I admit, but it does occur to me that we were much more than a hundred yards away from Mr. Fonders."

"You and Mercer are all right," Gerald growled. "A wife can't give evidence against her husband, even if she wanted to, and you're not likely to peach on your brother."

Benjy bristled up. "To peach on me! What the devil do you mean?"

"And what evidence do you think I could give against my husband?" I demanded.

He looked sullen. "I don't say you have any. I say if there was a—"

"'If you had a sister, would she like cheese?' in other words," Mr. Musson interrupted, as Addie came in with a cartridge to show him. "I think we may leave hypothetical cases out of it for the moment. Ah, thank you, Miss Stole, we are just wanting to see how Fonders could possibly be struck in the eye at extreme range. This does not help much."

He held up the cartridge, and she stared.

"Did you think it would?"

He shook his head. "This is a two-and-a-half-inch case, which would fire just the same charge as my twenty, which has a longer chamber. On the whole, I don't see your gun carrying all the way to Fonders's hide."

"The trouble to those of us who can think accurately and logically, Mr. Musson," Vanity said sententiously, "is that Mr. Fonders was shot in the eye. I know nothing about guns, and I have to take what you have said at its face value, but what is the good of saying that no gun fired to-day could carry the distance, when we know one *did*?"

He bowed ironically. "A logical mind like yours, Miss Doe, might remember that I made an exception. A brain of your calibre, even if you're not a gun expert, will be able to understand that a charge of small shot, such as one uses for birds, does not travel very far, as each pellet is light, and meets with friction in its flight through the air."

She bit her lip, and coloured up. "It may do so."

"It does do so. In a charge of one ounce of number six shot, there are two hundred and seventy pellets. In a charge of what I may call swan-shot, there are twenty much larger pellets, size SSSG. Have you got that?"

She said that she had, and he went on: "Swan-shot or buck-shot would undoubtedly travel a long way, and do damage at a hundred or more yards, even with a normal charge of powder."

"Why talk rot?" Benjy inquired. "Who is likely to come down here for swans or buck? And who wants the things, if they were here?"

"Mr. Musson is being wise as usual," said Gerald. "I shall show him the cartridges I have left, and insist on his dissecting them to make sure I didn't load up with buck-shot."

"Why should you?" said Musson, staring at him steadily. "I was merely trying to convince Miss Doe that a shotgun could have hit Fonders."

"Oh, by inference you were going further than that," Vanity said, thinking her logic had given her the advantage again. "You said it could only be done by swan-shot. It was done, so one of the guns *must* have done it."

Vincie nodded. "The real point is that no one was firing from an aeroplane at our party. So, whether it's possible or impossible, one of us accidentally shot Lionel."

"What about the keepers or beaters?" Addie asked. "I don't like the look of the Scotch one."

"Keepers don't carry guns at a drive, and the beaters had none, and were away in the woods to the south," Musson said.

I felt that there was a danger of the storm rising again. "There was an accident," I remarked. "The inquest will decide what its nature was. Or, if that is impossible, I suppose there is a suitable verdict?"

"There is," Vincie announced. "'Accidental death, though the jury were unable to say exactly how it was caused.' I think we had better leave it to the jury."

CHAPTER VII

GERALD Whick was driven off very early next morning to catch a train at the junction eight miles away. We breakfasted at eight, and Vincie, Musson and I set off at nine towards Theby Wood.

Musson had a long tape-measure and Vincie had a pad of paper and a pencil. We picked up Macpherson, the keeper, at the edge of the wood. Vincie went off to pace the wood, and make a rough sketch of its size and shape. I elected to stay with the other two.

They began by measuring the distance between the hide where Lionel was found dead, and that occupied by Vanity and Benjy in Little Covert. Then they measured from Lionel's to Whick's, and then worked through the others till they came to Musson's. All were over a hundred yards, except Gerald Whick's, which was about ninety, and Musson's was two hundred and fifty yards away. Vincie has marked the distances on his map.

Vincie was coming round the far horn of the wood when we finished there, and remarked to the keeper that he could not understand it.

"Unless one of us has a wonder-gun," he added.

"If it was no a saxteen she had, I wud say it was yon leddy in No. 5," Macpherson remarked, frowning. "Wha's to say, onyway, if she didna' walk a yaird or twa oot o' her hide?"

"No, no," said Vincie; "she was using number six shot. But I must get on with my sketch."

He had only gone on a few minutes, pacing solemnly, when the police turned up, in the shape of a large and intelligent superintendent and a stout but dull-faced constable. They had brought a map of the wood with them, enlarged to scale from the six-inch ordnance map, and greeted us with some surprise.

"Having a look to see what happened, sir?" Superintendent Brown asked Musson.

"We were measuring the distances between the hides," Musson said, passing over his notes. "We can't make out how the man was shot. Will you come back over the ground with us? We can go back to the hide where Mr. Fonders was found."

"Certainly. Who found him?"

"My husband, Mr. Mercer," I remarked. "He has just gone on to make a sketch of the wood."

Brown raised his eyebrows in some amusement. "I see. Waste of time really, you know, madam, for when you have shooting-parties you risk accidents. I shoot, myself, but not in company, I may say. All I want is just to look round, pick up the doctor again when he's done, and know enough to instruct the coroner privately. No need for anyone to get worried about an accidental death." He had reckoned without that typical Scot, the keeper, who was even more grimly logical than Vanity, and knew what he was talking about as well.

"Mebbe sae," he grunted, "but I'll juist draw yer attention, sir, to yin fact. A' the guns were oot o' range o' the bit hide where the man was kilt."

Brown smiled good-humouredly. "Macpherson, if I didn't know that you were a Scot, I should say that was a Hibernian way of putting it. A Saxon like myself would say that a man who was killed by a shot was not out of range."

"Weel, weel, ye'll know better when ye see," Macpherson bridled.

When Brown did come round with us, he saw. And made amends. "You're right apparently. Still we may take it that by some fluke, or balling of pellets, Mr. Fonders was accident-ally shot by another gun. It's obvious the doctor thinks the death was chance too. The shot would not have penetrated the body, or even the flesh of the face, deeply. But it went into the eye-socket."

We agreed, but Macpherson, having established his position as a man incapable of Hibernianisms on a serious subject, had not said all his say. He planted his feet apart, and stared at the officer.

"There's anither factor, sir, that ocht tae be investigated."

"What's that? You don't mean that it's most likely the shots must have come from Hides 1, 2, or 5?"

"*Or sax!* Nae doot o' that, and five, tae my mind, most likely o' a'; for yon leddy was in't! But it's nae that. Whaur did the ither shot, the stray pickles, gae, I ask ye?"

Vincie came hurrying back, was introduced to the superintendent, and asked what we were doing next.

"Mr. Macpherson here has suggested that we should examine the hide where Mr. Fonders was found, for signs of the passage of shot, sir," Brown remarked politely. "It is a good idea. It may be, but seems unlikely, that only one or two pellets went on. If so, we must search the trees and branches between that hide and the others, to see how, and where, they were intercepted."

"Good idea," Vincie agreed, "though it may be a bit of a job finding small shot in tree-trunks."

"We will make the attempt," said Brown, "but Hide No. 3 first. If we find any there, we may be able roughly to judge the direction from which they came."

I began to find all this rather fascinating, for, like the rest of us, I'm afraid, I had almost forgotten the man whose death had given rise to this search.

With six of us at work, aided by the keeper's keen eyes, we managed to do all there was to be done at No. 3 hide in half an hour. But not a branch or leaf, or tree-trunk, showed signs of having been struck by shot, and Brown became less airy in his manner.

It was lunch-time before we had done all the hides, and failed to discover a single clue to the manner of Lionel's death.

"Silly or not," said the superintendent, as we walked back to the house, "it must have been a shot that was falling from a height."

Musson did not reply to that. "Will you stay to lunch, superintendent?" he asked.

"I am sorry. I am very busy, and have taken too much time already. I can take the doctor back with me, if he's done his job."

Dr. Smith had just finished, and was surrounded in the hall by Benjy, Vanity, Bob and Addie.

I gathered that they were annoyed and disappointed, and the doctor very curt and firm. He had to make his report for the police. It was an official report, not something to be canvassed and gossiped about. I think he regarded us as a set of raffish Bohemians. At all events, he would not tell us what he had decided about the cause of death.

The superintendent supported him. He said that the report must be considered at headquarters. It would be learned at the inquest exactly what the medical verdict was.

"Ladies and gentlemen," he added, before he bore the doctor away in his car, "you will receive official notices this evening. But I may tell you that the inquest is fixed for a quarter past twelve to-morrow, and it is proposed to hold it in the old tithe barn on the estate. I do not want to detain you in the country longer than I can help, and I hope the whole business will not take long. There are good trains to London in the afternoon."

I must say that most of us found the doctor's reticence rather disquieting. Why was he so close about the matter? What harm would it have done to remark that it was an obvious accident?

"He can't have found anything, can he, Penny?" Addie asked me, when they had gone.

"I don't think so. What can he have found?"

"I am sure," said Vanity, "that the man was simply posing, showing his authority. He did not strike me as a man of brains."

Vincie laughed. "Probably it's the usual routine. The police must consider it first, and we can all wait till to-morrow to hear what he thought. I don't know what the rest of you are doing after lunch, but Penny and I propose to go for a walk, and see the countryside."

"I must study that tithe barn," Vanity said. "I was not aware there was one here. An article on tithe barns would suit my Review, I think."

Benjy said he would go with her, and Addie and Bob said they would play billiards.

"With muffled cues, I hope?" Benjy said.

Addie laughed. "The fact is the butler and that silly doctor think we are a lot of yahoos. You could see it in their faces. So we have no reputation to lose!"

As a matter of fact, we heard afterwards that the butler had told the other servants we were always quarrelling and sparring with each other and our late host. This got about, and caused some of the unpleasantness later.

Luncheon over, we set out for a long walk, leaving the others to do what they pleased. We had gone about a mile towards the river when Vincie wondered what had become of his petrol-lighter and, after searching all his pockets, produced and stared at a cartridge with a greyish case.

"Now, where the devil did that come from?" he asked. "It's a tracer. Just shows you, my dear, that I am not properly valeted. This waistcoat should have been shaken and brushed."

"I didn't like to ask the butler to do it," I replied ironically. "He looks too important. But what's the difference? I see it isn't the same as your others, in colour anyway."

"No," Vincie said, returning it. "I got it at the shooting-school. Blow it! I must have left that lighter at home."

"That doesn't matter," I said. "I carry *real* matches. Here you are."

The country was really delightful. A good many country seats, with their park trees and well-kept demesnes, were quite near, and we forgot all about Lionel, I am afraid.

Gerald Whick's absence kept matters on a less acrimonious plane that day. He had come down ready to quarrel with Lionel and with anyone else who crossed him, and he was obviously unhappy and worried when he heard there was to be a post-mortem.

"I wonder why?" I asked Vincie, that night in our room. "We know he made a nasty hit at Lionel in that cheap satire of his. People did recognise the original, and it caused some talk. But if that was to be taken into account, what about me? He had a go at most of us."

Vincie laughed. "The fact is that satire is the easiest job in the world, and is often mistaken for wit. Isn't it always a soft thing to make fun of people, and a hard one to point out their good qualities? But the police don't make cases against people just because they are known to have quarrelled with, or satirised, other people."

We had all been subpoenaed to attend the inquest, and Gerald would have to get an early train from town to be in time. After seven next day, police and workmen came and fitted up the empty old tithe barn as an improvised court, bringing a table and chairs on lorries.

Fortunately, the London Press had not thought it worth while to send down to report the proceedings, but three local papers had sent men.

The coroner was a doctor from Huckaby, a stout little man of few words. He was popular, not fussy or egotistical, and unlikely to turn the proceedings into a criminal trial or an unpremeditated farce.

Then there were the members of the jury, a mixed crowd of farmers, some shopkeepers, a veterinary surgeon and an estate agent.

We breakfasted at nine, and went down in a body at ten to watch the preparations at the tithe barn. The superintendent, with an inspector, a sergeant and some constables, was buzzing about. He came and talked to us for a little, and then disappeared into the building, as an aide came up with a bag full of papers.

"I don't know if we should take off our sporting rags, and appear in our bestest," Vincie said, when eleven came. "What do you think, Benjy?"

"Perhaps we should," Benjy remarked.

We went into the house and up to our room, and Vincie suddenly gave a yelp. "I do believe the valet service must have started!" he remarked. "Did the butler come up to our room this morning, Penny?"

"How can I tell, having been out with you?" I said. "Why?"

"Someone has shaken my cartridge out of this waistcoat," he replied. "If that doesn't hint at brushing, what does?"

"Then it must have been when you were at dinner last night," I said, "as you put on those tweeds the moment you got up."

He nodded. "May be so. One of the housemaids. I must ask what they did with my ammunition. Probably she removed the clothes, did not see that the cartridge had fallen out, and—"

"What do they cost?" I interrupted.

"Plain about a penny-ha'penny, rockets about threepence," he replied.

"Then forget it, and I'll give you the threepence!" I said. "Do hurry on, or they will be sending for us. And you might fasten this snickersnee for me; I can't get at it."

He did up the tiny catch-fastener, and went on with his dressing.

"This should be a lesson to us," I said. "The inquest, I mean. I have never been to one, but we could work in the details in a book later on."

"I had that idea too," he said. "Hateful, isn't it, that we can never forget our unholy job, even in a house of woe?"

"Terrible," I agreed, "but one doesn't feel the woeful atmosphere somehow here. Even the servants don't look much distressed. Lionel had the makings of a quite decent fellow, too, before he got into the Freudy set and went all nasty."

"True," said my husband. "It's no use saying that Lionel justifies many tears. Dying doesn't turn us into angels. Isn't retrospective, so to speak. Still, it is hard cheese being knocked out at his age."

It was now a quarter to twelve, so we hurried down and raced over to the improvised court. People had already taken their seats, and we were all herded together as witnesses, though we really hadn't witnessed anything material. At a little table there was a local solicitor, and also a grey-haired man in town clothes, who turned out to be Lionel's London lawyer. Gerald Whick came in with a rush, just as the coroner entered the court.

After a few preliminaries, the jury was sworn in, and its members went to "view the body". They came back, looking very serious, and sat down.

The coroner's introductory remarks were made in a quiet tone, and did not suggest much beyond the fact that Lionel Fonders had been shot dead while a member of a shooting-party, in circumstances which apparently led him to think that it might have happened to anybody rash enough to belong to a party carrying guns. He was not a sportsman but had, during his twenty years of office, held inquests on the bodies of at least two people who had been shot by reckless gunners.

"When we think how many of these shooting-parties are held all over the country during the season," he remarked, "and how many millions of cartridges fired, many of them by people who are neither expert shots nor careful in handling the dangerous weapons they carry, we may come to the conclusion that the death-rate from this cause is miraculously low. We are, indeed, in greater daily danger from the omnipresent motor-car."

CHAPTER VIII

"THE deceased gentleman," the coroner went on, adjusting his pince-nez, "was entertaining a shooting-party on the day of his death. Various members of that party are present here, and will tell us anything they know which may bear on the accident."

Those present turned their heads to stare at us, and the jurymen, who had been supplied with a sketch map of Theby Wood, passed it from hand to hand. The coroner resumed:

"After the last drive of the day, it had been arranged that the party should indulge in pigeon-shooting from separate shelters placed in the wood, technically known as 'hides'. There were seven of these and that occupied by the late Mr. Fonders was No. 3. Members of the jury will be able to follow the movements of the various guns by looking at the index numbers on the plan with which they have been supplied. Shooting went on for some time, and when it grew dusk the members of the party left their 'hides' and went towards that occupied by their host. Four of them reached it almost together, and when they went in they found Mr. Fonders lying dead on the ground, with a gunshot wound in the eye-socket of the left eye. I say eye-socket advisedly, since Mr. Fonders had been deprived of the use of his eye in the war, and had had an artificial eye fitted. Whether he removed this artificial eye before he was struck, or whether the pellet glanced in sidewise and forced it out, there is nothing to show. The point, in any case, is not important. Naturally assuming that the deceased had been accidentally struck by a pellet from one of the other guns, the guests had the body removed to the house, and very properly informed the police."

The coroner cleared his throat and proceeded: "A doctor made a rough examination that evening, and an autopsy the following morning. You will hear his evidence later, and draw your own conclusions. In ordinary circumstances, though I consider it unwise, an autopsy may be dispensed with, but there is one factor here which made an autopsy advisable. That, gentlemen, is the range at which the shot must have been fired. Most of you are familiar with shotguns. The hide nearest to that of the dead man was about ninety yards away; the others progressively farther; and all beyond the normal range of a normally loaded shotgun."

One of the farmers rose to make a remark. The coroner frowned at him. "Yes," he said, "I am well aware of that. But a shotgun pellet at the range you mention would not kill a man. If you will study the map, you will also be aware that there were numbers of trees between the various hides."

The officious farmer looked abashed and sat down hastily. The coroner then called upon Vincie, who had been the first to find the body, or to enter the hide. Vincie was sworn, and stated that he had been a guest at the shoot, and later occupied Hide No. 6, accompanied by his wife, to wait for flighting pigeon. When it was growing dusk, and shooting had ceased, he and I went off to find the other members of the party, those in Hides 4, 5 and 7.

"Miss Stole, Mr. Robert Varek, and Mr. Musson?" said the coroner, consulting his map.

"Yes, sir."

"You met them together, and returned towards Mr. Fonders's hide to see if he had any other plans?"

"Yes, sir. He had not told us when shooting would stop, but it had virtually stopped, so we went to see him."

"Tell the jury what you saw when you entered the hide, Mr. Mercer."

Vincie explained what had taken place, and the coroner nodded.

"It is obvious, Mr. Mercer, that Mr. Fonders was struck by a missile from one of the other guns, but difficult, on account of the intervening trees, to see how that missile could have had a low trajectory. However, before you stand down, may I ask you if you fired a shot at a low angle, and in the general direction of Hide No. 3?"

"No," Vincie said, "all the shots I fired were at a steep angle. I could only see such pigeons as passed almost overhead."

"In other words you were placed on the edge of a Hide in the wood. May I ask what size of shot you used?"

"Number five, sir, for the pigeons."

The coroner released Vincie, and called on Addie. She took the oath rather nervously, being conscious that some of her fellow guests were inclined to think her the culprit. The coroner asked her the same question about the angle of fire, and she admitted that she had shot a woodcock, which had flitted by.

The coroner had heard of woodcock, and the wild shooting for which these elusive and much-sought-after birds are often responsible.

"That shot, then, was fired at a low angle?" he said slowly.

Addie blushed. "Yes, sir. But the bird was flying towards the rough grass slope on the south of the wood, not near Mr. Fonders at all."

"H'm. I see. What shot were you using?"

"Number six, sir, and my gun is a sixteen-bore. It couldn't shoot so far."

"You heard a great many shots fired?"

"Yes, from time to time. I couldn't say who fired. They came from different directions."

"Did you hear Mr. Fonders fire a shot?"

"I heard a shot from that direction, and he had a pigeon down when we came to the hide."

Bob Varek and Mr. Musson were called in turn, and both said there were a good many shots fired. Benjy and Vanity and Gerald Whick also got into the box. None of them admitted firing in Lionel's direction. Gerald was very positive about it.

The jury were getting restive. I could see that they wanted to be off about their business, and did not see why an accidental death at a shoot should occupy so much of their time. But they settled down more attentively when the doctor went into the witness-box and began to explain what he had discovered as the result of the autopsy.

It appeared that he did not shoot, and was not familiar with shotguns or their missiles. He stated that a missile had entered the centre of the dead man's left eye-socket and penetrated the brain. He had found it embedded in the brain tissue, and had not the slightest doubt that it had led to Mr. Fonders's death.

The coroner asked a question: "Can you tell me, doctor, what size of shot you found?"

"I do not know, sir. It was not a pellet of the kind I have had shown to me by Superintendent Brown."

"Number five size shot, sir," the superintendent observed.

"Thank you. Can you throw any light on its type or nature?"

"No, sir. I believe it has been sent up to London for an expert opinion."

We all sat up and looked at each other. Had the coroner, or the superintendent, anything up his sleeve? What was it? The jury too began to stir in their seats, and the court was very quiet for a moment or two.

"It was not an ordinary leaden pellet, doctor?"

"No, sir, or so I am informed."

Superintendent Brown took the field for a moment. "May I say, sir, that I have examined the missile. It appears to have been made of copper and something like tin. It is difficult to say what was its original size and shape, but I should imagine it roughly to have been about three-sixteenths of an inch long, and about a quarter of an inch in diameter."

"It should have been kept, and exhibited in my court," the coroner said impatiently. "If you are unable to tell us the nature of the missile, the jury can form no conclusion without seeing it."

"I am sorry, sir," the superintendent apologised. "I really expected to have it back with an expert's report before the court opened, but it has not come to hand."

The coroner looked annoyed. "If the missile was not of a type used in such sporting guns as were carried by witnesses who have just now given evidence, it lends a new aspect to the case. Their evidence becomes irrelevant, and I may have to consider adjourning the inquiry until such time as we are provided with the further evidence necessary for the jury to reach a proper conclusion."

The jurymen glared at Brown, who apologised once more, and asked if he might get on the telephone to London and see if the report could not be expedited. "The pellet has been sent to an expert gun-maker, sir," he added.

"Very well," said the coroner. "I shall ask the doctor to stand down, and take the evidence of the two remaining witnesses, Mr. Fonders's head keeper and under-keeper. If you can get the report, I may accept that, even if the missile is not here to-day."

Brown hurried out, and Macpherson was put in the witness-box, and gave his views. He knew nothing of missiles apparently made of tin and copper. He had not been shown the one removed from the dead man's brain. But he did know that one of the guns had been shooting recklessly that day, and (having a prejudice against women in the shooting-field) determined to make that clear.

The coroner pulled him up once or twice, and finally asked if a missile of the size mentioned by the superintendent would fit a sixteen-bore gun.

"No, sir, it wouldna', nor a twenty. But this leddy—"

"That will *do!*" said the coroner. "The lady doesn't come into question in those circumstances, and we can see from the map that the intervening trees would have prevented the charge from her gun reaching No. 3 hide."

He called up the under-keeper, and was obviously anxious to keep the court in session until Brown returned. Then the superintendent did return, and in a deathly silence explained that the missile and a report were on their way from London. Meantime, he had spoken to the gun-maker, and been told the gist of the report itself.

"Well," said the coroner impatiently. "What was it? What did he tell you?"

"He said," Brown replied, looking at some notes he had taken, "that it was part of what is known as a tracer, or rocket cartridge."

I felt an icy finger down my back, and glanced at Vincie, whose face fell. But the jury must have heard of these cartridges, even if they had neither used nor dissected them, for they looked intelligent and knowing at once.

The coroner made a note on his pad. "Apparently you have heard of such cartridges, superintendent?"

"I have, sir; but I never opened one. People don't, as a rule, cut open cartridges. They may have shot all their lives, and never seen one open."

"Quite. But will you explain what the man told you?"

"It's this way, sir; people who don't shoot well may want to know where they make an error. So a cartridge was invented which contained a specially prepared pellet of a combustible nature inside it. When it was fired, the tiny flame in the air showed the track taken by the centre of the charge."

"I see what you mean. Will you tell the jury how this is effected?"

Brown again looked at his notes of the telephone communication.

"Roughly, sir, the thick felt wad, above the powder charge in the base, is pierced before loading, and the combustible pellet fits into it. I assume that this is set afire by the flame from the powder charge, and is then projected with the shot."

"The gun-maker had no doubt that the exhibit sent to him was the remains of such a combustible pellet?"

"He said he recognised it at once, sir. Gun-makers do know how cartridges are loaded."

"You need not explain the obvious to me, Mr. Brown! But you said this pellet was combustible. If that is so, there must be a limit to the time during which it is alight."

"I understand, sir, that is about seventy-five yards."

"Ah, the range? That is important. I shall recall the doctor for a moment."

The doctor was recalled, and denied finding any evidence of burning in the brain tissue. He was unable to say at what range the missile could have been fired, and stood down again. Then a member of the jury got up—naturally the officious farmer.

"May I say a word, sir?"

"If it is to the point, yes."

"I've used tracers, sir, and I know what it says on them?"

"On the cartridges?"

"On the packet, sir."

"Well, let us hear it."

The farmer was now conscious of being an important figure in court, and thrust out his chest imposingly.

"It says, sir, as well as I can remember, that it shouldn't be shot at rabbits or low birds, and not towards people even a long way off."

"Then it has its dangers?"

"Yes, sir, it says it mayn't fire."

"The cartridge mayn't fire?"

"The pellet mayn't catch fire, sir, and if so it goes like a buck-shot. That's a big shot, sir, that you can use for small deer and the like. Proper dangerous, that is, in a shoot."

"Thank you," said the coroner. "That does throw light on the subject. We have now to take into account the possibility that one of the guns engaged in shooting pigeons used a tracer cartridge, that the combustible pellet contained in it did not act as it usually does, but was carried on with, and past, the ordinary charge of small shot, until it reached Hide No. 3, and penetrated the eye-socket of the unfortunate man upon whose body we are sitting."

"Then the leddy—" began Macpherson, getting up.

"If you do not sit down and refrain from interrupting, I must ask you to leave the court!" the coroner snapped. "We are here merely to ascertain the cause of death, and no tendentious statements from any quarter will be admitted."

"I'm sorry, sir."

The coroner shrugged his shoulders. "To continue, it is evident that one of the guns present used a tracer cartridge. That in itself seems to be not uncommon, but we are anxious to settle the matter, so I propose to recall the witnesses. Mr. Mercer!"

Vincie got up, and I know I felt as if someone had struck me.

"Be good enough, Mr. Mercer, to tell the jury if you were in possession of tracer cartridges during the shoot?"

Vincie frowned. "I was, and I wasn't."

Now there really was a sensation, and the coroner threatened to clear the court. When there was silence again, he looked rather severely at my husband.

"What do you mean by that extraordinary statement?"

"I mean, sir," said Vincie quite steadily, "that I found a tracer cartridge in my waistcoat pocket yesterday. I was not aware on the day of the shoot that I had it with me. Further than that, it had not been fired. I showed it to my wife."

CHAPTER IX

THE coroner seemed surprised, but he was not impolite. "May I ask how it came to be there, Mr. Mercer?"

"Certainly, sir. I went some days ago to a shooting-school. I may say that the gun I was using here was one of a pair lent me by Mr. Fonders."

"Do I understand that you are a novice?"

"Yes, certainly. I had a lesson, and fired about a hundred shots at clay pigeons."

"Who supplied the cartridges, may I ask?"

"The school, sir, did that. I paid for a hundred, or whatever number I used, and after I had fired the first batch, the instructor said that he thought I was doing an unusual thing; that is, shooting in front of the birds. Most novices get behind, or below them. He handed me two or three tracer cartridges, and I fired them. After that I hit some of the clays, and I can only assume that I put the third cartridge in my waistcoat pocket, and forgot about it."

"Thank you. I quite understand what happened," the coroner nodded. "So far as you are concerned, the only point we want to clear up is the fact that the cartridge was unfired."

The court calmed down again, but Vincie did not. "I appreciate that," he said.

If he had stopped there, I think the coroner would not have asked him any further questions. But Vincie is painfully honest, and after a pause he added: "Unfortunately, sir, I lost it."

"Lost it. How was that?"

Vincie explained the incident, and the discovery of the cartridge when looking for his lighter, adding that he must have dropped it in the road when we were out walking.

The superintendent approached the coroner, and had a whispered talk with him. I saw what was coming. If Lionel had had an ordinary pellet in the eye, the inquest would have closed by now, but the strange nature of the missile, the length of the range, the intervening trees, not to speak of poor Vincie's loss of the cartridge, stirred up unpleasant doubts in the policeman's mind.

I saw the line of reasoning the coroner would adopt. The experienced Mr. Musson told Vincie afterwards that he had often mislaid cartridges in just the same way. But the coroner would ask himself how it was that the thing had remained safely for days in that pocket, or in a wardrobe, and just happened to tumble out after the accident.

The coroner finished his talk, and looked at us. "I think I shall just take the evidence of the other witnesses again, and then adjourn the court for a week," he remarked. "In the meantime, a search should be made for that cartridge. And I think I should have the actual missile before me when I sit again."

We were aghast, but there it was. Whick made some protest, but the coroner told him he could return to town, if he gave the police his address, and followed by taking him as the next witness.

"I understand," he said, "that you ladies and gentlemen belong to the literary profession, but that none of you could be called a skilled shot. Mr. Mercer has admitted himself a novice. What about you, Mr. Whick?"

Gerald growled that he was not exactly a novice, but had had no practice for a good many years.

"Have you attended a shooting-school?"

Gerald had not admitted that to us, but he reluctantly did so now. "Yes," he said, "I tried to brush up my shooting a bit."

"Did you use tracer cartridges?"

"Yes, but I did not take any away. The instructor doled the cartridges out to me."

"Thank you. Miss Stole, please."

None of the others admitted that they had used tracers, and while Musson remarked with a smile that he was too experienced a shot to need them, Varek and Benjy said they had never even heard of them.

The coroner adjourned the Court for a week, and we all set out for the house.

"Vincie," I said earnestly, as we went ahead of the others, "we have to find that rotten cartridge."

"But I showed it to you, darling," he said.

"I know, but didn't Gerald say that a wife couldn't give evidence about her husband?"

"But why should I have to call on you? I didn't shoot Fonders."

"My dear," I said, "that absurd policeman got it in the neck from the coroner. When anyone gets it in the neck, he immediately looks about for other necks. I'll see some of the staff the moment I get back to the house. The cartridge was more likely to fall out when the waistcoat was taken off than when we were walking, and you were upright."

"But it's absurd, my dear. Why should I kill Lionel?"

"We all loathed him," I said, "and I am not suggesting that they will think you killed him on purpose."

"Great Scott! You saw me shooting. Did I fire a single shot that could have hit him?"

"No. Still, I suppose they take it that a wife wouldn't say you did, even if you had. That was Gerald's contention."

"No, I see. In any case, my dear, I shall insist on it being thrashed out. I don't want it to be thought that I killed Fonders by reckless shooting."

"Quite. Well, I shall inquire in the house."

I saw the butler when we went in and asked him who was responsible for our room. He mentioned one of the housemaids, and I asked could I see her. The girl was intelligent enough, and quite understood what I wanted. She said she did our room, but had not brushed any clothes. She had not been instructed to valet any of the gentlemen.

I described the cartridge to her, and she had not seen that. The luncheon gong went, and I had to leave her, after asking her to tell the other servants about the missing object.

Mr. Jones, Lionel's lawyer, of course sat down with us to that very late lunch. He was very precise and dapper, and not used, I imagine, to the company of authors. He looked quite alarmed when Gerald Whick attacked him about the adjournment.

"It has nothing to do with me, Mr. Whick," he said. "I do not understand it. I have simply come down to look through my client's papers, to see if he left any testamentary dispositions, and so on. I have never shot, but I assume that the coroner sees some point which has eluded me."

"He has, but it's silly," Benjy remarked. "Mercer here had one of those rotten cartridges in his pocket, and didn't fire it. I had a try at a school too, but as I was never asked to fire off any tracers, and didn't know they existed, there was no need for me to say so. I admitted I was a novice. But Penny—that's Mrs. Mercer here—saw the cartridge after the whole thing was over."

The lawyer smiled dryly. "In this case, what the lady said is not evidence, Mr. Doe. Unless, of course, there was a witness, an independent witness."

"I'm independent enough," I said.

"Legally, no, Mrs. Mercer. There is a presumption that a wife will be prejudiced in her husband's favour."

"Anyway, it's rot," Gerald fumed. "If every accident is going to be worked over like this, the law will be more perfunctory than ever."

I could see that Mr. Jones did not like this, or Gerald. The law is not "a hass" in lawyers' eyes. "If things are not done properly, and in order," he snorted, "crimes go unpunished."

"What's that to do with it?" Gerald asked. "Who's talking about crime?"

"Don't get het up about it, Whick," Mr. Musson intervened.

But now Mr. Jones was roused. "You are under a misconception, Mr. Whick," he said coldly. "Every legal investigation has to take into account every human possibility. When a man dies a violent death, there may be the presumption of accident, but that is not automatically assumed."

"But a coroner's court is not a criminal court," said Benjy.

"Quite so," was the reply, "but in a violent death, if any circumstance hints that there has been foul play, it is the duty of the coroner to explore the possibilities. He is not to turn prosecutor, but he has to decide the cause of death, and to that extent may have to uncover acts and motives which may ultimately lead to conviction."

"There are no possible acts here," said Gerald.

"I do not agree with you. As I say, I do not shoot, but I do see that, with masses of trees intervening, it is difficult to say how the pellet reached Mr. Fonders's hide."

"There I disagree with you, Mr. Jones," Musson observed. "I have a good experience of shooting, and am a good shot. A buck-shot, to which this combustible pellet is the equivalent, is much heavier, and would carry farther than a small shot. It could descend at a steep angle, and enter the eye."

"What about Harold at the Battle of Hastings?" said Vanity.

Mr. Jones nodded. He began to see what a contentious crew authors are, and resented what looked like a dead set at his innocent self. "Well, I have nothing to do with the matter."

I tried to soothe him. "Don't mind them, Mr. Jones! They're only trying to suck your legal brains."

"That's all," Vincie said. "I suppose coroners were created for some purpose, and I shan't quarrel with ours."

And he engaged Mr. Jones in a conversation about the humour of the courts, which put the lawyer in a good temper again.

After luncheon, Mr. Jones went to work in Lionel's study. The others decided to take a drive in the Sunbeam, which had been put at our disposal. Incidentally, they were to drop Gerald at the station, as he had only brought a suit-case from town. The rest of us were to leave on the following morning.

Vincie and I went to our room, and made a thorough search for the cartridge, even in drawers and at the bottom of the wardrobe. But we had no luck. We were not frightened then, but were most anxious to clear the matter up.

Jones had called the butler into the study; I presume, to ask where Lionel kept all his papers. He was coming out when we came down again, and looked away when we met him. We heard afterwards that the old fool was quite seriously concerned about his master's fate, and had taken even more seriously than us our authorial quarrels over the dinner-table when we first came down.

It may have been that our backing him at luncheon had made Mr. Jones regard Vincie and myself as less savage than the rest of the tribe. Anyway, he opened the door of the study as we passed, and asked us to come in.

He had been sitting at a table covered with papers, receipts and bills, a box of Lionel's best cigars, and a glass of liqueur brandy. He invited us to sit down, gave Vincie a cigar, and asked him if he was aware that Lionel had made him his executor.

"Never!" said Vincie, quite startled. "So you found a will?"

"I did. He names you as one executor."

"Noli episcopari!" Vincie said at once. "Nothing doing! We were not great friends. I don't mind telling you that. And—"

"Excuse me," Jones interrupted. "You are still executor *de jure*, but may refuse to discharge that office. You were to be paid two hundred pounds on that consideration."

"I don't want 'em!"

"Then you will take steps to relieve yourself of the responsibility. Meantime, you are named executor, and I may tell you that Mr. Fonders's money goes to the Society of Authors."

"Is it a great deal?" I asked.

"It is not a great deal. Mr. Fonders seems to have spent a great deal of money each year."

"There is this place," Vincie said.

"It is heavily mortgaged. But we can go into all that later. I really called you in to ask for your help in a rather delicate matter. I have never met the guests before. I understand that they were not, shall I say, really friendly with their host."

"Dog bites dog in our crowd," I said.

Mr. Jones put on his glasses and looked at me.

"I suppose, of you all, Mr. Whick was Mr. Fonders's closest friend?"

We both laughed, without meaning to. Vincie then shook his head. "I admit that it wouldn't have occurred to me! To be frank, we have an idea that Fonders asked a much smarter party, got no acceptances, and fell back upon us. It may be difficult for you to understand why we came down to stay with a man we did not care for. But there it is. Put it down to the author's lust for new experiences that he can turn into material for a novel."

"You lead me to infer that Mr. Whick was not friendly with Mr. Fonders? Well, Mr. Mercer, as the present executor of the estate, may I ask you to let me have a chat with you for a few minutes alone. Mrs. Mercer will, I am sure, excuse me asking that."

I rose. "Certainly," I said, and went out.

About half an hour later Vincie came to me, where I was reading in the large drawing-room. "I don't like the look of this, darling," he said, with a puzzled look. "Fonders may have thought me honest beyond the average, and made me executor without my consent, but I'm damned if he and Gerald were as thick as that."

"You forget that I haven't heard the degree of thickness," I said.

"Well, that lawyer chap has been going through Lionel's pass-books and bank accounts, and it looks as if there had been some largish payments to Gerald," he said.

"What do you mean by largish?"

"Well, one sum of three hundred, and others less."

I opened my eyes. "I never knew Lionel to give, or lend, anyone money."

"Nor I. He might spend money on an impressive gesture, but not a gift or loan that no one would ever hear of."

"The lawyer doesn't think it was blackmail?" I said.

"He doesn't know what to think, but he dislikes Gerald at first sight, and means to have a talk with him about it. You see, if the sums were loans, they will have to be claimed on behalf of the estate."

CHAPTER X

IT WAS all very extraordinary. We met Whick at other people's houses, but we had never been in his—if he had one. We saw that he was well-dressed, but did not know what his income was. I took it that it was quite a comfortable one, or how could he pay for the publication of his long satirical poems? Why, indeed, pay for their publication when they created some stir? That was easier. Poetry is not a paying proposition, and Gerald was not a great poet; merely a malicious, and occasionally witty, one.

Blackmail is much commoner than most people imagine, but I felt sure that Whick did not make a living in that way.

"We have no idea what his income is," I told the lawyer. "He puts up a show outside, but may pig it at home."

"Well," said Mr. Jones, "he writes, doesn't he?"

Vincie explained. "So, you see," he added, "it must cost him something to pay for the printing of his stuff."

Mr. Jones looked blank for a moment, then he brightened up. "No doubt a literary light like my client would be anxious to foster talent?"

Vincie grinned. "Well, Lionel Fonders wasn't a literary light in the first place. In the second, he would not have fostered anyone he did not care for, and few that he did."

"H'm!" The lawyer was shrewder than we thought. "It just occurred to me that the sums in the pass-book might be in the shape of assistance to Mr. Whick's publishing ventures."

One wall of the study was lined with Lionel's books. I noticed among them copies of four of Gerald's satires. "That can soon be settled," I said, and got up to get them. "Here are four: *Outsiders on Olympus*, *Little Homers*, *Paddy and the Penwipers*, and *The Authoriat*. Full of venom, if you believe me."

Jones took the books in turn, and looked at the dates of publication.

"I suppose these could be printed and published in three months?"

"Or less," Vincie told him. "Do the dates fit?"

Jones compared the dates when the cheques had been paid out, and nodded. "Roughly, they do. I think, after all, Mr. Fonders must have admired Mr. Whick's work. I see one is marked: 'With the regards of the Author.'"

"A common phrase," I replied. "Fonders himself was satirised in the last one, and there was some unpleasantness about it."

Vincie had been plunged in a reverie. He woke up now, and looked at me, his eyes glinting. "I say—I mean to say, I wonder. You know, Penny, that there wasn't a blessed soul Lionel was up against but got it fair and full in the neck in those poems."

I started. "Why, of course. That's what made me wonder why he disliked Gerald. Most people would have loved a man who stuck a pin through their enemies, and put them in a collection of freaks for the public to see."

Mr. Jones rubbed his chin.

"Subsidised Mr. Whick, to get back on people he didn't like?"

"And pretended to be at loggerheads with him," I remarked.

"I am not so sure lately," Vincie said. "I think Lionel was not too fond of him—genuinely, I mean. But there may be a reason for that."

"You mean—?" Mr. Jones asked.

"It was the last volume which touched up Lionel himself," my husband told him. "It came out about a month ago—*Outsiders on Olympus*. We all took 'The Sooty Wretch profits by Dirty Labours, and laughs to see the Smut afflict his neighbours' to refer to Lionel."

"And what about:

'On Vice, not Virtue, long the pander ponders,
And selling sin's the ugly vice of—'?"

Mr. Jones sat up at my quotation. "Really. How very personal and nasty. But surely there was no question—?"

"No," I said, seeing what he meant, "Mr Whick is not a great poet. He was only trying to say that the person satirised made money out of rather mucky books."

"I understand. Well, of course, if Mr. Whick received these payments for services rendered, it is not my business. But I shall have to ask him. I am obliged to you both for helping me."

We rose and went out. Vincie was very thoughtful as we walked upstairs, and still silent when he turned on the tap in the hot-water basin in our room.

"What about it?" I said.

He lathered his hands vigorously. "I believe we've got it, darling. But, if so, there must have been a row before Whick turned on his blessed benefactor. By the way, you'll remember that he was the only one of us who got a formal invitation. May have asked him to come down and explain himself, mayn't he?"

"Yes," I said, "Lionel is dead, but it would be quite like Lionel to pay some 'ruffian stabber' to do the literary assassin for him."

"If there was a row, he has a motive," Vincie said, "but we must be jolly careful not to hint at it, darling. It's largely surmise on our part."

"Quite," I agreed. "More than that, Vincie, it isn't an adequate motive for murdering your host."

When we went down for tea, we found the rest of the party talking excitedly. They had driven in by the farther lodge gate, and noticed that a lot of police were strolling about near Theby Wood.

"I thought that silly inquest finished it," said Addie.

"Why, even that isn't finished," Benjy remarked. "But I say, Vincie, what do you make of it? Why make such a fuss of an accident?"

"The obvious answer is that they may not regard it as such," my husband said seriously. "In fact, that is my answer. Sure they were police."

"I never heard such a thing," Bob Varek blurted out. "Do they take us for a gang of gunmen?"

Mr. Jones had tea by himself in the study. We heard afterwards that he had rung up Gerald Whick who had, it appeared, a bed-sitting-room in the wilds of Highgate, and discovered that Lionel had indeed financed the venomous volumes.

"It's too late, or will be after tea, to go and see what they are up to," Benjy remarked, "but I vote we toddle round to the wood to-morrow to see if they have left any traces."

Musson smiled at me. "I have wired to a gun-maker in town to send up some sixteen-bore and twenty-bore tracer cartridges," he said. "Miss Stole very wisely suggested that the tracers for those sizes, the pellets I mean, must be smaller than those in a twelve-bore."

"I don't know, of course, but you would think so," I replied, giving him a fresh cup of tea. "How clever of you, Addie."

"But doesn't help us poor devils who carried twelves," said Bob.

We had hardly finished tea, when we had a shock—at least, Vincie and I had. The butler came in, and announced that Superintendent Brown would like to see us for a few minutes, in the study.

"But Mr. Jones is there," I said.

"He has gone upstairs, madam."

"You're both for it, good people!" Benjy remarked, as we got up.

"He probably wants private information about one of you," I said.

But it turned out that our role was not a vicarious one. The superintendent greeted us politely, asked us to sit down, and placed a quantity of cartridge-cases on the table.

"You and your wife occupied No. 6 hide, Mr. Mercer?"

"Yes, that's right."

"We found these empty shells buried there, sir."

Vincie forced a laugh. "I interred them, I'm afraid."

"May I ask why?"

"You may. The answer is an admission of human frailty, my dear fellow. I invited a lot of pigeons to come down, and they didn't. So I buried the doings, to avoid the scoffing of my fellow guests."

Brown seemed to see the point. "Ah, an average," he said.

"Yes, did you find any tracer cartridge-cases in the grave?"

"No, sir, I did not."

"And yet that is where you would have found at least one, if your suspicions had been justified."

"I did not suspect you, sir."

"Then why confront me with empty cases? I am several kinds of fool, but not that particular kind. It's your job to nose about, and I have no kick there. Only these cases seem a trifle irrelevant."

"I hope you didn't single us out, superintendent," I said. "Fairness even in exhumation is the correct thing."

He smiled faintly. "We are seeing to that. Thank you. I wonder if I could see Mr. Whick?"

"You can see Miss Stole, Mr. or Miss Doe, Mr. Musson or Mr. Varek," I told him. "Mr. Whick has gone home."

"I don't think I shall trouble the others at present," he said.

"Then you did find a corpse of a cartridge in his cemetery?" Vincie hinted.

"I shan't detain you any longer," Brown returned evasively. "It is largely a matter of form, you understand."

"That man's on to something," I said to my husband when we had left the room. "It's pure footle to think that any of us killed Lionel on purpose, but he thinks it, and that's as bad."

"Yes, I knew that when they adjourned the inquest," Vincie said more seriously than is usual with him. "I wish to Heaven I had forgotten that I had a wife, and taken Vanity with me. She could have given evidence on my behalf and been an enormous help."

"Thank you," I said, laughing. "But don't let it get on your nerves. You had no motive?"

"How do you know, and much more, how would a strange copper know that? Wounded vanity and jealousy make motives, and the world at large is apt to think that small authors like myself are fiendishly jealous of the best-seller—which is often true. Suppose I were a copper in this case; suppose you were one? What would you say to a cartridge of the kind which caused a death, being missing when you investigated? You're Caesar's wife to me, and I may be Caesar to you—"

"Not Julius for a parallel," I said. "At least I hope not."

"No, Julius was not all he might have been. But you take my point. Brown does not know us, and must regard us as quite possible suspects."

"Well?" asked Mr. Musson as we rejoined the party. "Did the man give you the third degree?"

"He was polite, but official," said Vincie, sitting down and lighting a cigarette. "I had to confess that I was a hollow fraud. I must admit it now. The fact is that I thought two pigeons to about thirty cartridges was a pretty poor show. I buried some surplus cases, and Brown went and dug them up with his little spade."

"But that was rather deceitful," said Vanity primly.

Musson roared. "My dear fellow, you are not the first, and won't be the last to do it."

"I didn't," said Addie.

Bob and Benjy also denied hiding the evidences of their shame.

"Very well. You are left crowned with undiminished virtue," Vincie said. "Mr. Musson's too hatefully competent to be asked."

"I could see Mr. Whick doing it," Vanity remarked sourly.

"Then your evidence will be useful," Mr. Musson rallied her.

"I mean that it would be the sort of thing he would do."

"For a precisian in words," I said, "you are not in your best form, Vanity."

We knew that it would come out later, and Vincie admitted that Gerald seemed to have committed a crime similar to his own.

"We thought so," Benjy murmured. "Earlier in the day I myself *saw* him kicking a cartridge under a bit of bracken."

"Grey, with a pattern in blue line?" Bob asked.

"No, it was one of a sort of maroon colour."

"Oh, let's give it a rest," Addie cried. "Do come and play life-pool, and hurry on to-morrow. I shall be awfully glad to leave this horrid house." We went. The butler met us on the way, and looked down his nose. The superintendent came out of the study, where I am sure he had been talking to Mr. Jones. He did not look down his nose, but nodded, and went away at once.

We all played vigorously, till the gong half an hour before dinner told us that we had to run upstairs to dress. The last night at Chustable Manor! The very thought was a relief. Mr. Musson was going up to town, too. He said he was to stay at the Sigma Hotel in Norfolk Street, Strand.

"It would have been the Savoy, if Fonders hadn't died on me," he added mournfully.

Mr. Jones was staying on till he had cleared up matters. None of us were really anxious to attend the funeral, though we all sent wreaths, but with no relatives to arrange things, the lawyer had to undertake it.

Even his momentary *tendresse* for Vincie and me seemed to have gone. He looked grave, attended to his food, and cut coffee afterwards, at least with us. I know he locked himself in the study later, and probably had a cup sent in to him.

When he had gone, Benjy looked at me. He really is a prize donkey at times, though well-meaning.

"This will be in the London papers to-morrow," he said. "I can see that. Vincie will have a headline to himself: 'London Author Loses a Live Cartridge'!"

"Authors are no news," I said.

"No," said Vanity with a little sniff. "Not in the sense that a fourth-rate actor or fifteenth-rate American film artist is news."

"I'm surprised at you calling them artists," Vincie said gravely.

Mr. Musson smiled at us. "Did it ever occur to you what the greatest problem of this age is?" he asked.

"Often," Benjy said. "What's yours?"

"This," said Mr. Musson. "If the American film artists were chosen after all the impossible voices and accents had been weeded out, how did the weeded speak?"

"You're getting away from the point," Benjy said. "Authors by themselves may not be news, but in a bunch, and in an inquest, they are. And Lionel was a best-seller. By the way, Vincie, old man, how did you mislay the cartridge?"

"Easiest thing in the world," Musson said.

Benjy would worry his bone. "No, it was in a waistcoat pocket, and waistcoat pockets are the very devil for retaining things. They lie close to you, and you don't disturb them with your fingers."

Vincie laughed. "Have a heart! Penny and I went for a walk, and I expect it dropped out on the way."

Bob Varek nodded. "It has always struck me," he said, "that the English police have extremely tidy minds. I am ready to bet that the superintendent will be fussy about that cartridge. You see, it's evidence, in a way, and the police are never happy when there's a missing piece in their jigsaw. Not to speak of the coroner. Old-maidish, I call him. He had the gun-maker's report, but he can't rest, or sit, or something, till he has the bally pellet on the desk before him."

"If I were you," Vanity said seriously to Vincie, "I should make a point of speaking to the superintendent to-morrow before you go. I should suggest taking him over the route you followed in your walk. If you negotiated a stile, you may find the thing, and so satisfy his tidy mind."

"Not a bad idea," I said.

Vincie nodded. "Right. Thank you, Vanity. I felt that your brain would be a standby to us all. If the fellow comes, I'll see him."

CHAPTER XI

THE superintendent did come bright and early next morning. He was fussing about that cartridge, and welcomed Vincie's suggestion that they should follow the track we had taken on our walk, and see if they could find it.

I admit that his reasoning about it was sound and justifiable. The butler had gabbled to Mr. Jones about us all, and especially Gerald Whick. Vincie had admitted possessing a tracer. If that tracer could be found undischarged, that would let Vincie out. Not that murder was alleged, of course, but the coroner was quite capable of having a further adjournment if everything was not shipshape at the next sitting.

"You see, sir," Brown said, before he and my husband set off, "whether you did, or did not, fire the cartridge that hit Mr. Fonders, it was an accident. It will be more satisfactory to you if we can show that you did not fire it."

"There's more than that in it," Vincie said. "I told you the cartridge was not fired by me. I can't afford to have an empty tracer case found, can I?"

While he was away, the parcel postman arrived, and with him a package sent (illegally) by the gun-maker to Addie Stole. It contained a packet of five sixteen-bore and a packet of five twenty-bore cartridges of the tracer variety.

Mr. Musson led us to the gun-room, and sat down to dissect the cartridges. He cut the cardboard case off, about an inch from the base, in the neatest possible manner, lifted out two felt wads, and showed us the combustible missiles neatly set in the middle of each.

"Exhibit One is no doubt in the hands of the police," he said. "Here are Exhibits Two and Three. In case we have to go, Mrs.

Mercer, before Brown returns from his quest, I shall hand them to you. Also these filled cases."

"I am sure ours must be smaller," said Addie.

"As you have not seen the other, it is impossible for you to know," Vanity remarked.

"Everything is relative," Musson suggested.

"Look first on this pellet, then on that."

The butler came in, looked at us coldly, and remarked that the cars would be round in a quarter of an hour. From his voice, you could see that their advent would be thoroughly welcome to him.

I took charge of the ammunition, and the others hurried away to get ready for the journey. I buttonholed the butler.

"Do you know of a convenient train for my husband and myself later on?" I asked.

"I will ascertain, madam," he said.

When I said good-bye to the party, and the care drove off I felt very much alone, and rather worried. Mr. Jones was at his papers, and Vincie had not returned. So I took a newspaper which had come, and sat down at the fire in the morning-room to see if Benjy's prophecy had come true.

It had. There was an obituary notice of Lionel, and an account of the inquest, forwarded by a local correspondent and embroidered by a London colleague. There was an informative article on tracer cartridges, and a sub-title mentioning the fact that Vincie (a novelist of some repute) had a tracer in his pocket, but denied having used it. "The cartridge, however, has not been found, and a search is being made for it," the account added. "The accident has caused regret in literary circles, in which Mr. Fonders occupied a position peculiarly his own."

The last statement was a fine mixture of the true and the untrue.

It was nearly lunch-time before Brown and my husband returned. They had not found the cartridge. Mr. Brown went off to interview all the staff about it, and Vincie and I had a talk.

"Considering that we did not lay a paper trail on our walk," I said, "how could you expect to find a bit of cardboard, about two inches long, in four miles or so of country?"

Vincie felt in his waistcoat pocket, and took from it a red twelve-bore cartridge.

"I put this in the same pocket before I left with Brown," he said. "It is still here. I don't think I can have dropped the other, for I had my coat buttoned up."

"Then it must be in the house," I said.

"Not necessarily now," Vincie remarked grimly.

"It couldn't walk out," I said.

"No, but it may have been walked," he returned.

I stared. "You mean someone pinched it?"

"I mean that I think it was there when I came home, and it is not there now. I am not going to let this rest, even if Brown does. And I am not so sure that he will. I was the only one to admit having a tracer."

"You think someone else may have had one?"

Vincie looked troubled. "Between you and me, old thing, I don't like this Whick complication. He raced off to town as soon as he could, he undoubtedly used tracers at the school, and he and Lionel were at loggerheads. And, also between you and me, I don't think Gerald is the world's most high-principled man."

"You think he got the wind up and denied the fact, though he did use one? But do you think he would pinch yours to throw the blame on you?"

"I hope not, but there is this about it. If he was engaged on some funny business with Lionel, and Lionel was shot, he might fear that it would lead to serious trouble. Since I was never subsidised by Lionel to blackguard his enemies in verse (and then have a stab at my patron), it would seem pure accident if I shot Lionel. In other words, as Sir Philip Sidney said: 'His need was greater than mine.' You can see that Mr. Jones is not preju-diced in his favour."

"But how could Gerald, who was not a good shot, shoot Lionel ninety yards away, even with that pellet?"

"His hide was the nearest," Vincie explained. "Ours next; and Benjy next to that. But whereas our hide and the others were separated by more than a hundred yards of wood, Gerald's and Benjy's had an open space of about seventy to eighty yards between them and Lionel in No. 3. It would be easier for a shot to find its way through a few yards of trees than a long bit of wood. Then Benjy had Vanity with him. Vanity is the last word in self-conscious braininess, but inveterately truthful."

I saw that. "I wonder why Gerald and Lionel quarrelled," I said.

"My dear, they were both engaged in a very nasty business. Lionel wouldn't respect his paid assassin, and the assassin wouldn't have much respect for his employer. If I have an idea about it, it is this: Lionel either found the revenge unsatisfying, or too expensive, or thought he had had enough of it. Perhaps he refused to finance further ventures, or Gerald tried to blackmail him over the first volumes. He daren't admit that he paid the fellow to scarify all his acquaintances and rivals. So Gerald may have touched him up in the last satire, and been invited down to hear what Lionel thought of him."

"But it would be perfectly swinish to put it on you," I said.

"Admitted. I'm not out of the wood yet, darling. On my own admission I was the only person to have something which could have killed Lionel. And I can't find it. Think what the *Daily Wash* will make out of it. They won't forget that you hit them in the eye in that novel of yours. The one that had no click and ended in a woolly way."

"I pulled the wool over some eyes," I said. "That's all."

"At any rate, they will see if they can nose out something against us. And we know half a dozen people who will recognise you as 'Penny Pumpernickel'."

"And they all know I don't mind criticism, if it isn't merely spiteful, Vincie," I said. "Of course, if Gerald was paid to do it, I should. But neither of us knew."

The butler had told us that our train left at a quarter past three. So we went to luncheon, and there was Mr. Jones, looking a little more friendly, perhaps because he was anxious to tell us something.

"If you really refuse to act as executor, Mr. Mercer," he began, "will you take steps to get that settled at once?"

"Yes, when I reach town I'll ring up my lawyer about it. Any more about the Whick complication?"

Jones saw that the butler had left the room, and nodded. "I rang him up this morning. He was inclined to be unpleasant about it. But he calmed down when I wanted particulars of the matter. He admits that Mr. Fonders financed his books. He does not admit the reason alleged. He says his poems had begun to sell."

We exchanged glances. "The last may have done," Vincie said. "It always pleases people to read what nasty people others are. And I must say that only growing sales could have encouraged Whick to slang his patron in rhyme."

"But why should he wish to?" said Mr. Jones.

"Lionel was his paymaster," I said, "a situation in private life that often leads to unpleasantness. Not so bad as lending people money, but bad enough."

We were having coffee when that ubiquitous Brown turned up. He accepted a cup, filled a pipe, and regarded us with a professional eye.

"Pity about that cartridge," he said, when I invited him to light up.

"Isn't it?" I agreed mildly. "Makes everything so negative, doesn't it? But that reminds me: Mr. Musson and Miss Stole were anxious to help. They sent for some tracer cartridges. Mr. Musson cut them open, and asked us to hand the results to you."

I got up to fetch them, and he turned to speak to Vincie. When I came back with pellets, wads and filled cartridges, Brown put the pellets on the table, and then examined the cartridge-cases. "H'm," he murmured; "very thoughtful of them."

He was evidently impressed, for he left a half-empty cup, bade us good-bye, and went out hurriedly with his prize.

Mr. Jones lit a cigarette and looked at us doubtfully. Again he glanced at the door, as if to assure himself there was no chance of an eavesdropper. Then he took a letter from his pocket.

"As you are still an executor, Mr. Mercer," he said, "I think you should see this. It came from Mr. Whick."

Vincie took the letter, read it, frowned, and passed it on to me. There were only a few lines.

"DEAR LIONEL,

"Mercer's been chewing the rag about Penny. He heard you were telling everyone who it was, and making some comments. I hear he told Swayne that he had a good mind to go down and give you a kick in the pants. Apparently it's the 'narsty way you said it.' He used to play full-back at Rugger!

"Yours,

"GERALD WHICK."

"Vincie," I said severely, "were you vulgar enough to make that remark? If so, you never told me. I wasn't worried enough to care."

He nodded. "Well, I was—at the time. But"—he turned to Mr. Jones—"I may suggest that a kick in the pants is not quite the same as a pellet in the eye."

"I took it merely to suggest that there was bad blood between you."

"I don't deny it. I hardly know a writing man or woman who hasn't expressed similar views about Lionel's nether garments at one time or another. But this is the first time he's been shot."

"I gathered from the butler that there was a certain amount of hostility displayed to your host."

"The butler is a blather," Vincie remarked, "but fundamentally right, though the fact means nothing from a police point of view. We did wrong to come. In rejecting the two hundred offered with the executorship, I can repay the cost of our entertainment here. But it's too late now for regrets."

Mr. Jones nodded. "I only told you, Mr. Mercer, because I have an idea that the superintendent is not satisfied. These officers, with no experience of murder, are apt to attach too much importance to trivial details. The butler has been talking too much, and I also imagine that he repeated remarks made by Mr. Fonders, prior to your visit, which suggest that he disliked his guests almost as much as they disliked him."

"Probably more, if he paid to have all his rivals slandered," Vincie said, "but who's talking about murder?"

"The word was not mentioned," said our companion cautiously, "but I could see that it was in the man's mind."

"Did it never occur to him," I asked bitterly, "that no one would have known of the tracer cartridge my husband had, if he had not mentioned it at the inquest? All he had to do was to keep quiet, and let it go at that."

"But he had lost the cartridge," Mr. Jones said.

"He showed it to me after the tragedy," I said.

Vincie laughed bitterly. "Mr. Jones is quite right, my dear. You are my wife, and the cartridge is lost. I might have thought it advisable to make the admission, in case someone found the thing."

"But how would they know it was yours?"

"There would be fingerprints," Vincie said. "Well, Mr. Jones, I see what a stink there is going to be about this, and I shall do a bit of investigating myself. As for Brown, he can just get on with it. A man like that is a public danger."

Before we left, Vincie had a word with the butler. "In the ordinary course of events," he said, "I should have left you something. I do not intend to, unless it is a word of advice and caution. You have been talking a bit freely, and unwisely, about us. When this business is settled, if you continue to do so I shall take you into court about it."

The butler looked hurt. "Never, sir, did I—" he began.

"Well, don't do it again," said Vincie. "You are entitled to give evidence about what you know of the case, which is exactly nothing. But when you suggest that I might have a motive for injuring your master, you are becoming libellous."

We did our duty by the other servants, and went off to catch our train. So ended our visit to Chustable Manor, if you can call it an ending, in view of the fact that we had to attend the inquest when it was resumed, and listen to a verdict which said, by inference, that someone might have shot Lionel, though it was uncertain whether the affair was accidental.

We were quite aware by then that the verdict of a coroner's court runs parallel with, but does not collide with, ordinary criminal processes of investigation. In other words, when the coroner's train stops, the police train running alongside it does not necessarily pull up.

I may admit now that we were unjust to Superintendent Brown. He did not himself clear up the case, and he involved some of us in serious trouble in his attempts to do so. But there would have been a serious miscarriage of justice if he had rested content with the verdict of the coroner's jury. The trouble with him was that his mental processes were not very clear, and his methods of investigation crude and clumsy. He had started by thinking that Vincie had shot Lionel by accident, and when the cartridge was not forthcoming, began to wonder if there was not malice as well.

Addie came to see us after the second sitting, and was full of sympathy for us, the more so that the expert consulted by the police had decided that the pellet could not have come from a sixteen-bore cartridge.

"I always prefer a sixteen," she added, with a strange lack of logic, as if her sporting preference had some sort of prevision about it. "I wish you had used one that day," she added to Vincie.

"As I had to depend on Lionel for arms," he remarked, "that hardly comes into it."

Addie is the least atmospheric, the least intuitive, and the least subjective of authors. Her novels are all fierce action, or exotic love-making, in a void. But she is sure that she is a definite "sensitive," with mental antennae that quiver frightfully when anything mysterious is in the wind.

"I do think," she said, "that I knew it would happen from the first. The house was electric, wasn't it? I mean to say, it crackled with hostility. There's something in one of my books like that.

A lot of quiet people are sitting about talking, and one of them suddenly feels there will be murder done. *And it was!*"

CHAPTER XII

"So you think murder was done?" Vincie asked, with a faint smile. "Go on! Who killed Cock Robin?"

"Don't laugh," she said seriously. "I have no idea, but I know we all hated him."

"He made me his executor."

"Sounds so ominous," I murmured.

Addie shook her head. "I know. But if anyone had said that they fired at something low down in Lionel's direction, we could have imagined it an accident. I said I had shot a woodcock, but not in that direction. Still, Lionel was shot."

"Q.E.D.," said Vincie.

She regarded us dreamily. "No one could have been blamed then. You don't think—that is, if you have shot at all—"

"Leaving out the novices," Vincie said.

"—that you can hit a man a long way off, in a wood," Addie continued her sentence, "so you would not mind admitting it."

"It would depend not only on your respect for your oath, but the state of your *amour-propre*," I commented. "One hates to look a careless fool."

* * * * *

Four days after that, Vincie met Mr. Calyn in his club, and asked him up to dinner. Calyn is a fat little man, and very good-natured. He is, or was, Lionel's literary agent. He is not ours, but we get on very well with him.

"Well, our poor friend is gone, Mrs. Mercer," he said when he came. "And I must say that the tragic event has made his English sales spurt a bit. All this publicity, you know."

"For us all," I said. "Even Vincie and I have been treated to nibbles from publishers. But we wish we had stayed away."

"Naturally," he said. "By the way, Fonders never told me he was making you his executor, Mercer."

Vincie scowled. "He never told me, and I am retiring."

"Is that so? I don't blame you. By the way, I heard this morning that the *Daily Wash* is sending down one of its so-called crime experts. The paper isn't satisfied."

"It never is," I remarked. "From the doings of prime ministers, to the price of bacon, it considers a change necessary. How that little squirt the proprietor can believe he knows so much about everything beats me."

"Which may account for the activity at Chustable, Mrs. Mercer. He may be a donkey, but he has long ears, and a longer memory. The trouble is that, while his omniscience is a joke to you, it's a basic belief with him. By the way, did someone say that Fonders had appointed a new American agent?"

"You ought to know," Vincie remarked.

"I? My dear fellow, I never did his U.S.A. business. He took it out of my hands from the first. England, and the Continent, was my job. I think he worked the United States himself.

"I hear you're his executor, Mercer, but don't want to take over," he added. "I bet you'll have trouble first, for you become one on the death, and you are supposed to make an inventory, or something, of his effects, pay debts, and so on. Frankly I know he didn't like you, so that may have been his idea—to give you some worry."

"We're going to have some worry with the newspapers," Vincie said. "I know the *Wash* will be on our trail."

"And the *Splash*," Calyn grinned. "If anything is to be started, the *Wash* will do it; if not, the *Splash* will. They're both experts at scratching an irritable spot till it becomes a sore one, or goes septic."

"They're both septic papers," I remarked, "but I don't see what they can do down there."

Calyn looked at me. "Seen their evening rag? The crime expert has collected the local unemployed, and set them searching for the missing cartridge. The *Splash*'s evening effusion is quite envious. They aren't sending anyone down, but relying on the genius of a consultant to show their readers the solution."

"Who?" Vincie asked.

"Mr. Feenie Solan, the actor-manager," Calyn told us. "They say he is a first-nighter at every criminal trial, so to speak, and we know he took the part of the detective in *Not for Nuts*. He'll larn you!"

Mr. Calyn was quite right. The *Wash* had sent down a man to scour the country for a missing tracer cartridge. It told all about it, but it did not mention the fact (communicated to us later by Mr. Jones) that Macpherson had caught the crime expert leading a flock of searchers through a pheasant covert, and bestowed on the unfortunate man that "kick in the pants" which most people would have applied to his late employer.

That was not enough. The *Splash* sent a man round next day to talk to us. Jones had returned to town, and sent for Vincie. I saw the pressman, and told him that we had nothing to say.

"But you must see the importance of our help, Mrs. Mercer," he said. "We detest the methods of our yellow-press rivals, and especially this offensive business of searching for a cartridge your husband was alleged to have dropped."

"No 'alleged' about it," I said. "He dropped it. Now you drop this! We are not at all concerned in the matter, and if we were, I think we would both rather die clean than survive splashed, or washed, in yellow."

He looked annoyed. "It may be a very serious matter for your husband if the cartridge is not found."

"So you allege," I returned, "but whether the 'alleged' cartridge is found or not, is a matter for ourselves. And please understand that my remarks apply not to you, but to your paper, and all its rivals and circulation-chasers."

The next person to ring up was Mr. Musson. He said cheerfully that he had been harried by the Press, but had done his best to make them see that none of the party had anything to do with the affair. As the man remarks in the song, an arrow had been shot into the air, and come down somewhere. He added that Bob Varek had told him some of the papers had a "down" on us. Fortunately for himself, the gun expert had decided that his twenty-bore could not have fired the pellet.

The crime hounds down at Chustable did not find the cartridge, but did what they were expected to do, in the shape of gathering gossip, half-truths and innuendoes about the shooting-party, its quarrels, jealousies and incompatibilities. It repeated something Macpherson was understood to have remarked to the under-keeper, in the presence of a beater, and, as we received seven copies of the paper from unknown friends, we knew all about it.

Public opinion, which is what newspapers call their own views in many cases, does move the authorities to consideration, and occasionally action. Superintendent Brown was surprised to find that the accident was so speculative, and no doubt wondered if such a temperamental crowd as we had seemed to him might not find motives for murder in what the calm countryman would only consider provocation to profane swearing.

No doubt, too, he received copies of the papers, and underneath all the "allegeds" and other protective adjectives, received the impression that there might be more in the case than met the eye.

His Chief Constable was a reader of the *Wash*, and called him into conference about it. Here was a dead man, and a pellet which could only have come out of one cartridge. None of the shooting-party admitted having fired it. The only admitted specimen was missing. The former possessor of that cartridge was the dead man's executor. But he had said that he was going to renounce probate, and refuse the two hundred pounds contingent on his doing the job. He had said that he disliked the dead man, he had even spoken once of a possible assault. The assumption in the Chief Constable's mind was that an author of whom he had never heard (therefore a beggarly one) must have deeply hated anyone from whose estate he had refused to benefit.

"These fellows have got to live," I could imagine him saying. "I expect two hundred would be a little fortune to him. Shows he's got a conscience of sorts."

It would be, of course, an artistic conscience. He had read novels about writers, and they had seemed very extraordinary fellows, their lives and loves conditioned by ideas and desires which had never entered into his own head. Melodramatic, that's what they were!

The crime man of the *Wash* had a go at him. The Chief Constable did not give anything away. He was a conscientious and high-minded official, even if he was one of the *Wash*'s readers. As with creeds, so you often find a man better than his newspaper; a man quite capable of enjoying the respectable journals if he tried.

In his tribulation, the Chief Constable remembered an old messmate at New Scotland Yard, a Deputy Assistant Commissioner, and called on him in town. He laid the facts before him and was advised that there was matter for investigation. He was also advised by his experienced friend not to pay too much attention to what the papers said.

He remarked that investigation of that kind was rather above the head of his superintendent. The party at Chustable Manor had been an odd one, and the birds at it were not of a type familiar to the officer. They had apparently scrapped among themselves, and with Fonders, and artistic folk like that might fly into a rage about nothing, and poop off a gun into their host's eye before they came to their senses.

His companion had laughed, and remarked that he knew a few of the kind. They were pretty ordinary, and no more likely to burst into murder than a gang of fishmongers.

The gist of this conversation was given to us later by the Chief Constable, when he made the *amende honorable* and admitted that we were more normal than he imagined.

"However, old fellow," the D.A.C. had remarked, "it can do no harm to have the matter ventilated, and if you ask for our help, we can put a very sound man on it, and set your mind at rest."

So, two days before we were sufficiently worked up to apply for legal help, and after dinner one evening, we had a visitor. He sent in his card, and Vincie read it out to me:

"Chief Inspector Voce."

"Has he got the 'Kitten' with him?" I asked.

"Show the inspector in," Vincie said to the maid, and added to me: "The Kitten?"

"Detective-Sergeant Bohm," I said. "Don't you remember, they persecuted poor Mr. Montgomery Brace in the book I saw through the press for him?"

"The 'Cat' and the 'Kitten'. So they did!" said Vincie.

Mr. Voce came in, the same tall, good-looking and cheerful man Brace had encountered. He greeted us most politely, beamed when we gave him a seat and a cigarette, and remarked that the weather still held.

"It looks stormy to me," said Vincie. "Depression advancing from Scotland Yard, eh?"

"Well, no, sir," said our visitor, laughing heartily; "not even a high-pressure system. The fact is that we have been asked to look into this death at Chustable, and calm the fears of our rustic colleagues down there. That's all."

I smiled. "It seems enough. Well, we haven't seen that cartridge since we left Chustable."

Voce nodded gently. "Bless your heart, madam, that cartridge may have nothing to do with it. The fact is that there has been gossip about your relations—I mean Mr. Mercer's relations with the dead man. I am sure he will not mind me asking him to define them."

Vincie laughed. "I didn't like him. He was not my type, though I had known him for years. But I have to meet many people I dislike, and they have to meet me."

"You threatened him, according to a note from another member of the party, sir. I do not attach much importance to that. But I would like to know the reason for it."

Vincie explained about the satire, and Lionel's comments on it. Voce smiled again. "A storm in a tea-cup, sir. I wonder would you explain to me exactly what happened this day of the shoot, and where you were all placed."

Vincie got out his rough sketch, and showed it to him. Voce studied it thoughtfully, and remarked that the trees complicated matters.

"Mr. Doe and Mr. Whick seem to have had the clearest field of fire," he added. "There is one thing the local police do not seem to have worked out—the time when Mr. Fonders was shot. Of course a doctor can't tell to half an hour, but they don't seem to have made a shot at it."

"Well, it was an accident," I said.

He beamed at me. "Yes, of course. Still, we like to be exact. Now Mrs. Mercer, you were with your husband, but not occupied in actually shooting, so your mind would be more free to take in anything that happened."

"I did not see anything happen, except the death of two pigeons."

"Quite. Let me say that your ears would be more free to notice sounds. You were within a hundred yards or so of Mr. Fonders's hide. Did you hear him shooting? If so, roughly, when?"

I was rather puzzled to say. "There was a lot of shooting all round us. It is not so easy to trace shots in a wood. I did hear shots from what I imagine to have been his hide, but they might have come from Mr. Doe's, or Mr. Whick's. I rather lost orientation going to our hide. It's one thing to see the places on paper, and another to walk, as we did, to one horn of the wood, drop some of the guns on the way, and come to our own hide without having emerged from the trees again."

He laughed. "Well put. I can see that. But you could eliminate some reports: the lady had a sixteen-bore, which would make less noise, Mr. Musson had a twenty-bore, which would make less noise still, and he was farther away."

"That sounds common sense," Vincie told him, "but I advise you to go down and make the experiment. We were not listening for, or trying to place shots, or speculating about the degree of loudness of different bores. And this was our first real shoot."

"You would be naturally excited, and on the look-out for birds passing over your ride, sir. I quite understand. And if one of the party"—here he looked at us hopefully—"*did* fire the shot that struck Mr. Fonders, *and* said so, it would obviously be an accident; considering how you were placed, and the trees between, and so on."

"Only that I didn't fire it!" said Vincie. "Go down, Mr. Voce, get the keepers and some beaters with guns, and stage the scene. I'll bet you an even five bob that you won't place one shot out of every five fired. And I can only assure you again that the cartridge was in my waistcoat pocket after the tragedy, and unfired."

Mr. Voce rose. "There you are, sir. I wonder if I might borrow that nice sketch of yours. It's a wonderful help, a thing like that. What information we had from the locals was a bit confused."

"Take it with my blessing," Vincie told him. "I have a copy. Is Sergeant Bohm well?"

Evidently the chief inspector did not read fiction. "Sergeant Bohm, sir? Yes, he's in good form. Did you know him?"

"By repute," said Vincie grimly. "We heard of your joint efforts in the Bryham murder case."

Mr. Voce looked at my husband sharply, bit his lip, then beamed again, said good-bye, and went out.

"The tongue is an unruly organ," I told Vincie. "It does no good trying to score off the police."

CHAPTER XIII

"It was unfortunate," Vincie admitted. "Voce is no fool, even if he fell down over the Bryham case. I know he has had a dozen successes, and a chief inspector in the C.I.D. is a man of parts. He will see one thing that I can see—this case and the Bryham one were hocussed up by gossip. He'll be more careful whom he listens to this time."

"But has he a case at all?" I asked.

"I think so, though whether he carries it farther will be for others to say, my dear. The Director of Public Prosecutions is a wary gentleman. Men have been shot for getting other men's wives lampooned. It was not an uncommon thing long ago. But, after all, none of the other fellows had any stronger motive than

I, or, at least, none that I know of. And someone did hit Lionel in the eye, accidentally or otherwise."

"Do you think it could have been Gerald Whick?" I asked.

"By accident, yes. If he did that, and knew he had fired a tracer, he would get rid of the case. But I can't see him killing Lionel in cold blood, even if they had a row over this nasty lampooning business."

"Would Scotland Yard be called in if it was supposed to be an accidental death?"

Vincie shook his head. "I don't think so. That means that the local man believes it may have been intentional *or* accidental. Eliminate the accident, and you have murder. But I must get help at my end, Penny. I won't put off seeing Robinson any longer."

"Mr. Robinson does not strike me as a clever or sharp man, and that is what you want," I said. "He is a good lawyer, of the office type."

"Well, I'm not going to fee one of those private detective fellows."

"And Mr. Robinson," I went on, "knows nothing whatever about any kind of sport. He told me himself that he never takes exercise."

Vincie smiled. "Perhaps you'd like to take it on?"

"Mr. Power!" I said. "He's in town with a firm now. Mr. Brace seemed much impressed with what he did at Bryham, and there he was up against the 'Cat' and 'Kitten' together."

"That's a brain-wave," Vincie replied at once. "Horace knows him. I am inclined to ring up Horace now, and see if he can put me on to the fellow."

"Do," I said. "I have some proofs to correct and post to-night."

I was still busy with my proofs when Vincie came to tell me that he had been able to speak to Mr. Power himself, at his flat. He was going out to a dance, but promised to call to see us next day.

"I asked him to come to tea," said Vincie. "He seems to have read the account of the inquest, and thinks that there are some elements that justify Voce's suspicions."

"I almost feel as if I know him," I said. "I hope he has some ideas about guns, though. If he thinks a shotgun is like a rifle, he won't be much help."

I must confess that I found Mr. Power as stimulating as Mr. Brace, and as attractive as Miss Alice, the anonymous-letter writer, had done. He was breezy in every sense, but behind his good humour and cheerfulness there was a hint of drive, subtlety, and imagination, a rare combination.

He told me he had read the account of the Bryham case, and modestly disagreed with Brace's estimate of his cleverness.

"Bless you, no, Mrs. Mercer," he laughed.

"You knew Brace well. I only met him shortly before he went abroad. But no one with an eye in his head and a scrap of grey matter behind it could see Brace either besieging another man's wife, or corpsing her husband. Why, the poor chap was half balmy, I think."

"He had a disarming naïveté," said Vincie, passing more hot muffins to Power, who appeared to have a passion for them.

"Symptomatic of the balmy," Power said.

"When a man talks of being sophisticated, it means that he enjoys dirty-doggishness nowadays. The normal lies between him and the naïve! Brace was too much of a fool to be guilty of anything."

"What do you think of *our* trouble?" I asked.

He grinned. "Don't know that it is trouble yet; I only know what two papers think it is. But no one takes them for the news. All I will say, and I hope you will forgive me, Mrs. Mercer, is that if you gave up writing you would be able to attend to the first duty of women—shaking and brushing your husband's clothes."

"He's a nasty Hitlerite, Vincie," I said.

"But so right with it all," Vincie agreed. "That cartridge spoiled me. A further joke, with a nasty edge to it, is the fact that I was not conscious of pinching it when I was at the shooting-school."

"'Satan and the Idle Hands'!" he said. "There's a title for your next novel. But, meantime, I advise you to keep your hands in your pockets when you go shopping with your wife. The magistrates are not as easy birds as they used to be."

"At any rate, I saw the cartridge, and it was unfired," I said.

He nodded. "Good. Now tell me what a tracer is. I don't know a thing about shooting, except the fact that a shotgun has a smooth barrel, and a rifle a rifled, or grooved one."

Vincie explained the tracer, and Power looked regretfully at the hot, empty plate, and selected a cake. "Right," he said. "Extraneous details apart, it is like some brands of baccy—goes farther. You say it burns out in about seventy-five yards?"

"The carton it comes in says it does."

"How far will an ordinary charge go?"

"It might, if the gun was well elevated, go up to a hundred, but with no murderous force," Vincie said.

"There was no sign of burning in the brain tissue, so that suggests the pellet had either been burned out in its flight, or failed to catch fire?"

"I suppose it does. If it caught fire, as you call it, it would obviously have been burned out by the time it reached Lionel Fonders's hide."

"But it would reach it, in any case?"

"That I can't say," Vincie replied. "The metal, or composite metal, of it was found in the brain."

I fetched the cigarettes, gave Power his fourth cup of tea, and said that the gun-maker to whom the pellet had been submitted had discovered its use from the nature of its composition.

"'There was a little man, and he had a little gun, and its bullets were made of lead, lead, lead'!" Power chanted. "Only a nasty changeling got in among them. I shall buy a few of these cartridges, and have a look at the filling. Anything odd about your gun, Mercer?"

"No, it was one of a pair Lionel lent me. Oh, that was rather odd. He had two pairs; lent me one, and another chap another, and then changed about with one he was using himself."

"No jiggery-pokery about getting your fingerprints in that, I suppose?" Power asked.

"I can hardly think Fonders wanted to prove who shot him before he knew he was going to be shot," I said.

"He was like a man foozling at billiards," Vincie replied. "Always thinks he's got the wrong cue."

"I see. So the gun was one he might have used himself. The papers, by the way, have some yarn about a woodcock. Linked up with some beautiful lady, who writes of the sons of the desert, and their white conquests. The lady, fired by the powder-play of the Arabs, shot low at a skimming woodcock, and was only saved from homicide by the fact that she carried a sixteen-bore. What is a sixteen-bore?"

We explained its meaning and relevancy, and Power nodded.

"I am learning. Then there was a joss with a twenty-bore. As these sizes seem to increase in numbers so they grow smaller. I take it that the twenty is still less likely to have inflicted the fatal injury?"

"We don't know much more about it than you," Vincie said, "but the theory I think is that the combustible pellet in the 'sixteen' and 'twenty' cartridge must be smaller than in the twelve-bore. It would crowd the charge of small shot too much, I imagine."

"I'll get the three sizes, Mercer. I like to see things for myself. Meantime, there were seven of you, poked away in wigwams under the palms. You all blazed away when you saw a pigeon fly over. You might see more or less of them than the other chaps, of course, but there was a lot of promiscuous firing, anyway."

"Mr. Voce asked about that," I said.

"Voce would. Had you any idea who fired what shots you did hear? Confusing, I know, but have you any ideas on the subject?"

"Very few," I said, and told him what I had told Voce.

"I understand. But tell me one thing: did you notice that the report of one gun was fainter than the others, and another fainter still?"

Vincie fetched his copy of the sketch of the ground. "Here we are, all nicely numbered. I think I did notice some shots of that kind. I know Miss Stole's gun made a sharper, but fainter, sound, and Mr. Musson's was hardly to be heard."

"Not only because of the smaller charges, but the fact that those two guns on this map," Power said, looking carefully at the sketch, "were at some distance from you. Does anything occur to you, as it does to me, in that connection?"

We both leaned over, and stared earnestly at the map. "No," I said, "I can't see anything in that."

He grinned. "Mightn't Musson's small bore sound about as loud as Miss Stole's gun, if he was in her place, and she in his?"

"Surely," Vincie agreed. "That would level up the sounds. But she was not in his place, and doesn't claim to have been."

"True," said Power, "and there is no reason why she should, unless Musson and she were palling up for some nefarious purpose."

"Even then," said Vincie, "Musson's gun could not have fired that particular pellet, though the range would have been one hundred yards instead of over two hundred. It's a long range for his weapon. Finally, there were hundreds of trees to intercept the missile."

"True again, but the moral remains. By coming nearer than a hundred yards, Mr. Musson's gun might sound more like a twelve-bore, I suppose. According to Mrs. Mercer, you were not as attentive to the sound of other guns as to the chances of letting off your own."

"Yes," Vincie agreed, "I suppose if the twenty was fired two hundred yards away, and then fifty, I might have taken the latter sound for one made by a larger gun."

I had been listening very intently, and ventured to interrupt. "Mr. Power, if you mean that Mr. Musson could have crept up and shot Lionel Fonders, how is the fact to be accounted for that there were no traces of the rest of the shot charge—the leaden pellets, in other words—found either in the face or body, or in the branches of which the hide was built?"

He bowed to me. "Only by the fact that this is the first I heard of it. It seems to move the peripatetic Musson right out of the picture."

"I made inquiries about him all the same," my husband remarked. "He is a wonderful shot, and superciliously refused to come out with us for the pheasant drives. What he did that day was this: he asked for the American contracts of Fonders's former novels, and the correspondence with the United States generally. He worked on those till lunch. The butler brought him in a drink at eleven. His lunch was taken into the study at half-past one, and coffee at two. He only left the house to join us before the pigeon-shooting."

"Perhaps he has a contract to deal with royalties on past works," said Power.

"No, he hasn't. He was to take over from now on."

Power nodded. "I see. But to get back to our real muttons: you went into the hut, and saw Fonders. Where was his gun?"

"Lying up against the side of the shelter."

"Your fingerprints are on the butt of that gun," said Power.

"What? Oh, so they are. He changed with me. Didn't think he had got his favourite."

"Didn't he change again with Bob Varek, when he found he hadn't?" I asked.

"I forget," said Vincie. "Anyway, his gun was leaning up."

"Which showed it wasn't in his hand when he was shot," I said. "It would have fallen with him."

"Not necessarily," said Power. "I mean that it may have been picked up—though that is unlikely—and put that way. It seems out of the question, though, so we'll pass on to his artificial eye."

"How odd that sounds!" I exclaimed.

"It's really no more out of the way than an artificial hand, or leg, Mrs. Mercer. Thinking makes it so, that's all. It was unbroken, you said. Now, he had an eyeglass to cover it. What about the eyeglass?"

"Quite intact," Vincie told him, "but the ground was not hard."

"The pellet would be, my dear fellow. Let me see: the pellet enters the eye-socket. That suggests that it did not strike the artificial eye. You see, there was the eyeglass undamaged too."

"But, Mr. Power," I suggested, "the eyeglass was no help to him. It was just camouflage for company. Why should he wear it when he was sitting by himself, and about to shoot?"

"Oh, he had it on a ribbon or cord?"

"No. He put it in his waistcoat pocket, on the one occasion when I saw him take it off."

"Quite," said Power with a smile, "and I submit that that is what he might have done if he meant to dispense with it for an hour or so."

"But it was removed, and it was not in his waistcoat pocket," Vincie objected.

"Agreed. Had he a shooting-stick?"

"We all had."

"Then what the thing suggests to me is this: for one reason or another, Mr. Fonders decided to remove his artificial eye. He was sitting on his stick. He took off his monocle, and placed it on his lap, since he was in a convenient position to do that. It was while he was polishing the artificial eye, or perhaps attending to some irritable spot on the rim of the socket, that he was shot."

It did seem a very reasonable explanation to me. I could imagine Lionel doing it, then collapsing when the pellet penetrated the brain, and tilting his monocle on to the ground as he fell.

"I think you are right," Vincie said slowly. "That would account for his gun being placed upwards. He would stand it that way before he attended to the other job. That's a brain-wave of yours."

"And it points to murder," said Power, seriously.

We both started violently. "Why should it?" I asked.

"Because," the lawyer said, "Harold and his arrow are irrelevant, if Mr. Fonders was sitting with his artificial eye in his hand."

CHAPTER XIV

WE BEGAN to see how it was that Mr. Power had gained a reputation for mixing the detective with the lawyer. And we got a shock.

"Suppose Mr. Voce knows that too?" I said in a hushed voice.

"It doesn't follow, Mrs. Mercer, and we shan't tell him—yet. He may have spotted a point I have ignored, but I may have got on to something he hasn't seen yet."

"I hope not. Still," Vincie remarked, "I think I have witnesses to prove that Fonders changed guns with me."

"His gun doesn't come into it, Mercer. If the gun-maker says that none of the guns—twelve, sixteen or twenty-bore, could have fired that pellet by itself, and only the twelve-bore could fire it in a tracer cartridge, we may have the presumption of murder, but are not much further on as regards the method, or murderer."

"What will you do next, then?" I asked.

"The first thing is to steep oneself in the technicalities, and not at second-hand, Mrs. Mercer. I'll tootle out to a shooting-school to-morrow, take some lessons, and personally inspect guns of the three calibres. You have done your best to explain, but I have to see the works for myself before I can talk guns with confidence. By the way, what sort of fellow is this Whick? I gather from you that in literary circles the chance of loving your neighbour in the same game is round about minus ten; but why did the insect lampoon Mrs. Mercer here? You think that was due to Mr. Fonders's instructions?"

"I think it may have been," said Vincie. "It wasn't really a very vicious skit: just something about her sucking other people's brains."

"Exactly how?"

"Well, using stories given to her by other people, instead of making up her own."

"It only amused me," I added. "If you write, you are fair game for criticism. Only the swollen-headed object seriously."

"I see. But who is he?"

We exchanged glances, then Vincie spoke. "Funnily enough, we don't really know. You meet a lot of your own kind at literary dinners and lunches, and get to know them, and occasionally you realise that you don't know them at all. We heard from someone that Whick had to pay to get his long satirical poems published, and took it that he was well-to-do. Only the rich, or the ambitious young, pay for publication."

"But he isn't rich?"

"No. Hearing that Fonders financed him, to work off private spites, and also that he has a room in the wilds of Hampstead, I assume that he is pretty poor."

"And he was in a foul temper at your party inspired, apparently, by Fonders?"

"Absolutely," I said, "but I think, Mr. Power, I can tell you something which puts him out of the running as the successful gun-man."

"I shall be glad to hear it."

"Well, my husband and Mr. Varek had to borrow weapons from our host. Whick brought his own gun, and said in the train going down that he had brought it to shoot Lionel Fonders. I remember that we joked about it, and the targets at Bisley. Now, if he went down intending to do that, he would never mention it, or make such a remark."

"A fool wouldn't, Mrs. Mercer. A smart man might, anticipating the way people would react to it; your way, in fact. Then there is the man with the odd name—Varek. What is he—Rod, Pole or Perch?"

"He's a Varek by deed-poll," I said. "He writes gossip articles, and also short stories."

"Prosperous?"

"Seems to do well, though he is not very well known as a writer. But, of course, he may have private means."

"Gossip-writer? I'm going to make a note of that." Power helped himself to another cigarette, and rose. "Well, I have to see counsel for the defence in another case, Mercer, so I will get home and change. I'm dining with my man, and it's the devil of a complicated business, which may keep us busy till the small hours."

When he had gone, we agreed that we had done wisely to retain him. He was not infallible, but he had shown a grasp of the case, and given us fresh confidence.

"So it looks like murder," Vincie said thoughtfully, as the maid came in to clear away. "Thank goodness, it isn't left to us to investigate the affair. On the other hand, we must be prepared to have Voce play the 'Cat and Mouse' act with us. Which is a pity."

Writers are all more or less self-centred, but I think my husband and I did both realise that most of the members of the shooting-party would be as apprehensive and anxious as we were, and with some reason.

"We know you didn't do the dirty deed," I told Vincie that evening after dinner, "which is a consolation of sorts. But Bob Varek, Mr. Musson, and Addie Stole, not to speak of Gerald Whick, were alone at the time of the tragedy. One of them must be feeling pretty bad."

He frowned. "I was thinking about Whick. Do you make anything of Mr. Power's reference to gossip-writers?"

I did, and said so. "The chief grouse against them, my dear, is the fact that some of the Society gossip they get is legitimately gathered, and some is communicated to them by people who have a grudge to work off."

"Well?"

"Some of it," I said, for Vincie seemed unusually dense just then, "is probably libellous and daren't be used."

Vincie grinned. "I've heard that much myself."

"Mr. Power," I suggested, "may have meant that a gossip-writer, being the destined recipient of news which the senders hope to get into the papers, and the libel-conscious writer won't use, may come to hear some very odd things."

"Oh, you mean blackmail. It might have occurred to me if Varek had looked that sort of hound."

"That's why it did not occur to me, until Mr. Power stressed it," I confessed; "and I am afraid Mr. Voce, if he has similar ideas, won't judge Varek by his face. The police daren't."

"That's true, Penny. There are several shady professions, including crooked share-pushing, in which a nice honest face is an asset. But Bob Varek's hide was between Addie's and Musson's, about two hundred yards from Lionel's."

"And it is more usual for a blackmailer to shoot, than be shot, though neither crime seems common," I said.

"As a hypothetical case, we might say that Bob had some nasty bit of information about Lionel."

"That would be easy," I said. "We know he had a bad reputation."

"Well, Varek thinks he sees a bit of stuff coming to him if he can hush it up. He touches Lionel, and is a bit heavy with the retouching. Lionel gets fed, perhaps adjures him to 'tell and be damned,' and hints that he may show Varek up to the paper he is on. Varek decides to wash him out before any more is heard of it."

"It might be," I said, "though all my instincts are against it. Then there is Mr. Musson. We don't know a thing about him, except that he was to be Lionel's agent in the United States. He is a jolly good shot, as he showed us, and—"

"And had trees in the way as we have," Vincie interrupted, "but that was an obstacle to us all, so we'll analyse Musson. He refused to come out with us."

"He was known to be working in the house, and Lionel was alive when Musson joined us before the shooting," I said.

"Granted. But suppose just before we started out Lionel took one of his nasty turns, quarrelled with Musson, and said he'd take his blessed agency elsewhere. Musson was obviously counting on it to get into a profitable business, and thought he had been let down."

"He didn't seem to me a hot-headed type, Vincie. Bit of a bully, if you ask me."

The maid came in suddenly and announced that Mr. Gerald Whick would like to see Mr. Mercer. Vincie remarked that Mr. Whick had better come in and see us both.

"Got the wind up," he murmured to me, "but what does he think I can do for him?"

Fear makes some people timid and servile; others show it by temper and arrogance, and Whick was one of the latter. He greeted us with a face like thunder, and a voice which was surly, to say the least of it, and he accepted a cigarette with the air of taking tribute from a conquered subject. We knew at once that he was trembling in his shoes and felt sure we would think he wasn't.

It was really difficult to get to the bottom of that man. I feel sure even now that he loved poetry, and did attach some importance to his own satires.

I know he had a small talent which, very naturally, he believed to be a large one, and I am still inclined to think that he would never have accepted Lionel's dirty commission if he had not seen in it the only hope of getting his rhymed acidities into print.

"I wanted to have a talk to you alone, Mercer," he said to Vincie.

"So I assumed," Vincie replied. "Sorry you can't. Penny knows as much as I do, so you'll have to put up with her."

"That's right, Gerald," I remarked; "and do try to look bright. We get enough thunder in summer."

He shot a hostile glance at me. "I suppose he told you that the lawyer had been on to me?"

"Yes," I said; "it wasn't pretty hearing, but I forgive you."

He hadn't come to be forgiven, but to bully Vincie, I suppose, into keeping it dark about the subsidised satires. He scowled, and then looked at my husband.

"What right had he to talk over my business with you?"

"Lionel had the bad taste to make me his executor. I believe I am still that, until I can get out legally. So I had a right to know. By the way, was the Penny Pumpernickel incident part of what he paid you for, or your own sweet idea?"

Whick glanced at me, and saw that I was smiling. I think he hated me then. There is nothing more foully provocative than to inject your venom into somebody, only to find that their system has what the doctors call a toleration for it.

"I still think it's true," he snapped. "I bet she does too."

"Partly," I told him. "Only you're entitled to suck brains if you have the owners' permission, as I had. I wasn't hurt by your little jokes. I am disgusted to hear that you were paid to make them. Bravos aren't a bit romantic, outside the Middle Ages."

"Anyway," he growled, "this has got to go no further. I won't have it. A damned detective called on me this morning: fellow called Voce."

"He called on us," said Vincie. "By the way, don't throw your cigarette ash on the carpet. It can't hit back."

Whick's nerves were all to pieces. He coloured up, and threw his cigarette into the fire. "And I suppose you told him all about it," he said.

"Why suppose it?" said Vincie. "Come off your perch, Gerald, and don't try to bully us. And don't get into a state like that, if Voce comes again."

"It would put any man in a temper," Whick said.

"Yours isn't temper, it's sheer funk-effervescing," I said. "Voce has an eye for that sort of thing. The fact is that you know we don't like you any longer, and you hate to come and ask for our help. You want to bully us into giving it."

"You're a liar!" Whick shouted.

Vincie began to laugh. "This is where any nice husband would rise in his wrath and throw you out of the window, Whick. But I don't feel a bit like that. I'm sorry for you. I don't like you, but I am really sorry."

Whick squirmed. He would much rather have been thrown out of the window.

"Well, are you going to keep that private information to yourself?"

"Can't say yet," Vincie told him. "I'll decide the point, not you. Will you have a drink? You need one by the look of you, and a bromo-seltzer at that."

Gerald Whick suddenly collapsed. Not that he burst into tears, or begged my, or our, pardon, or said he would try to do better in future. But if you have ever seen a cat attack a grey squirrel, and come away with a smack on the face, you can imagine Whick at that moment. Crest-fallen—though cats don't have crests—describes him best. He sat and looked at each of us in turn, moving his lips silently, and wondering what he should say next.

Vincie got him a drink, and passed the cigarette-box again. "You see, what I say, or don't say, depends on what the detective asks me. But you aren't going off the deep end like this just because you happened to be at Lionel's rotten party."

"What do you mean?"

"There's something against you that will look ugly, if it's known that there was a rumpus between you and Lionel; or that he asked you down to tell you off, Whick." Vincie said, following a method sometimes adopted by the police of appearing to know more than they do.

"How do you know he did?"

"Well, for one thing you went down to Chustable in the same sort of ragged temper you came here with. You knew there was something unpleasant coining to you, and that's the way you meet difficulties. Bluster, my son; silly bluster that gives you away."

"It was only that I gave him a touch-up in my last," Whick growled very sullenly. "There wasn't anything of a row."

"We've just got your word for it," I said, "but even the 'touch-up' had a genesis, hadn't it? Unless you make a habit of taking-off your patrons as well as your acquaintances."

"I put it in because people might wonder if he was behind my stuff."

"I don't believe it for a minute," said Vincie. "You went for him with a club, not the fool's-bladder you used on Penny here. We're not your friends any longer, but we are not going to take sides. Voce scared you, because there is something you did, or left undone, *or left about*, at Chustable, didn't he?"

Whick's voice denied it, but his scared eyes did not. "No. Look here, Mercer, you think because you had a tracer, everyone else might have had one."

"As we are on the subject of tracers—" Vincie smiled—"had you one?"

"No," said Whick.

"He had!" I cried, as I saw how he looked down. "He had, and he got rid of it. No wife, you see, to show it to. And he was in such a hurry to get back to town."

He did not reply to that, but started another hare. "I was told, Mercer, that the blooming police at Chustable were digging up all round the hides. Do you think they were?"

He was climbing down, and more anxious than angry now. Vincie nodded.

"They turned up a little cartridge cemetery of mine from under the sod. Mercifully, the grey cartridge was not among the shells. Did Voce confront you with one?"

"No, he didn't fi—" Whick began, and stopped aghast.

"A word of four letters, beginning with 'fi' and signifying 'discover'," I murmured. "Perhaps they won't come on it now."

"I fired the damn' thing at a pigeon," he said bluntly, "but I did not go back to town to get rid of it. Don't you see, none of us knew it was a tracer-pellet until that came out at the inquest."

"One man did," I said.

"How could he?"

"The man who fired it," I said. "He knew."

"Not if it was an accident," Vincie remarked.

"No," I said, "not if it was an accident."

Gerald Whick looked relieved again. "I went round later, and there was no sign of it."

"Hard luck," Vincie murmured.

"There was no sign of yours either, Mercer."

"I've mentioned mine in the proper quarter," Vincie replied. "We're not in the same boat on that point. By the way, it may help you if I say that the very agreeable detective suggested something. If any of us did fire the shot by accident, and says so, it may let him out."

"I didn't fire it near Lionel. And what rot that is! How can I say I did, if I denied it at the inquest?"

"And still deny it?" I asked.

"Of course I do, in the sense that I did not fire a tracer near Lionel."

Vincie got up. "Well, Whick, we can't bear your burdens as well as our own, and your emotions have a way of being weary-ing to others. Drink up, and clear out, there's a good fellow. I've given you the tip about Voce. If you can't take his advice, the next thing is to see who has your missing cartridge. There, I am afraid, we can't help."

"I wonder," said Vincie dreamily, when Gerald Whick had gone out, "if the silly ass thinks I pinched his tracer, and am holding it up on him for purposes of my own? The one I showed you, I mean?"

"I wouldn't put it past him," I said. "Someone has got it."

CHAPTER XV

THERE was something rather unpleasant to us both in the thought that someone—be it keeper, beater, police, or a fellow guest—might be the present possessor of our tracer cartridge as well as Gerald Whick's.

We imagined that it could not be the police. Their methods, if not admired by the criminal, are fairly straightforward, and I think Voce would have told us if he had made that discovery. For the shell could only be identified by fingerprints on it, and even Voce dare not at the moment ask us for them.

"Mercifully, darling," I said, as we got ready for bed that night, "I think, even if some nasty person had pouched the two, Gerald's plight is worse than ours."

"In what way, Penny?"

"Ours was unfired."

Vincie regarded me with concern. "Sure all this upset hasn't dulled the bright brain, sweet-heart?"

"Should have," I said, "but hasn't got into my stream of consciousness yet."

"Why, you little juggins!" began my husband.

"Now then!" I cried. "You're not Gerald."

"You ineffable donkey," he said. "The gentleman who may hope to harry our nerves, and play on our fears later, has only to get a gun, put on gloves, and fire the beastly thing off. Then he has a nice, empty shell with my fingerprints on it."

"I am sorry. I overlooked that, Vincie."

He grinned. "Well, conscious virtue and innocence will help me to sleep to-night. Let others worry! And let me help you unship that garment, or dawn will surely break over Lethe before we get to sleep."

Nothing, I am happy to say, worries me when I work. The piano can play, the radio expound, the larks sing, or the rooks have a conference in caws, but I concentrate. I worked all the next morning. Vincie went out to see his publisher, and lunched with him. I began again at two, turned on a radio-gramophone selection from *Rigoletto*, and plunged once more into one of those placid descriptions into which dramatic music from the operas perversely urges me.

At three, Addie Stole was announced. You can work when there is a noise, or a running melody, or even a conversation to be overheard, but I defy anyone to work with Addie in the room.

She asked me to finish the bit I was doing, and I tried. She walked round and round the room, like a caged gazelle out of one of her desert stories, looking at all the books and pictures, and treading so softly when she passed my desk that the break in the tramp had the quality of a passing bell.

"What a nosy person you are, Addie!" I said, slamming the lid of my desk down, and turning round. "You've seen those pictures forty times. Has the detective been biting you?"

He had. She sat down, and began to puff nervously at a cigarette, while she told me about a nasty, slinking kind of policeman, who had come and asked her a hundred and one questions. Somehow, I gathered that this must be Voce's satellite, Sergeant Bohm, the "Kitten" of Mr. Power's naming. Did that suggest that Addie was one of the minor suspects?

"He wanted to know all about the dinner the night before," she said. "My dear, that too cherubic butler! You would think we had fought all the time with chicken-bones, or hurling plates at one another. I admitted that Mr. Whick was flying out at Mr. Fonders, and then at Mr. Musson. I didn't mind saying that he seemed to have a down—a purely literary down—on Miss Doe. But I explained that she was a reviewer."

"Who would more suitably figure as a corpse among authors," I said. "Well, even that doesn't hurt you."

"It puts me off my work," Addie complained. "I had just pulled myself together, and was going to start an entirely new line, when he came."

"Deserting the desert?" I asked, astonished.

"Well, it's getting worked out," she said. "These young girls nowadays would be more likely to give a sheikh a knock in the eye than let him carry them off."

"Well, we can't expect to work through the beginnings of a murder case, can we?" I asked. "At any rate, not so well as usual."

She jumped. "Murder? Who said it was?"

"No one but me, so far." I evaded her as well as I could, if not as truthfully. "But all you have to do is to stick to your story. You had no tracer, and no gun to take one of the right size— the pellet, I mean. So, wherever you fired, you didn't make a bull's—I mean to say, you're out of it."

She looked relieved. "Do you know, I have been wondering about Mr. Musson. He seemed to be bossing Mr. Fonders about, didn't he?"

I reflected. "I thought he treated him as rather a joke, which is uncommon, or was uncommon, to his face."

"That's what I mean. If they hadn't—I mean to say, if I hadn't known it was Mr. Fonders, I should have said Mr. Musson was our host."

"And rude to a guest?" I murmured. "Lionel Fonders told me next day that Mr. Musson had a good heart."

"Mightn't he mean that as an insult? Some people do?"

Addie was improving. I nodded. "Did you tell the sergeant about that?"

"Yes, I did. He wanted to know, and I think one is supposed to be truthful if one gives evidence don't you?"

"Oh, one is obviously *supposed* to. What did Mr. Bohm say?"

"He told me they had a new witness, one of the beaters who was working home round the far end of the wood, having got his money and given the keeper the slip. It seems that Mr. Musson saw him, and called him over to ask what he meant by disturbing the pigeons coming in. You know Mr. Musson was just outside the wood."

"Yes, I know. But what is the point?"

"Well, no one could place the shots very well, but comparing what we all said, the detective believes that Mr. Fonders only fired at the beginning; I mean, soon after we all settled in. And it was about a quarter of an hour after that that Mr. Musson black-guarded the man for walking outside the wood, and alarming the pigeons coming in."

"I see. Didn't fit the times. In any case, he was farthest away. And of course, if a beater was crossing the open, that would spoil it."

Addie got up. "I am glad I came. I don't feel so worried now. I may be able to work."

I understood, and felt sympathetic. "Quite. It's the suspense that is trying. Almost worse than waiting for Partridge's great detective novel to come out. But don't run round saying that you suspect Mr. Musson, my dear. He may have you up for criminal libel."

When Vincie came home for tea, he was interested to hear about Addie's visit. He said he had had a bad lunch, but good news. His publisher thought all the publicity was helpful, and wanted something quick. And he had asked if I had anything ready.

"Next to being shot, which only brings posthumous, not prof-itable fame," Vincie remarked, "it is a good thing apparently to be mixed up in a tragedy. I would sooner have stayed out, but as it is, so it is. Capitalise the publicity while it's fresh, is his advice."

"A horrid necessity, till one is as rich as Lionel was," I admitted.

"Addie's view-point," he reflected, "is better than I expected from her. I don't suggest that all novelists of the sheikh tradition have no brains, but that is what I gathered about her from the only novel I read. I do agree that Musson treated Lionel rather airily. Now if Lionel had been a sucking author, an agent might do that. But best-sellers are rare birds, and he was at the top as far as sales went, the kind of proposition which would be taken to lunch at the Ritz, or Claridge's, according to taste."

"Do shooting hosts allow their guests to arrange things for them?" I asked.

"Not usually, I imagine, but of course, Lionel was fresh to it. Like a new M.F.H., who has to get used to cursing his field, and may go slow at first."

"There is another thing," I said. "Gerald Whick, as we both know, gets in a bate when he has the wind up, and is most likely to be offensive when he is afraid of you."

"Like a nervous dog," Vincie murmured.

"Yes, I agree there. He snaps when he's worried or anxious."

"He snapped Mr. Musson as well as Lionel," I said.

"So he did. Also Vanity."

"I leave that out," I remarked. "Vanity simply waits for his satires to come out, to parse and analyse them, and correct the scansion. I don't count bite for bite as an indication of anything out of the way. But he bit Musson at the first time of asking."

"Are you suggesting that he was afraid of Musson?"

"He may have been. Musson's our mystery man. We don't know a thing about him, and we don't know what Lionel may have told him."

"I may be dull," said Vincie, "but I do not really think that Mr. Musson's attitude to Lionel suggested a desire to murder. More like that of an aggressive, domineering fellow."

I agreed that it might be so. "At the same time," I went on, "the whole business in nine out of ten cases would have looked like the semi-yearly shooting accident. If it was murder, it was meant to look like an accident, followed by the usual casual inquest and an innocuous funeral."

Vincie keeps a file of *The Times* in his study. He went for it now, and fossicked for ten minutes, letting his second cup of tea get cold, before he stopped.

"I knew there was an accident at Ferdisley Park two months ago," he said. "Branker's cousin was there, and told me. No, I don't want any more tea. I'll have a cigarette, and see just how casual it was."

"Absolutely casual," he said, when I had finished my tea. "A lot of stockbroking merchants out, and one shot by a gun with the beaters. Doctor just said he had been shot in the head, everyone said the party was a normal one, the coroner commented on the care everyone should exercise at a shoot, and that was that. You see, it's taken for granted that a shoot would be the silliest occasion on which you could determine if you wished to commit murder. So public, and so difficult to get your man in the right place with a shotgun."

"In this case there was the tracer pellet."

"Quite so, but tracers are occasionally used at shoots, or there would not be the cautionary notices on the cartons they're packed in. That thought would occur to the murderer, if there was one. He might take it that the doctor who did the autopsy would just dismiss the missile found in the brain as part of a charge. Our man even confessed that he did not understand guns. It was just bad luck for someone that the thing was sent to a gun-maker to examine."

I could not get any further along those lines. "What suggests a murderer to me most of all," I said, "is the fact that your cartridge vanished. I am convinced that it didn't fall out during our walk. If it fell out in the house, someone must have seen it. I doubt if a carpet-sweeper would pick one up. If it did, it would make a noise. Then the girl sweeping should have seen it, or heard it."

Yes. An odd coincidence, too, if Whick's also vanished.

"Yes, it sounded like an afterthought," he agreed. "I must say that I was convinced by his denial that he had one at the inquest. He didn't sound as if he were lying."

Vincie put the file of papers away, and came back. "We'll tell Power about that, and about Musson too. Oh, blow! There's the bell!"

Visitors! It turned out to be Benjy and Vanity Doe. They both looked worried, and Benjy had hardly sat down before he said they had seen Inspector Voce, who wanted to know all about Mr. Musson.

"We informed him of course that the man was a stranger to us," Vanity cut in. "Why should he want to know?"

"He's asking each of us about the others," Vincie hinted. "Sort of suspects' symposium, don't you know! We authors are usually more anxious to talk about ourselves than about others, but not when there is any responsibility to be shifted."

"I admit that Mr. Musson impressed me rather favourably, after I had grown accustomed to his manner," Vanity commented.

"He didn't me!" Benjy shot out. "Throwing his weight about, I thought. Still, it would be tripe to say he had a chance to shoot Lionel."

"And his motive is more than obscure," Vanity added. "Definitely so."

"Most motives are," Vincie said rather testily, for Vanity is somewhat irritating in her sententiousness. "None of us, otherwise, could have any for murdering Lionel."

I had made the bloomer before with Addie. Now Vincie followed suit, and the Does started simultaneously. Apparently Vanity must have had the idea in her mind, but had not adopted it as a possible fact, so that his blunt mention of murder was as good as new to her.

"Did the detective think it was murder?" Benjy asked in an awed tone.

"I can't say what he thought, my dear chap. He didn't say so," Vincie replied lamely. "I suppose I shouldn't either."

"I certainly think it unwise," Vanity remarked severely; "very unwise."

"But you remarked on motives, and Benjy talked about a chance to shoot Lionel," I objected.

"If that meant anything—"

"It must," Vanity interrupted me, "have been a voice from the subconscious."

"Then your subconsciousness isn't as definite as you," Vincie said.

CHAPTER XVI

WE WERE almost surprised, after the brother and sister had left us, to receive no visit from Mr. Musson and Bob Varek. Consorting with us for mutual help and comfort appeared to be the order of the day.

But Mr. Power came in after dinner, and sat down to talk matters over with us.

"I have seen Voce," he told us. "I thought it wiser not to split ourselves up into opposing camps. He can make things nasty, and he has sufficient respect for me, after the Bryham case, not to, if he believes I can give him a tip."

"I think you were wise," Vincie said. "We aren't at odds with the law, whatever the inspector may think."

Power lit up, and produced his copy of Vincie's sketch, which he laid on the table near his cup of coffee. "There's one ray of hope in this dirty business," he began. "So far, there is no suggestion that the murderer, our hypothetical friend, has tried to throw the blame on anyone else."

"The missing cartridges," said I, and told him about Gerald Whick.

He shook his head. "I think not. I believe the fellow was up to some nasty work with Fonders, and it may be that he decided, or thinks of deciding, to admit that he fired a tracer, and accidentally shot Fonders. That would settle the business, and he would hope there would be no publicity thrown on his subsidy from the dead man."

"I don't see that," Vincie objected. "If he said he shot Lionel Fonders, he would have to prove it was an accident."

Power swallowed the rest of his coffee, and smiled. "Not a bit of it! The lie of the land does that for him. Look at this sketch of yours and you will see."

We stared at the map, concentrating on Gerald's position in the second tiny wood which was part of Little Covert. He went on:

"I haven't visited Theby Wood yet. I am going down, with Voce's permission, to-morrow. But to get within close enough range to shoot Mr. Fonders, he would have to cross the open between the two coverts."

"What about all the trees?" I asked.

"Quite possibly that open space was absolutely hidden from all the hides by trees," he said, "but it may have been visible from Hides 4 and 5, from Hide 1, and under distant observation by any beaters who were scaring the pigeons out of woods to the south-east of Little Covert."

"But they may not have seen him," I said.

Power nodded. "No. But there is a human tendency you have to take into account. You see the idea in the new United States political slogan 'Don't Get Out In Front!' If you were going to commit a murder, would you walk out into the open, and hope that all observers were blacked out by the trees? Wasn't it Shake-speare who made some suggestion about the fears of those who thought each bush contained an officer?"

We saw that, of course. A murderer simply could not afford to take a chance of being seen crossing the open with a gun. It wasn't even that he knew where every possible spectator was placed, for there were the beaters and keepers to be reckoned with.

"But most of us would come under observation from another hide," I said at last.

"You were in the best position to corpse the man," he replied airily. "Voce sees that, and so do I."

"But would I have admitted the cartridge in court?" Vincie asked.

"You might, if you thought the police had it," he said, "just in case they had picked it up. But let us get down to tin-tacks. Mr. Musson was busy till tea-time, and then came down to show you how to shoot. Coming from the house in the morning, to drive pheasants, most of you had your guns and cartridge-bags carried by the beaters, or keepers. Did you know that Macpher-son, the head, was not aware that Musson was staying at home? He brought Musson's gun with him."

"Who told you that?" Vincie asked.

"Musson had it under his arm when I first saw him arrive."

"Can't help that. Macpherson left it in the keeper's hut, near where you had tea, and fetched it out, with the requisite ammunition, when he heard from his master that Musson would join the pigeon-shoot. Voce told me so."

"I wasn't looking for Macpherson," Vincie said, "so that may be true. But what does it suggest?"

"It suggests that Macpherson had a chance to see what cartridges the man had, Mercer. Voce thought that was important, if negative, evidence."

"I suppose Musson had waistcoat pockets," Vincie murmured.

Mr. Power grinned. "We can't settle the case on the mere evidence of this map, but the lay-out does suggest to me that you, Mr. Varek and Mr. Musson would have had the easiest job," he said. "There may be two minds with but a single thought, though that thought would hardly be murder. Besides, you're my clients, and it would be rude to go back on you."

"But Varek and Musson were the two farthest away," I cried.

"Quite"—he nodded again—"but you will be the first to admit that those two are nearest the northern rim of the wood, that is to say, farthest removed, and better concealed, than any of the others, not only from the view of the guns, but of the beaters to the south."

"I have an idea of your theory," Vincie said. "It involves one of them creeping eastwards along the northern fringe of the wood, then turning south and so getting within shooting distance of Lionel."

"It does."

"But just before, and just after, he turned south," I objected, "he would be within about thirty yards of our hide."

"At the inquest, Mrs. Mercer, your husband made rather a feature of the fact that your hide faced south, so that the back would be more or less presented to the danger-point. The murderer would, of course, walk softly."

"You remember there was a horn-shaped rhododendron cover north-east of us," I told Vincie.

"So there was," he agreed. "Anyone could have stolen along behind us, if we hadn't heard him."

Power lit another cigarette. "He would take care that you didn't. Besides, each of you was expected to keep his place, for safety's sake, and you would not associate any soft rustling sounds with one of the guns."

"There were plenty of sounds like that from time to time," I said. "What with rabbits, and pheasants which had escaped the beaters."

"And the fact that you were busy watching for pigeons, and shooting pretty often. People working in cities don't think of traffic noises, unless they are asked to, and then they hear them all right."

"Just a moment," Vincie said slowly. "Miss Stole had been rather reckless, and shot a bird across Benjy Doe. But she hadn't actually done that for Mr. Varek. When we went into the wood, however, he seemed very windy, and insisted on reconnoitring between her hide and his before he settled in."

Power studied the map again. "That is to say between No. 4 and No. 5. And moving in the general direction of No. 3?"

"Yes."

"Well, that's an idea, and I'm glad you told me. It might have been to see if he could be observed from her stand, or to help in laying out his own route through the wood."

"There is a ride cut in the wood between them, about here." Vincie put his finger on the map. "We didn't see her hide when we crossed it."

"He may have noted that, gone up the ride northwards to the edge of the wood, and turned east, and so round behind your stand."

As we only nodded agreement, he went on: "I have made some inquiries about Varek, and hear he isn't liked. For one thing, though there may be nothing in it, there was talk about his change of name. Then a journalist who is a pal of mine says he isn't very particular how he collects his gossip. I've known of blackmailers with better public characters than that."

"Possibly," I admitted, "but Mr. Varek has been much less disturbed than Mr. Whick since the thing happened."

"Talking of Whick," said Power, putting the map away in his pocket, "I got a sharp clerk of mine to make some inquiries about these great satirical poems of his. The opinion in the trade was that about seven hundred and fifty copies of the first poem would be as much as were printed, and some were remaindered off."

"Poetry does not sell well, Mr. Power," I said.

"Does poetry cost any more than prose to print?" he asked.

"I never wrote any," I said. "Very little more, if any, and even these long satires wouldn't contain nearly as many words as a book—a novel."

"So that the cost of composition, setting-up, printing, binding, and paper, would not be as large?"

"Of course not," Vincie cried. "I remember the first one wasn't much advertised, either. Advertising does cost money, but the nasty quips and sneers in the book would be circulated among friends of the victims. A book of the kind gets advertised gratis in that way."

"All I am suggesting is this," Power said. "Do you think the sums Fonders paid Whick represented the cost of publication only?"

"If I remember the figures the lawyer showed me," Vincie said, "I think the sums were grossly excessive. But, of course, that may have been partly payment for services rendered—lampooning, in short."

"Let me have a large sheet or two of paper," Power said; and added while Vincie was fetching it: "Voce isn't going to be content with what you thought was a thorough search of the wood. By the time he and his helpers have done with it, they'll have a census of dropped feathers. I know his methods."

He produced his fountain-pen when Vincie supplied the paper. "I am going to draw up a motive chart, with your help," he said. "You see, I am observant, but I don't know the characters of your friends."

"Do we?" I asked. "Dubious. Still, we'll try to help."

"Hide No. 1," he said. "The male and female Does."

"Male Doe," Vincie said solemnly. "Normal human dislike of being patronised, combined with the decent man's aversion from a writer of sticky books."

"Female Doe," I said, as Power finished writing that down. "Temperamental dislike of the type, and the work, knowledge that Fonders made game of her kind, and was blistering about spinsters. Justifiable dislike of a man who made a lot of money with such cheap stuff."

"Hide No. 2," Power said. "Mr. Whick?"

"Had been apparently paid by Fonders to lampoon, evidently had a quarrel with him, and gave him a dose of his own medicine," Vincie remarked. "I should say he was envious of anyone who did well as an author, and he certainly is afraid about something, though that can't count as a motive."

"Fear is a motive," Power said, "but now for Hide No. 4—Mr. Varek?"

"That beats me," I said. "Unless you allow speculation, and admit the possibility of blackmail, I can only think of dislike."

Power wrote that down. "Hide No. 5—Miss Stole?"

I tried again. "She never met him until that visit, so I can't suggest any animus against him. She did hint to me that Fonders had tried to be a bit amorous, which she resented. But I don't think that was a strong enough motive for murder. In fact, I can't see Addie killing anyone."

"Visibility in motives is usually bad," said Mr. Power. "Hide No. 6—Mr. and Mrs. Mercer?" I left that to Vincie. He reflected for a moment. "Put down justifiable enmity for us both; on same grounds as Miss Vanity Doe, and resentment on the part of male Mercer at some remarks, made by Fonders, with regard to the lampoon on his wife."

"Also dislike of Fonders's manner, books, ostentation, weight-throwing, and general conduct," I said.

"On the part of female Mercer," Vincie went on, "dislike of Fonders for his 'Old Turk' ideas about women, sort of feminist inferiority complex."

"Hide No. 7," said our recorder. "Mr. Musson?"

"Man unknown, motives speculative," Vincie remarked. "Tendency to bully Fonders, or treat him with irreverence. May be sign of dislike, whip hand, or just arising out of the fact that Musson has a talent for organisation, and a desire to organise everyone and everything. He practically took command of the arrangements for the shoot."

Power read what he had written. "Rotten lot of motives for murder, if we were dealing with ordinary human beings," he commented, "but we're considering a crowd of authors."

"Not *prime donne*," I said.

"Next door to, Mrs. Mercer. Imagine a lawyer paying someone to write nasty verses about a rival firm! Books are all a bit out of drawing, you know. No matter how realistic they try to be, they aren't like life. You have, as the stage folk say, to get it across."

I laughed. "I admit that. No person really talks all the time as he does in a book. You see, the characters have to be a little larger than life to be taken for life. The art consists in making unreal talk, and unreal action, seem natural and inevitable to the reader."

"Quite. Then the motives of the characters as a rule take so much explaining that, away from the book, you realise how shaped and adapted they are to fit your scheme, Mrs. Mercer. Now I believe that you can never be quite detached from anything you do constantly. I have a feeling that, in time, an author himself tends to be moved by fictional motives, at which he laughs, but by which he is occasionally moved. I don't think a party of ordinary business men would have regarded Fonders as you people did."

"No," Vincie said, "I agree there, but it isn't a parallel. A lot of more or less unsuccessful business men might feel envious and ratty if they were invited to a party by a pompous and ostentatious millionaire."

"Right. Seems sense. Still, you got worked up and irritable over something that was really trivial. Some of you live on your nerves, and it is nerves that are behind many murders. Analyse the figures as regards murder in this country. There aren't many, but only a very small proportion is committed for gain. Drink, jealousy and fear are behind most of them. That is why the police task is difficult here. They can't handle the amateur as easily as the professional. Amateurs aren't in their records. What puzzles me in this case is not the motive really, but the technique. I think most of you could have committed murder in haste. But how the dickens that tracer pellet got into Fonders's brain, I don't know."

"Did you go to the shooting-school?" I asked.

"I did. I spent two guineas and a good many hours there. I fired tracers at all kinds of marks, including some dead rabbits, and I tried guns of the three calibres for half an hour. I had them all taken down and explained to me. Was your gun an ejector, Mercer?"

"It was," Vincie said. "Most of the guns used were."

"You had a tracer cartridge in your pocket, and did not know it was there. You abstracted it absent-mindedly at the shooting-school, before you went down. Could you say that you did not take two?"

"I couldn't remember," Vincie said. "I do not think so."

"You had two barrels to load," Power said. "You instinctively take two cartridges, one for the right and one for the left. You didn't remember taking one, so you wouldn't remember taking two, if the action was so automatic, unconscious, as that. Do you look at the cartridge as you put it in the breech?"

"No, not if you are watching for birds to come over. But wait a moment. Tracers have a sort of milled edge that the others haven't got. I should have felt that by touch as I loaded."

"Possible, but doubtful. You would, if you had it in your mind that you must not fire one. But I noticed at the school that one soon loads and fires away without conscious thought."

"In any case," I said, rather indignantly, "what can it matter?"

He smiled, and got up. "I was only wondering if Voce and his merry men might find an empty tracer shell that the ejector had shot into the branches of your hide."

"But *my* ejector didn't!"

Power corrected himself. "Which would appear to Voce," he said, "to have been ejected into the framework of the hide."

Vincie looked shocked. "You mean that someone might try to wish the crime on me?"

"Not necessarily a murder. But if the cartridge was found in your hide it would prove accident, or seem to. You would not be expected to murder Fonders, carry the shell back, and place it in your hide. And, of course, if it is held to be accident after all, you won't suffer."

"Even then, why put it on me?"

"Because you were too officious, my dear man, with your unnecessary honesty at the inquest. Never try to be more honest than others. It leads to trouble!"

CHAPTER XVII

THOUGH I had not liked to tell Vincie, for fear of upsetting him, I had been somewhat worried by the idea that his missing cartridge had not walked off by itself. If not, it had been kept as a threat or a warning, or a bit of camouflage to screen the real villain. To be useful in the latter role, it would have to be fired before it could be presented.

Mr. Power, I think, believed that we were victims of circumstances in that matter, and argued on my lines. The only place where the empty shell would be a shield for murder would be in a hide which might possibly lie within tracer-pellet reach of Lionel Fonders. That meant ours, Whick's, Addie's or Benjy's.

I admit that I would not have minded the thing being officially judged an accident. We were in for a lot of trouble otherwise, and were anxious to avoid that. But we were not anxious to have it said that Vincie *had* fired towards Fonders's stand, and told lies at the inquest about it. My lying in support would be excused as wifely duty, but I have enough real faults to be blamed for, without chastisement on account of these I haven't committed.

If Vincie is at home in the mornings, we both work with our pens. We were silently scribbling at ten next day when Inspector Voce was announced.

"Nice to see you again," Vincie said, as the man sat down.

"And sorry to disturb you both, sir, I am sure," Voce replied cheerfully. "I can come another time, if you wish."

"No," I told him. "We would much rather have a nice chat with you than earn our bread and butter. And we're naturally curious to hear if you have made any discoveries."

"Thank you, madam," he said. "I have made one discovery. In fact, that is what I came about this morning."

"The missing cartridge," Vincie grinned.

"Yes, indeed, sir. How did you know that?"

"And how do you know it is mine?"

"I don't, sir, but perhaps you will help me to identify it."

He produced a cartridge-case from a box, and I was horrified to see that it was empty.

"And I can't do it better, can I, than by pressing my fingers on it?" my husband said, as the thing was held out to him. "Or mayn't I?"

Voce laughed. "That's for you to say, sir."

Vincie nodded. "Then I will. Allow me."

He took the cartridge by the base, as if removing it from his pocket before loading.

"I presume, Mr. Voce, that it has been finger-printed before you came along with it. There were prints on it, eh?"

"There were, sir."

"Now, if you have the necessary doodahs with you," Vincie went on, "why not let us have a demonstration?"

Voce had an attaché-case with him. "Why not, sir? Saves time, and may perhaps prevent me from troubling you again."

"Though, of course," said Vincie, with the utmost gravity, "the comparison of the prints will be only relatively valuable at this stage. They will have to be photographed and enlarged before you can talk definitely."

"That is so, sir," remarked our friend, as he drew on a pair of rubber gloves and sprayed the case with powder. "This, however, will bring out the main lines, and if you and your good lady care to listen I can tell you something of the method. It isn't an official secret, but you may not know how it is done."

"We should love to," I said. "I am sure, Mr. Voce, that criminals must love your frank ways."

"Not that I've noticed, madam," he laughed again, and blew off the surplus powder. "Take my glass, and have a look for yourself."

We might be the victims of his well-known cat-and-mouse act, or merely having a taste of the man's natural bonhomie. I took the magnifying glass, and he withdrew a large envelope from his pocket, and a sheet of paper from that, with photographs of fingerprints.

"Those to the right were on the base of the cartridge, sir," he said, pointing two out to Vincie.

"Now these are what are called ridges."

I put down the glass while he gave his little lecture, and was rather grimly fascinated when he showed us that a certain loop or whorl was repeated on the cartridge-case where Vincie had held it last.

"The presumption being," he said, in his most light-hearted tones, "that this cartridge was the one you missed, sir."

Vincie pursed his lips, and nodded. "I think you are right. At least, I have never doubted the fact that no two prints are alike."

Voce seemed pleased. "Very good, sir. You are quite correct there. And from the position of the prints, with the impressions of the index and second finger-tips, and a partial impression of the thumb, it could be assumed that you were in the act of loading when you gripped it. The fingertips, as you see, point away from the base of the shell."

"Most interesting," Vincie murmured, though I guessed that he was a bit disturbed. "What are those other prints on your sheet?"

"They were also found on the case, sir."

"But round the case, not pointing away from the base, I imagine?"

"You're a good observer. They suggested that the cartridge was picked up by the middle."

"That was when I fished it up from my waistcoat pocket," Vincie suggested. "You see, a solitary cartridge is like some of our heavyweight prize-fighters. When you put it in your pocket, it adopts the prone position."

Voce's smile was as good to see as sunlight on a wintry day. "You're very helpful, sir. That seems to explain the position of the second set. The first are not so easily explained."

I thought that was dismally true, but Vincie did not appear dismayed.

"I learned more from your demonstration of the method of taking a print than I would have done from reading about it," he replied. "I always feel that modern educational methods nowadays shine because they are practical. Children are shown things."

He took the cartridge by the base. "When I purloined a cartridge for the first time in my life, I was at the shooting-school. If I remember rightly—and you can check that with the gun-fitter who accompanied me—the cartridges were in cartons, in fives, standing up with the milled bases only visible. I don't say that I made those prints then. But as I must thoughtlessly have transferred the thing to my waistcoat pocket, and forgotten it, I assume I did it like this."

He threw back his jacket, and pushed the cartridge into his waistcoat pocket base upwards.

"Damn the thing. It will fall down!" he said.

"Take it out to show me now, Vincie," I said. He fished it out by the middle, and smiled.

"But your wife did not take it from you when you showed it to her, sir?"

"No. I exhibited and returned it. By the way, where did you find this pretty little thing?"

"It was found by Sergeant Bohm, my assistant, in a bit of furze which had been used to build up your hide, sir."

"Apparently ejected by the gun?"

"That was our conclusion after some experiments."

"And didn't you take me for a cursed fool not to remove it?"

Voce was positively sugary now. "Why, sir, if Mr. Fonders was shot by accident, it wouldn't occur to you. You wouldn't know he was dead."

"My dear Voce," Vincie said, "we love your frankness. Give us a chance to admire it. Scotland Yard is too busy to waste powder—even fingerprint powder—on cases of accident in the country. There is a presumption that Fonders was murdered. Let's save time by talking with that in view. I lost that cartridge; the local police did not find it. I think it must have been fired by someone wearing gloves, and then ejected into the furze, or placed there by hand."

Not even the most prejudiced assert that men of the C.I.D. only give consideration to one side of a question. Mr. Voce nodded.

"That occurred to us, of course. It may be the explanation. I admit that what you have said a few moments ago does help me."

"That pleases me immensely," Vincie said. "I should, in fact, love to expound further. Our visit to Chustable was cut short. Neither my wife nor myself saw enough of the place. How would it be if we ran down, stayed at the manor—I am not sure if I am not still an executor—and acted as assistants, unpaid?"

"An admirable idea, sir. I am afraid we shall have to have all the party down later. I could perhaps telephone to the butler, who is still in charge, and make arrangements. Could you go down to-day?"

He had turned to me, knowing that it is the woman who dictates household arrangements. I nodded.

"Of course. I'll look up the trains."

Chief Inspector Voce made a charming gesture. "I have the use of a fast car, madam, if you and your husband do not mind travelling down with me after lunch."

"That will suit us very well," I said. "We're not often taken for a ride. Of course, you must get back to have that last set of prints photographed."

"At two, then, madam"—he bowed, and collected his things—"I shall call here for you."

"I don't like this, Vincie," I said when Voce had gone.

"Well, it doesn't give me any pleasure," he replied, "but the lor's the lor, my dear. And I think at bottom Voce is honest, if oily. I could see that my demonstration did impress him. Meanwhile, if you get on with your work, I'll telephone a message to Power's office."

I lit a cigarette, and went on. Like Addie, and many other authors, I make a change sometimes, and now I was doing a story about a little place in the country. It was not a story of the country-man's country, but of a rustic Eden where every prospect pleased, and man was excessively sentimental over the earthiness of the earth and the unusual miracle of the flowers emerging from it. Sermons burgeoned from stones, books from the running brooks, and I hoped that it would create a profitable nostalgia in the minds of my town readers. The difficulty lay in not being too realistic, but I am ideally fitted for that, since my knowledge of the real country is practically nil.

Power had already gone down to Chustable, but Vincie's message would be relayed on from the office. At two, with a brace of suit-cases, we were called for by Mr. Voce, in a nice car, with a driver in plain clothes.

"But how considerate," Vincie remarked, with a gesture at the driver's stolid back. "Plain vans provided for quick removals."

Then Mr. Voce became a man, a householder and a husband. He told us about his own first house, and how he had furnished it. He was a handy man, it seemed, and could even do a bit of cooking if the wife was ill. The car was not five miles from London before he and I were exchanging recipes, and he had explained to Vincie, who loved the flesh, but loathed the smell, of onions, how to peel them inodorously.

But he was most lyrical, I think, about a date pudding he had evolved. His wife had never heard of such a thing. He made it, and converted her. Then there was a furniture polish of his own creation, a quick way to deal with pancakes, and a trick I had never heard of for dividing the whites from the yokes of eggs.

He was busy jotting down one of my favourite recipes in his official note-book, when Vincie asked him if he had ever made a mistake.

"Yes, sir, many," he said. "You ask your lawyer, Mr. Power, about one of them. A nice gentleman, but sharp as a razor. You couldn't have done better than get him."

"I hear he went down to Chustable this morning," I said.

"I heard he was coming, madam, so we shall have a nice friendly little gathering."

"Something to look forward to," Vincie murmured. "By the way, about that convenient furze bush, or branch. Left it *in situ*, I hope?"

"Exactly, sir. Bohm is an experienced man. And photographs have been carefully taken of all the hides, from several angles. You have something in your mind about that?"

"Vaguely, yes. I may expand the idea when we get down."

"You shall have every opportunity to demonstrate it. Even Scotland Yard doesn't give us a new pair of eyes, or prevent that occasional tired feeling in them."

"Optically, we all have a blind spot," Vincie said cheerfully. "If that man of yours pushes on a bit we might come in for a late tea."

Mr. Power had got our message and was waiting for the car before the porch when we drove up.

"Tea is just ready," he announced, and I could see the pompous shape of the butler in the hall behind. "Had a good run?"

"Topping," said Vincie. "Mr. Voce is an ideal host."

"He generally entertains vicariously," said Power, with a grin. "Don't you, Voce?"

CHAPTER XVIII

CHIEF Inspector Voce betrayed an admirable modesty, refusing to share our tea, on the grounds that he had better consult one of the men who was, apparently, taking the house to pieces.

"And you may wish to talk privately to your lawyer," he added, with a sly smile at Power.

The butler, now become a wooden image since we had been brought down in a police car, did not actually spy about for the gyves on our wrists, but he brought in tea as if it were an early morning breakfast in the condemned cell.

"Old fool's got the wind up," Power commented, as the door closed. "He talked so much and at large that he is not sure if he is in for official commendation, or an action for criminal libel. But he did favour us with hot cakes, I see. Do you mind letting me know how you stand with the 'Cat'?"

Vincie told him what he had said to Voce, and Power nodded. "Good man! You have your wits about you. Firing practice is fixed for ten to-morrow, I hear. I have been allowed a squint at the photographs of the furze in which that tracer shell conveniently, or inconveniently, stuck, and see a hope there."

"What is it?" I asked eagerly.

"To be inconspicuous it had to be almost out of sight, or appearing to blend with the furze, Mrs. Mercer. If you had fired it, you would not be such an ass as to put it there by hand. It should not be too hard to prove that the ejector couldn't project it where it was found. That is the line I advise your husband to take to-morrow. Ask to fire, eject empty shells in the hide, and note their fall."

Vincie nodded, and took a hot cake. "I meant to, when I heard where the thing was found. I expect you noticed, Power, that the ejector is only a spring arrangement, just strong enough to throw the empty cases out, not to force them into tight places?"

"Absolutely. The shooting-school bloke said if the paper of the case was even damp the ejector might fail to throw it out. But hot cakes are too good to be wasted. Let's postpone the discussion till tea is over."

Mr. Power has a healthy appetite, but tea was over at last, the wooden image answered a ring and removed the tea things, and Power pulled up an occasional table, cleared some knick-knacks from it, and drew up chairs for us.

"Voce is being nice this time," he said, as we all lit up. "Our last encounter bred a mutual respect which is bearing fruit. So

I can tell you that the fragments of pellet, first submitted to an ordinary gunsmith, are now going to Hendon police laboratory."

"To be really scientifically treated?" I asked.

"Yes. Meanwhile, as the result of my own hard firing the other day, I have a few exhibits of my own."

He took a box with a glass lid from his pocket, which we afterwards learned was a receptacle for holding dry-flies for fishing. It was divided up into about ten tiny compartments.

He opened the lid, and indicated a division containing an unfired pellet from a tracer cartridge.

"This is the article, untouched, virgin and un-fired," he said. "I will go through the series. As none of the attendants volunteered to help me reconstruct the actual murder—too fond of their eyes, perhaps—I tried rabbits—dead, of course. Now, No. 2 pellet was fired into a bunny at thirty yards. It had ignited in the gun. No. 3 was a pellet specially loaded for me by the school, which would not ignite. Over fifty yards I missed the bunnies' bodies every time, so an expert marksman took over, and produced pellets 4, 5, 6 and 7, alternately igniting and non-igniting."

We examined his exhibits through a glass he handed us.

"Nos. 8 and 9," he went on, "were hit by the expert at the extreme ranges of eighty and ninety yards. After that, even he could not hit the bunny. He agreed that a shot, fired without aim at a high angle, might do what was done, but that was not proof."

"Have these helped?" I asked bluntly.

"I cannot be sure yet. I think so. Let us go back to the earlier series number. Being no shot, even at a standing mark, I did not often centre the charge of shot on the object. But every time I hit the rabbit with a tracer pellet, there were sundry lead pellets in the rabbit as well."

"The theory," Vincie remarked dryly, "is that at extreme range the pellet will carry on after the lead shot has lost its momentum and fallen. So close range firing would not help."

Power smiled oddly. "H'm. You never know. Voce at least believes in the minutest examination. Believe it or not, he has had men examining the trees as if they were woodpeckers looking for ants under the bark. The Othello who coloured himself black all over is nothing to a C.I.D. man when it comes to thoroughness. So far they have eighteen pellets, all knocked out of shape, garnered from tree-trunks and branches."

He replaced his precious box, and laughed.

"Do you still believe that Mr. Whick had a tracer that day?"

I nodded. "He said so. Couldn't he have fired it, and stuck it in the furze?"

"Not without your husband's collaboration, Mrs. Mercer, unless he stole into the room when Mercer was asleep, and gently pressed his finger-tips over the case."

"You mean that he decided to take Voce's tip that we handed on to him, and admit accident, rather than have the association with Fonders investigated?" Vincie said.

"It looks like that to me. As I told you, if he fired it, it was an accidental shot that killed Fonders. Voce and Bohm agree with me that it is so. Whick was up to something, and does not want it known. When I get on to that something, I will begin to see light."

"Still leaving the manner of, and the reason for, the murder unsolved?"

"Neither, I hope, though I can give no guarantees," he told me. "You see we have now two human factors: Mr. Whick, who tells a lie to prevent an exposure; and the gentleman unknown who shot Mr. Fonders. Were they connected in any way? Was that connection irrelevant to the murder? Did Whick know that Fonders was murdered, or going to be murdered? Why was that extreme measure necessary? Pretty questions I have to ask myself."

"And a lovely chance you have of getting them answered," Vincie murmured. "How can you dig into the private lives of at least seven people?"

"Voce will do that," Power returned. "It's his job, and he has the men and the apparatus. He can get answers; and I can't, except by favour and kindness on the part of those I question."

"The clever brain behind the murder will have covered up," I said.

"The clever brain behind the murder spent all his ingenuity in faking an accident. If he had thought there was the slightest chance of the thing being investigated as homicide by the C.I.D., he would have let Mr. Fonders live. It was a gift for him, or so he thought."

"I wonder if you are trying to link up Whick and Bob Varek?" I said.

"Gossip arm-in-arm with lampoons," he said quizzically. "I wonder. Sorry, both of you, but the whole party will be down here again one day, and I don't want any of them to see the Mercer family studying them for outward signs of the inward homicidal tendency. You would try to be discreet, I know, but murderers develop cats' whiskers."

"Will Voce dine here?" I asked.

"I am going to ask him to," he said. "Why?"

"I was wondering if he will investigate Mr. Musson's past," I said. "After all, the man came from the United States, and might find it easier to cover up than we do here."

"Voce has already communicated with the American police, Mrs. Mercer. It was the first thing he did. Quite rightly too."

"Then I hope he will question the old donkey of a butler about Musson's relations with Lionel Fonders before we came down," Vincie said. "He may have overheard something."

Power grinned. "The butler is in a delicate condition. He blabbed and talked most unwisely at first; then he began to wonder."

"We told him what we thought," I remarked.

"Quite. Well, the result is that he is afraid to open his mouth. Between fear of being sued for libel, or drawn by the police into making some statement he can't substantiate, he is positively dithering."

"Petrified, rather than dithering, by his appearance," I suggested. "It seems to take him that way. I think he was always a bit of a ramrod; now he's gone all statuary. At any rate, he just says 'Yes' or 'No' to everything."

"Voce can make him talk, surely?"

"No. The police here can't force some answers. If they try, the defending counsel will comment on it, and it makes a bad impression on judges. Men are released every month over legal technicalities. That is what is called British justice, even if it isn't always equitable."

Mr. Voce did join us at dinner, but not officially. After one or two attempts to get him to use his mouth for other uses than the reception of food and drink, we settled down to discuss the London theatre. It seemed that Voce and his wife were addicts. They rarely went to the cinema. I gathered that Voce disliked seeing detectives who wore their hats in the houses they had to visit.

When we had had our coffee, he woke up, and suggested a visit to the gun-room. We retired there, and he opened some of the glass-fronted cabinets and smilingly removed two guns, which he laid on the table.

"The gun on the right, Mr. Mercer," he said, "is the one you used during the pigeon-shoot."

"Are you sure? I used two guns that day."

Voce nodded genially. "Even a pair of guns are not exactly the same," he said. "Not to a scientific eye. As you see, the striker hits the cap at the base of the cartridge, and makes an indentation. This pair has been tested, and there is a fractional difference in the depth and size of the indentation on a cap. One corresponds to the marks made on the caps of the empty cases you left at your stand in the wood."

"Very neat indeed," Vincie said. "I'm no scientist, so I'll accept that."

Power leaned forward with a grin. "Well, Mr. Voce, did the mark on the cap of the tracer you showed us correspond with that also made by the gun Mercer used?"

Voce smiled rather unwillingly. "It did."

"So, if it can be proved that that was not fired during the actual pigeon-shooting, it might have been fired during the drives earlier in the day?"

"That stands to reason, sir."

"It could not have been fired by Mr. Varek, since he was not using this gun at pigeon?" Voce shook his head. "You are trying to prove, sir, that someone must have planted that case in the furze to confuse the issue. It was either fired at the drives, at the pigeon-shoot, or later."

"Or—later?" I asked.

"Certainly. That is the *real* alternative, madam. If someone planted that case, to put the blame on your husband, he had first to get his print on it. We will assume that he placed a loaded cartridge in the waistcoat pocket of your husband's jacket. If it was fired at pheasants, or at the pigeon-shoot, it would be an empty case your husband showed you the next day."

"No, it was loaded," I said. "Do go on."

"That sounds reasonable," Vincie remarked.

"I must say I never knew that I had taken a tracer from the school. I only assumed I must have done. Still, if that is so, my fingerprints—"

"Just a moment," I cried. "There were two sets of prints, weren't there, inspector?"

He looked at me approvingly. "Just two."

"There, Vincie," I said. "You picked the cartridge from your pocket, holding it by the middle. When you put it back, you stuck it into your pocket base up. I did see that."

"Good," Power intervened. "You held it in the same position as if you were loading it into the gun. That would account for the second print."

"Taking all that for granted," Voce remarked, "it would suggest that the cartridge was afterwards abstracted from your pocket, and fired from this gun. But I think the guns were examined here, and I have not heard that any shots were fired after the tragedy."

Vincie and I looked discomfited, but Power was not at all impressed. "I gather that the guns were only cursorily looked at," he said, "since there was nothing to suggest murder at the time, and when the tracer pellet was discovered the police knew any twelve-bore could have fired it without leaving any mark on the gun-barrel itself."

"But we did not hear any shot fired," I said. "I think we should have done if it had been fired here; and no one would dare to go out with a gun under his arm to fire it off."

Mr. Power raised his eyebrows. "Come, Mrs. Mercer, you mustn't act as witness for the prosecution. May I see the cartridge-case, Voce?"

"Certainly, sir." Voce produced it.

"And another empty case, if you have one?" The inspector took out another, one of those found in our hide. I could see that he was puzzled. Power lit a fresh cigarette, took a glass from his pocket and sat down on the edge of the table to look carefully at each case in turn. Presently he passed both back to the inspector.

"I think, if I were you, I would send that case to your police laboratory, Voce. Have a good look at the inside of the case—both cases, and tell me if you notice any difference."

Voce certainly took pains. It was some time before he put down the exhibits, and looked hard at Power. "Yes, there is a difference. I am not sufficiently familiar with shotgun cartridges to say what, but there is some."

"I have steeped myself in shotguns and their ammunition," Power laughed, "giving up my night's rest to everything technical I could read about them."

"And?" said Voce, rather impatiently.

"And the result is an idea, my dear fellow. The cardboard of the case, which is turned in over the top wad, shows signs of nicks, as if it had been tampered with. I may be quite wrong, but if you people will go back to the drawing-room, I shall conduct an experiment which may throw light on the question."

"I should like to see it," Voce returned dryly, "but with all respect for you, Mr. Power, I can't leave my exhibits for you to play about with."

"Nobody axed you, sir," Power laughed. "I don't even require the same gun. You can take that away if you like. All I want is one gun, and one common or garden cartridge."

"Very well, sir. I think there is ammunition in one of these drawers. Ah, here we are. As Mr. Varek's gun could not have fired the tracer, you can use that. I shall take away the other."

We must have looked a strange trio as we went off to the drawing-room, Voce carrying a gun under his arm.

"Varek is out of it?" I said as we went.

"It seems likely," Mr. Voce replied.

During the next quarter of an hour we discovered that, while you can confide things to the police, they do not reciprocate. Voce wanted to know what we thought, but kept his own thoughts and conclusions strictly to himself. At the end of that time he was beginning to look impatient, and glance at the door. A few minutes later Mr. Power came in, carrying an empty cartridge-case. "Is this the one you gave me?" he asked.

The suspicious Voce had evidently made a private mark on it before he handed it to our lawyer.

"Yes," he said, with a rather startled air, as he examined the thing. "You fired this?"

"I did."

We started now, too. "We never heard a sound," Vincie protested. "Where were you?"

"Where you left me, in the gun-room."

"How did you work it, sir?" Voce asked, more practically.

CHAPTER XIX

"No, I am not a conjuror," Power remarked, "but it occurred to me that there are two explosions when a gun is fired. The cap explodes first, and ignites the powder, but both are so closely synchronised that they appear to merge in one."

"It is the powder that makes the big noise," Voce said slowly.

"Yes. The marks on what is called the 'turn-over,' above the top wad, made me wonder if the thing had been opened from the top, the charge extracted, and so on. I managed to do the same with your cartridge, and loaded the gun with the powder-less shell. When I pulled the trigger, you did not hear the sound because it was so faint. Fulminate is powerful stuff, but there is very little of it in the cap."

"Bravo!" cried Voce, and his voice did sound quite sincere. "It struck me when I compared the cases first that one was more blackened and rougher inside than the other; caused by the loaded one sending the shot charge out with great velocity, I suppose."

"That was my idea," Power replied. "It proves that someone could have fired the cartridge with Mercer's prints on it, without making a row in the house. And, of course, Mercer dressed for dinner. His shooting-suit would be in his bedroom."

We overwhelmed him with congratulations, and Voce also added his approval. "The laboratory would, of course, have seen that," he said, "but you are one up on me. It is rather important, too. I'll have them give it a careful examination, and make a covering note of what you say."

"Mr. Gerald Whick," Power remarked presently, "didn't leave a similar empty case near his stand, did he, Voce?"

"No. And he can't produce one. Except for his word, there is no proof that he fired a tracer."

"Then why admit it?"

The inspector looked blank; it was a studied blankness. "Ah, that's a question I can't answer, sir. But, of course, I shall go into it."

Power nodded. "When you admit some small fault you did not commit, it may be to burke inquiry into a larger one that you did commit."

"It isn't so easy to burke police inquiries, sir, as that suggests," Voce replied dryly. "We are taking every factor into consideration."

"And I shall take myself off to bed," Power grinned. "I read myself blind on small print last night. Why are technical articles so often put in the most blinding type?"

Voce only smiled for answer, and presently Vincie and I retired, and settled down to sleep in a much more serene frame of mind. We had begun to see that a clever detective may be a good advocate, as well as a pertinacious and dangerous pursuer.

Voce did not breakfast with us, but at ten we were all back in our hide in Theby Wood, Vincie carrying the gun, and Voce a bagful of ammunition. Sergeant Bohm was also there, looking big and heavy, but ever so innocent and mild.

Voce indicated the furze which was part of the camouflage of the hide, and an empty case was placed in it in the position indicated in the police photographs.

"You must not put yourself in any abnormal attitudes," Voce told my husband, "but stand close enough for your gun to eject shells into, or near, that furze. No; not so close in, please! You were looking for, or firing at, pigeons overhead."

Vincie began to fire. Ten, twenty, thirty, fifty shots, and not one spent cartridge stuck in the furze. Some bounced off it, some went over, or under it. Voce took a turn, moving back, altering his position, but with no better luck.

"I did not hope for much luck after your experiment last night, Mr. Power," he admitted, "but I think we can be sure now that the shell was placed in the furze, not ejected into it."

"Cheers!" I cried. "Now to find out the kind gentleman who wished the accident on us."

Voce did not reply. He consulted with Bohm and left for the house with the guns and ammunition. When we got back, we found he and the sergeant had left in the fast police car.

Power smiled. "I find a cup of tea stimulating at this time of day." He rang a bell, and added: "Give the wooden cherub something to do, too!"

The butler came in, and received the order.

"And lunch a little later: perhaps a little after half-past one," Power told him.

"Very good, sir."

"In addition"—Power wagged his finger—"keep your head. No one is going to bite you!

"Now," he said to us, "tea, and then another walk through the enchanted wood, eh? I have asked Macpherson to join us at noon. He is to take the part of Miss Stole. You, Mrs. Mercer, can be Mr. Varek, Mr. Mercer is Mr. Musson, I am Mr. Mercer."

I laughed. "What about players for Whick and the two Does?"

"We will leave them on their wooded islands," he said. "This is just my rehearsal to get the lie of the land. You can be sure that the producer, Mr. Voce, will have a dress rehearsal when he wants one."

The tea was good on that dry wintry morning, and when we had lit cigarettes afterwards, and walked across the crisping grass, there was a cheerful glow about us. The police had momentarily suspended their operations in Theby Wood. We met Macpherson at the corner, and Power saluted him.

"Well, Mr. Macpherson, we are a party of six guns, a skeleton battalion, as it turns out. We began by dropping Mr. and Miss Doe at their hide, then Mr. Whick at his—both isolated coverts. You must imagine that Mr. Fonders is with us, and we are now five guns and a lady spectator. You were not with the party during the later afternoon, I understand, so Mr. Mercer—Musson for the occasion—will demonstrate what happened. Mr. Musson!"

Vincie stepped out, and the rest of us followed him to Addie Stole's stand, No. 5. He paused there.

"Here Mr. Varek saw that he would be next to Miss Stole," Vincie explained. "He was rather nervous about it."

"And nae sae wrang, either," muttered Macpherson.

"At any rate, he insisted on studying the natural obstacles between her gun and his brains, afterwards going on to his hide. We followed him, leaving Miss Stole—that seems to mean you to-day, Mr. Macpherson—at the place she was to occupy for the shoot."

"Once we are out of sight, you can go," Power told the keeper, "and thank you for your help."

Our stage party now consisted of myself, Vincie, and Mr. Power; Lionel Fonders being what one might call with us in the spirit. I was dropped at Bob Varek's hide, and before going on Power put a question.

"Mr. Fonders is still with us. What did he do next?"

"He sent Mr. Musson—sent me," said Vincie, "to the hide on the horn of the wood, and then he told you—that is, me—to come across to your—"

"Let us be ourselves in speech, if not in character," Power said. "He told you to come with him to your stand, No. 6?"

"Yes, we were at Stand No. 4; he said we could cut across to No. 6."

Power turned to me. "Well, good-bye for the present, 'Mr. Varek.' Look at your watch, and join us in Hide No. 3 in a quarter of an hour."

I did not know what all this portended, nor was I to know till Mr. Power, with Voce's connivance, staged the full-dress rehearsal later. I stayed fifteen minutes in my place, then went across to Hide No. 3.

As I approached it, and while it was still hidden from me by the trees, I heard the sounds of a noisy, but not unfamiliar, voice speaking. I knew at once that Gerald Whick had followed us down to Chustable, and must therefore be more uneasy than ever.

"The villain still pursues us, Gerald," I remarked, as I came up to the little group, "or did you really not want to see us, merely Mr. Power?"

"Good morning." He scowled at me. "I don't know Mr. Power! I came down to see Mercer. They told me he had come here."

"We never speak except in the presence of our lawyer," I replied primly. "Mr. Voce has disappeared. I expect we can get our pet butler to scratch up some lunch for you, too. Let's go back and see."

I observed that Power was studying Whick, with a semi-humorous twist of the lip.

"That's what Mr. Whick wants most," he said. "A spot of lunch. I see he's one of those people who never settle down till the lions are fed."

"Mind your own business!" Gerald snapped.

"Haven't time for it," said our friend. "My time's hired out at present to Mr. and Mrs. Mercer."

"Quite right," Vincie said firmly. "If you want to talk, Gerald, you must put up with him."

Gerald stalked off ahead of us across the grass. Mr. Power winked at me, and we followed the offended one to the house, where the butler was told to lay another cover and make preparations for a fourth guest.

The butler presently served our lunch and left us to it. I decided to open the ball.

"Have you told Voce?" I asked Gerald Whick.

"He doesn't believe me."

"Detectives are naturally suspicious persons," Power murmured, "but that's surely good news for you."

"You don't know what you're talking about," was the sullen answer.

"I like this cold pheasant," said Mr. Power.

"Perhaps one you shot, Mr. Whick?"

Gerald laid down his knife and fork, looked black, opened his mouth, shut it so violently that his teeth clicked, and went on eating.

"Look here," Vincie said. "No use pretending that Mr. Power isn't here, or is going away after luncheon. He isn't. You told Voce that you really had fired a tracer cartridge. He can't find any trace of it. What's the idea?"

"He can't have looked everywhere."

"He's done his best."

Power sipped at his glass, and smiled at Whick.

"You never saw such a man as Voce. He says he'll turn over every stone, paper, and bit of grass till he finds what he wants. He doesn't care two hoots whose private life he exposes: in fact, he hopes to dig into the affairs of everyone who shot here. Among those present will be Mr. Gerald Whick."

"What's that got to do with me?"

"I am only giving you a hint, in case there is any little matter unfit for polite—I mean for police ears, Mr. Whick. Your hasty rush down here, your demand for Mercer and privacy, suggests that you were in urgent need of a father confessor, but don't care for three. Meantime, it may reassure you about the other little matter if I say that Voce does not think you shot Fonders, accidentally or otherwise."

"If I hit Fonders, it was accidentally, and I can't blame myself for it," Gerald Whick growled. "I never knew the damn' things would shoot so far."

"Possibly not. But Voce has eliminated you there."

"And I suppose everyone else?"

"Merely, I think, the two Does, Mr. Varek and yourself," Power said soothingly. "Acquitted of the act, you know. Detectives are notoriously reticent, but I understand that he is digging into the private life of Mr. Fonders, his work, his assistants, proteges, and so on. With fellows like that there is nothing like frankness. If you'll take my advice—"

Gerald interrupted him by turning violently towards Vincie. "Mercer, I want to talk to you alone."

"Nothing doing. You can talk to us three, or talk to Voce."

Gerald rose, and left the table. He slammed the door, and made a bee-line, I think, for his hat and coat.

"He's in something up to the neck," Power said gently. "Not murder, I think. Leave him to me. I'll make a point of seeing him when I go back to town. Something is bound to bubble over, if he keeps on the boil like that long enough."

"You think he'll talk?" Vincie asked.

"I think he'll be glad to take my advice before I have done with him. And I think I shall hint to Voce that a little grilling will do no harm to the joint."

The butler came in with the second course, looked surprised to find that we were now three again, and retired. Mr. Power looked at us.

"Mr. Musson went to the study that morning with Mr. Fonders's papers and book contracts. Now why?"

"He was to be the new agent," I said.

"But he wouldn't draw commission on the old contracts?"

"No, but he might wish to familiarise himself with the terms."

"Apropos of Mr. Musson," I ventured, "you don't see him as the murderer, do you?"

"Why not? In the absence of any evidence to the contrary, he is quite as capable of killing Fonders as the rest of you."

"To kill his own job at birth?" Vincie asked.

"From my own slender legal knowledge of infanticide, Mercer, I should say that it is done because the owner of the bantling sees no other way out."

"One evening Musson is bantering or bullying Lionel, the next day he slays him," I said. "Too sudden, surely?"

"It depends what happened in between, Mrs. Mercer."

"Then it was something he saw in Lionel's papers; for no one came to the house. No visitor, I mean, that day. Would Mr. Fonders let him have any papers which would breed thoughts of murder in the man who read them?"

"Unlikely. The whole thing is a hypothesis. But you are all merely hypothetical murderers so far, and there is no harm in examining this one. Suppose something did happen which decided Mr. Musson to murder his host. Either his former attitude was a bluff, or that something happened during the period between your party leaving the house in the morning and Mr. Musson joining it for the pigeon-shoot."

"The telephone!" I cried excitedly. "Is that what you mean?"

"It may be. We'll ask the butler when he comes again."

CHAPTER XX

"WE WANT to ask you a question or two," Power said, when the butler came in at last. "You can serve coffee when we have done with you."

"Yes, sir." The man looked alarmed now.

"Cast your mind back to the day of the tragedy. Your master and the party had gone to shoot. Mr. Musson was in the library, or study, or whatever it is. Did he get a telephone message before he left the house, or a telegram?"

"No, sir, he didn't."

"What about the post? Have you a second post?"

"There is generally one between two and three, sir."

"There's the telephone-bell now," I said, hearing a shrill sound from the hall. The butler hurried out, to return in a few moments.

"For you, ma'am."

I got up and went out. Vanity Doe was on the wire. She said she and Benjy had been asked by the police to go down to Chustable Manor. They had rung up Addie, who had also been summoned. This official gathering of the clans looked ominous.

I went back to the dining-room, to hear the butler assuring Power that there had been no afternoon post on the day of the tragedy.

"Very well. We'll have coffee," Power said.

"You look grave, Mrs. Mercer."

I told him that Voce's dress rehearsal appeared to be fixed for an early date. "I did not hear if Mr. Varek, Mr. Musson and Whick were coming, too," I said, "but the Does and Miss Stole are starting."

"Then I shall have a stroll after my coffee," Power said irrelevantly. "I may be some time, but you can amuse yourselves without me."

"The butler knocked your theory on the head," I remarked.

"He stunned it momentarily, but it isn't quite dead, Mrs. Mercer. I remember staying once in a country house—in an official capacity, of course. I was drawing up a contract, went out to the front for a breath of fresh air, and was handed a bundle of letters by the postman. It's wonderful what a tired man will do to save himself walking a few yards."

"And the meaning of the parable?" Vincie asked.

"Oh, just that history may repeat itself, and a stroll to the post office won't hurt me."

"There was no mention of letters at the inquest."

"Why should there be? They were inquiring into the cause of death, not the non-delivery of mail. It's only a chance shot, but it looked like a chance shot that did Fonders in. Whether it was one is my particular pigeon just now."

Vincie and I exchanged glances of indulgence.

"And Mr. Musson did not give any letters to Lionel Fonders," I remarked.

"That seems quite likely," said Mr. Power, dryly. "It struck me too."

While he was away we had another telephone message, and again from London. Lionel's solicitor, Mr. Jones, wanted to know if Vincie would advise him on a literary matter with which he felt himself unable to deal. Among an accumulation of rubbish he had sorted out at the manor there was the ragged and dirty manuscript of a novel entitled *The Jumping Jane*. The title page and name of author was missing; the title was above the first page of the script. This might, for all Jones knew, be a manuscript of great value to the estate.

Vincie suggested our reading it, and sending it to Fonders's literary agents in England for negotiation if it proved worth while—though, of course, a bestseller's worst work is worth while, commercially. Mr. Jones thanked him cordially, and said he would send it at once by registered post.

"The thing may be a studio scraping, or it may be the manuscript of a novel that has already appeared under a different title," Vincie told me.

"At any rate, I can skip through it, to see."

"Do you think it is a sea story?" I asked.

"The name suggests a saucy schooner to me."

"Sea, my hat! Lionel went to America once, but he knew nothing about the sea. He travelled on a luxury liner."

Mr. Power came back looking very cheerful.

"You can't be too careful," he remarked as he joined us. "I value that adage more every day."

"Don't tell us that you were right," I said.

He nodded. "I was right. The postman called. He saw no one about, except for a tall gentleman smoking a cigar. As only gentlemen smoke cigars on week-days, he handed him a letter."

"It was an American letter?" said Vincie.

"It had a United States stamp, if that is any good to you."

Vincie laughed. "So the postman did not go so very far wrong, after all?"

"Not at that stage. But the letter was addressed to Mr. Fonders."

"Horrors!" I cried.

"Not necessarily. Mr. Whick has something on his mind, too, but not a murder. Mr. Musson received a letter. He should, of course, have taken it down to the shoot, and handed it over. Did he? I doubt it. If he did, Mr. Fonders must have torn it up into tiny pieces and swallowed it; an action more common among secret service agents than novelists."

"Shall you tell Voce?" Vincie asked.

"Yes. Dangerous not to. But I may talk it over with Mr. Musson first."

"What do you think it means?" I asked.

He grinned. "I have no idea. I have nothing to go upon."

We talked it over excitedly for some time, and finally gave it up. As Power said, we were not mediums, or media, and the interception of a letter might have a thousand interpretations.

We knew that Addie, and Benjy and Vanity Doe were on their way. To our surprise, Mr. Musson turned up before they did. Still more to our surprise, he was carrying a gun-case. He greeted us with his usual breeziness, was introduced to Mr. Power, and explained that the police had asked him to come down.

"As guns figured in the unfortunate accident the other day," he added with a smile, "I thought the sleuths would like to have a squint at mine. The London men will be more thorough than the local cops."

"Terrifically," Power agreed, as we went to the library, and the men lit cigars. "Evidently Mr. Jones, the lawyer, has arranged for the party to stay here again. Voce is away somewhere, but will be back. What they are chewing the rag about now is a missing letter."

I was glad that Vincie and I were able to repress the outward signs of the shock this mis-statement gave us. If Mr. Musson shared the shock, he too managed to conceal the fact.

"What letter?" he asked.

"Well, it seems the postman brought one up to the house, the day Mr. Fonders was shot."

"Oh, that one?" Mr. Musson laughed. "But that isn't—wasn't missing. The postman gave it to me, and I took it down with me and handed it to Lionel. I guess the police must have found it on the body and—" He paused, frowned, and added: "But if they did, why are they kicking up a schemozzle about it?"

"It appears that they didn't find it," Power said genially. "Lucky you saw it and can perhaps describe it."

"I saw the envelope, of course, Mr. Power. It was addressed to Mr. Lionel Fonders, and had a United States stamp. That's all I—Wait a moment; the address was typewritten."

"Did you see where it had been posted?"

"No, I wasn't as curious as all that. But I know the stamps by the colour, without peeking at the postmark."

"Naturally, since you live there. Did Mr. Fonders read it?"

"Not while I was there. I just slipped it to him, and he put it in his pocket, the inner breast one. I wonder where it's got to."

Mr. Power shrugged his shoulders. "No idea. Better tell Mr. Voce all about it when he comes. It's his business to look."

The two Does and Addie Stole arrived just then; Vanity full of the tyranny of officialdom, and thankfulness that the totalitarian state had not yet reached this country.

"We are ordered about sufficiently as it is," she said indignantly. "I wished to refuse to come, but Benjy insisted, though we have nothing whatever to do with the affair."

"Don't be an ass, Van!" said her brother, who looked white and nervous. "Just the way to convince 'em we were in it. But it's a bore."

Addie had been staring at Mr. Musson's gun-case. "They don't think you did it, do they?" she demanded. "Are they going to test it?"

Musson grinned. "I hope so. Every trial and test permitted, so that the article will give satisfaction."

"I find your facetiousness very distressing," Vanity told Musson. "I am sure it is out of place."

He bowed ironically. "Your hat, Miss Doe, if you will not think me rude to say so, is a *mite* on the wrong side."

Vanity's hats generally were, but she glared at him, straightened it, and left the room with the small suit-case she was carrying.

"Goes up in the air mighty easy," murmured Mr. Musson.

Benjy looked at him with distaste, then turned to Power. "What's up?"

Power tried to explain. "I am representing Mr. and Mrs. Mercer, and the inspector does not really confide in me. But bringing you all here does hint that he is hoping to stage a reconstruction of the scene."

"Going all Frenchie," said Musson. "Glad I brought my gun. Like the fellow in *The Mikado*, I am all for verisimilitude."

"Not a bad idea," Benjy said. "It will show him that I couldn't have hit Lionel from where I was."

Vincie nodded. "I am for the idea, too. All the theorising in the world won't tell half as much as the detective can learn from seeing us do what we did that day."

"What I wonder at," Mr. Musson said, "is the remissness of the police in not taking footprints. If Fonders was shot by someone who left his hide, surely casts could be taken of all footprints near it. It seems to me that this country is so proud of the fingerprint system that it neglects others."

"What about that?" Benjy looked at Power.

"Well, two things. In the first place, the leaves and fallen twigs and stuff, and the frost, make footprints not so easy to take or compare."

"And the second thing?" said Mr. Musson.

"The fact that Theby Wood was beaten for pheasants earlier in the day. There are plenty of mushed-up beaters' footprints all round the stand where your host stood. Voce looked into that, and gave up trying."

"Well, I'll give up trying, too," said Musson. "This has me beat. Let the trained sleuths get on with their job."

Benjy got up. "I'll take my bag upstairs, and see where I'm housed," he remarked.

When he had gone, Mr. Power asked if he might see the gun. "I have been reading up fire-arms, with a view to saving Mr. Mercer's neck from the noose," he pointed out. "Twenty-bore, isn't it?"

"Sure," said Mr. Musson, opening the case. "While you're having a look at it, I'll go upstairs, too, try to locate the butler man, and find my room. I could do with a wash."

We sat beside Power as he took the gun from its case, and when Vincie had put it together for him he examined it with loving care through his magnifying glass.

"Stock's a nice bit of figured walnut," he said, "kept in good condition. Maker, Thorp and Thorp, of Bond Street, London. Not a new gun, but a good one."

"It looks good to me," Vincie said. "He's a crack shot."

Power took the gun to the window, opened the breech, and squinted through the barrels. "Keeps the barrels clean and well polished," he murmured. "Let's go into the gun-room, and see what the barrels of Fonders's pair are like."

Fonders's guns, though much newer, were not so highly polished. We returned to the library, and Power noted the number incised under the right barrel near the breech.

"Messrs. Thorp and Thorp are an old firm," he said. "While Musson washes his hands, I'll try to get them on the telephone. Firms who sell expensive guns usually keep a record of them."

"But we were told that this size of barrel would not fire the pellet," I said.

"Quite true. Still, information is always useful, and sometimes precious. Hold the fort, and the gun, till I come back."

"He's a clever fellow," Vincie murmured to me a few moments later, "but a bit theatrical, eh? Too much patter for the simplest trick."

"I don't care how much patter there is if he gets you clear of this, darling," I replied. "I can't see anything odd about the gun myself."

We took it to pieces and inspected it for a long time. It seemed to us both that it was just a fine gun, with nothing to distinguish it from other fine guns of the same bore. Power afterwards told us that this was correct.

He came back in twenty minutes, just five minutes before Musson came down to us with clean hands.

"It was ordered four years ago by a Mr. Braithwaite. Not Thorp's 'best gun,' which costs a hundred and eighty guineas, but their second best. Price, one hundred and twenty. It is a twenty-bore ejector. They sell thirty or so of the type each year. Obviously Musson bought it second-hand."

"Then it tells you nothing?" I asked.

"What tells who nothing?" Musson asked, suddenly reappearing.

"Your gun," said Power. "I was looking for gore on it."

CHAPTER XXI

SURE enough, Bob Varek and his dog turned up before dinner. The dog seemed supererogatory, but Bob explained that having had it with him in his hide on the day of the tragedy, he brought the beast.

"Conscientious man," said Musson. "If we have to have *all* the properties for the staging, I'm sunk! I left my shooting-stick behind, and you know I had it here that day."

"By the same absurd logic, I should, I suppose, have brought the book I was reading," Vanity sniffed. "I hate all this clowning! It is a very serious business, and the aim, as I understand it, is to discover how the man was killed."

Power restrained a grin, but some flickers of amusement showed about his lips. "We must play about a bit to relieve the strain, Miss Doe," he said. "That's sound psychology."

"I was not aware that you were a student of psychology," Vanity replied loftily. "I am well aware of the value of what is vulgarly called a safety-valve, but I maintain that Mr. Musson's facetiousness is out of place."

The butler was serving the second course, and looked perturbed again. You could see that he still thought us capable of anything.

Mr. Power relieved the situation by starting a discussion on psychology with Vanity. He was able to sustain it by allowing her to do most of the talking, and to score all the points. Musson,

Vincie and Benjy Doe began to discuss the foreign as against the English method of criminal investigation, and Bob Varek turned to me.

"I don't know why I was asked down at all," he grumbled. "Do you know?"

"To cloud the issue," I returned, "and then everyone wanted another look at your dog. No chance, I suppose, of his having wandered away, and accidentally knocked over Lionel's gun?"

He smiled wanly. "It might be so, if he put it back again. But, really?"

"Really, I suppose, the police daren't single one out," I said, "until they have definite evidence. And each of us remembers much better what he did that day than he could put into words. When we start through the wood to-morrow we are sure to see a tree, or an opening or something which we had forgotten."

"That's true," he remarked doubtfully. "It may come back. But I did not see anyone that day in the wood."

"Possibly the police are hoping someone saw you," I said. "We shall all be cross references for each other, if you know what I mean."

"But suppose someone says he saw me. What about that?"

"Your bad luck," I told him. "Did anyone see you leave your hide?"

He glared. "Of course not. Are you suggesting that I—"

"Children, children!" Mr. Power heard the raised voice, and chided the speaker. "Dogs delight . . . you know!"

The butler had just come in again, and looked palpably nervous.

"I meant," whispered Bob, pausing to scowl at Power, "that the murderer might say he did."

"Obviously a murderer would say anything," I rejoined. "No inhibitions, you know. I wonder if he saw you?"

"What do you mean? I wasn't near Lionel."

"Then why are you worrying?" I asked.

He bit his lip, and tried to join in the Power-Vanity Doe discussion, only to be shooed out again. He attacked the sweet which had just been put before him with simulated eagerness.

The fact is that we were all nervy and quarrelsome, and before the evening was over all of us, with the exception of Power, who had stolen away, and Mr. Musson, who preserved an Olympian calm, quarrelled and argued all over the house. And when there was a scene, because Bob Varek called Vanity a "tinpot pedant," Vincie and I decided to go to bed.

If Inspector Voce and his sergeant had returned, they did not show up at the house, and we saw nothing of them till break-fast-time next day.

Then the inspector came in, told us that we were to muster near Theby Wood at half-past three in the afternoon, and vanished like a jack-in-the-box when the lid is put down.

It was generally agreed that the wait would be nerve-rack-ing, and to avoid any more trouble Benjy and his sister went for a walk, Musson and Bob Varek vanished in another direc-tion—with dog—and the arrival soon after of a registered parcel addressed to Vincie gave us something to do.

"So your work even follows you here?" Power asked, as Vincie produced the tattered manuscript.

"This is part of Lionel's estate," Vincie replied. "I am going to read it."

"Then I'll be off to see if I can get hold of Voce. I have a new line, dear friends, so once more unto the breach!"

"Is that a shooting pun?" I asked.

"It just happens that it is," Power replied. "Well, good hunt-ing."

The way a professional writer or reviewer reads a book is very different from the fashion in which it is read by the layman. His expert eyes know how to skip and where to cut in and cut out without losing the thread.

We established ourselves in the library with a box of ciga-rettes, and Vincie divided the manuscript into two parts, of which he gave me one.

"You begin at the beginning," he said. "I'll start in midway."

Only half-way down the second page, I sat up. "Vincie, 'through' is spelt 'thru'."

He had looked up simultaneously. "Listen to this: 'Gosh! I should say that jane has considerable gall!' So Jumping Jane is merely a high-spirited filly, not a saucy schooner."

We plunged again into our scripts, and read on for half an hour.

"British muck is mucky enough, but American muck is rawer," said Vincie at last. "In addition, this is semi-illiterate, and obviously written by someone who does not know the ways of the American richer classes. He writes about them from the outside."

I agreed. "Perhaps it's a parody."

Vincie put down his script. "Tell me the gist of your bit, darling? Mine reminds me strongly of something."

I gave him the plot up to the half-way line, and he whistled.

"Golly, sweetheart!" he exclaimed. "This is *The Girl from Gehenna* in embryo."

"It had begun to dawn on me," I murmured. "Lionel's third big hit. But why did he not destroy the traces of the crime?"

"They don't," Vincie replied. "They seem fated to keep something they should dispose of. That is how so many are caught."

I went to the book-shelves and took down the original copy of the novel.

"We must put Power on to this," I said. "You get to work and write a précis of the stuff, and I'll see if I can find Power."

One of the detectives, a plain-clothes man, was near the house when I went out. He believed Mr. Power had found Sergeant Bohm and gone with him to pick up Voce, who was at Theby Wood.

I hurried towards the wood and met Mr. Power coming thoughtfully back. He raised his eyebrows comically when he saw my excited face, and asked if I had found a clue.

"I have no idea," I said, "but Vincie and I have found something. The lawyer discovered it in his paper-hunting, and sent it on to—"

"Oh, you mean the manuscript that came this morning. What about it?"

"It's a sticky tale, written in the cheapest Americanese by someone who never heard of Edith Wharton or Willa Cather," I told him. "In other words, some uncultured chump with a vivid, but nasty, imagination."

"There are such, I believe, even in America," he said judicially, "but they're out of our jurisdiction."

"The point is this," I said. "The hand is the hand of Jacob, but the plot is the plot of Mr. Fonders's big hit, *The Girl from Gehenna*."

"You mean that he pinched it?"

"Well, he had the manuscript here, and it has that appearance. Vincie is making a précis for you, and you can read Lionel's novel for yourself."

"Can't I take your word for it?" he said.

"Have you to see Mr. Voce again?" I asked. "If so, of course, you may not have time to read it before we assemble at Theby Wood."

"Voce has rushed off to town," he said. "Bohm will have to be stage-manager this afternoon. I suppose I can skip the thing?"

"Oh, yes," I said. "Better to, I think."

When we got indoors, Vincie handed over his précis, and said he needed a breath of fresh air. He and I went out and came back to find Mr. Power packing up the manuscript and précis in a bit of brown paper.

"I'll borrow this, if I may," he said. "Now for a cigar to take the taste out of my mouth." When he had lit up, he looked at us thoughtfully. "Do people send their manuscripts to famous authors?"

Vincie laughed. "Do they not? Even to those not so famous. Some want an opinion, most want praise, some have an idea that authors already in print have a pull with publishers and editors, and want you to push their stuff gratis for them. Lionel Fonders's first hit in America was a big one. If you ask me, this stuff came in with what is horridly called his 'fan mail'."

"And he did not send it back?"

"No. I should say he saw how foully it was written, but approved the idea, liked the plot and pouched it. He made the characters English, and laid the scene in Italy."

"Instead of making them Americans on holiday in Florida?"

"Yes."

"And he expected to get away with it?"

I smiled. "It has been done. One of my own ideas for a plot has been exploited in other novels twice since. It may be chance, or anything you like, but in this country it isn't at all easy to copyright a plot. Our judges are so fiendishly careful."

"In this country, Mrs. Mercer? Is it easy anywhere?"

"In the United States," Vincie said, "some authors say it has developed into a ramp. Some amateur has written something you never read, but which might be twisted into a resemblance to your work. You get a threat of legal proceedings, and unless you have money, patience and a cast-iron defence, you pay up and get done."

Mr. Power's face now wore a pleased expression.

"That is new to me. But how helpful! You may be threatened in good faith by a person who imagines you have stolen his plot, or in bad faith by someone who thinks he can scare you into paying up rather than endure the American law's delays, and dollar expenses. If you have money and patience, you fight. If you 'have the goods on you,' as our American friends say, you are in a hole?"

"You are sunk," Vincie said. "That is if someone knows that you have the manuscript."

"Why did Fonders keep this?"

"We authors are often untidy people," I said. "The other day I was wading through an old trunk, and came on a lost manuscript of Vincie's. Yet we are more methodical than some."

"That seems reasonable. Fonders mislaid the stuff, or didn't worry, since the author was some semi-illiterate person living in the wilds of America. But wouldn't that person ask to have it back?"

"He might," I agreed, "but I know two people who refuse to send back unsolicited stuff, or even to acknowledge it. That doesn't matter here, for it's evident Lionel did pinch the plot and keep the manuscript."

Vincie frowned. "I wonder if this fits in anywhere?" he asked. "Our friend is dead, but his reputation was unsavoury. He was not such a bad cuss once. We take it that he did the dirty on an unpleasant amateur. But that may be a thing apart from his murder, Power. Or do you think not?"

Power shook his head. "I think it may have some connection, Mercer. If it has, you have to postulate knowledge of the trans- action on the part of someone else. As I see it, the script might have been forwarded to Fonders's agent, to be sent on—"

"Mr. Musson wasn't Lionel's agent then," I said.

"I forgot that. Still, he is the only link with the United States in your shooting-party, Mrs. Mercer, and he is a literary agent. Suppose he knew what had happened. He may have been in a small way of business, and thought he would like Fonders on his books. The bestseller would, I think you said once, be a profit and an advertisement?"

"Absolutely."

"Very well. He comes over here, gets in touch with Fond- ers, and tells him that a big action for infringement was to be launched against him in the United States, and would cost him a mint of money. I noticed that your script was a carbon copy."

"Go on!" I cried eagerly.

"When I had the privilege some time ago of meeting a party of American lawyers," he said, "several of them told me that one problem they were up against over there was the 'shyster' lawyer. In America a fellow who may be a cheesemonger's assistant will read up law, and presently stick up his shingle and practise. The cheesemonger's assistant is an honest man, and often a clever one. But this taste for law brings in others who don't know anything about cheese, except as a bait for mice. The shyster lawyer takes up cases on the chance of making a bit by fair means or foul."

"We have heard of them," Vincie said.

"Very well. We'll put it that Mr. Musson, whatever his profes- sion, gets to know that Fonders stole the plot. He may, for all we know, have been given the top-copy of this *Jumping Jane* novel to negotiate, when the writer found that Fonders did not reply to him. And, like you, he may have seen the resemblance to *The Girl from Gehenna*?"

"Why," I said, "I read an account of a similar case some time ago, and the plaintiff won, though there wasn't anything like the similarity of plot and character we have here."

"Right."

Vincie agreed. "You think Musson may be a shyster lawyer?" he added.

"No, I don't," Power returned, "because he is not an American citizen, and I assume they do not allow aliens to practise without being naturalised. I think he is very probably what he says he is."

I started. "A thoroughly unpleasant idea."

"He was dealing with a very unpleasant man, Mrs. Mercer: one who was willing to steal other people's rotten refuse to turn it to his own account."

Vincie nodded. "Every time. But how could Musson square his own client?"

"It's easy. The writing suggests someone living in a poor district, who has got some local, but absurdly glaring, colour from reading cheap American magazines. He might rely on his agent to tell him what was what. He may even have been offered, or paid, a small sum to square it. Three or four hundred dollars might seem a lot to him."

We saw that, and said so. Power went on.

"So it is quite on the cards that Musson came over to tackle Fonders if there was money in it."

"There was a case some years ago where the damages claimed were huge," Vincie said. "Over there you can be dragged from one court to another, and legal fees are high."

"Very well. Musson put the fear of death in Lionel Fonders, but said he could wash out the plaintiff, if they came to some agreement. For his part he was ready to take the agency, without any ready money passing, and get his client's signature to an agreement not to proceed with the threatened legal proceedings."

CHAPTER XXII

"You have almost convinced me," Vincie said.

"It is quite on the cards that Musson is not as open and nice as he appears. His breezy talk may be really a sign of dirty weather, and his frankness bluff. But how do you fasten the murder on him?"

"I don't yet, and may never do," Power sighed.

"But though the prosecution need not prove motive in a murder case, the poor defence had better discover one—to settle on someone—if the client is to be saved. I cannot, as a human and fallible being, say who killed Fonders, and it will be darned hard to show how Musson could have done it. Still, I think this manuscript is a help. We have seen that there are possible circumstances in connection with it which suggest Musson could have wished Mr. Fonders away."

"I think so, too," I agreed, "but you will forgive my saying that unless Mr. Voce has some evidence to help you out, you may be hard put to it."

Power laughed. "Voce takes possession of anything which he can use for an exhibit in the case. He does not know of this script, but he has already taken the fragments of the pellet."

"Will he make any thing of that?" I asked.

"I am pretty certain he won't tell me what his police laboratory think, unless he decides to make a mark of Mr. Mercer here," was the cheerful reply. "I have an idea about that too, but, unfortunately, I am not a scientist. I can't say if my idea is a bright one, or plain bunk. Of course, I shall try to tap Voce, in exchange for information supporting a motive for Musson. But he is quite entitled to ask me for anything which is germane to his investigation, without promising to let me in on his own nice little ground-floor."

"It doesn't seem fair," Vincie said.

"We won't debate that, Mercer. Sheer waste of time. But there was something I wanted to ask you about shooting. You didn't give me a verbatim report of all that was said the day

Fonders was killed. But I think you said Musson came vainglor-iously on the scene in the afternoon, and, a providential pigeon appearing, was enabled to show off there and then."

Vincie nodded. "It was a high pigeon, he just flicked the gun up, and I wondered if it was a fluke. I don't think so now. He wouldn't risk missing when he was trying to impress us."

"No. He's evidently hot stuff with a game-gun. But I asked my shooting-school instructors, and they said wild pigeon needed some bringing down. Whatever there is in its favour, a twenty-bore cannot hit quite so hard as a twelve."

Vince looked blank. "Well, he hit it, and down it came."

"Wait a moment," I interrupted. "We had some talk about that. We were, or the men were, dud shots, and there was a discussion. You remember, Vincie, don't you?"

Vincie looked suddenly intelligent. "I remember, of course. That was in the house, my dear. Musson explained that you can partly level things up. By having a chamber to take a longer cartridge, you could fire a twenty-bore with a full sixteen-bore, or a light twelve-bore, charge."

"Oh, I see," Power said, rather cheerfully, "and I suppose Musson would know."

"He had the longer chamber in his gun, and that is how he was able to shoot high pigeon with it," Vincie said.

"What chambering is available in his size?"

Vincie reflected, then. "Three, I think. Three-inch case, two-and-three-quarter-inch, and two-and-a-half-inch. The last is the normal. But he was using the second size of chamber."

"Two-and-three-quarter inches?"

"I remember him saying so," I remarked.

"The length of chamber would not affect what was fired from his gun," my husband remarked. "Whatever it is, the actual bore of the rest of the barrel is the same."

"So I understood," said Power, "but I must get on the tele-phone before lunch, and try to work that out."

We went to our room to prepare for the next meal, and Vincie was still somewhat doubtful about the value of Power's clues, though he admitted that there might be something in it.

"I wondered at the time why Lionel did not appoint a well-known American agent," he said. "His agency would be so valuable, and so on. Any of them would have been glad to get it."

"Have you considered the possibilities of that letter?" I asked.

"Jove! no," he exclaimed. "The one Musson said he took down to Lionel? We can't swear that he didn't, even if none of us saw him hand it over."

"No, we can't, but it hasn't been found, my dear," I reminded him. "It doesn't, follow that Musson expected one to come, and stayed at home to intercept it. For one thing, he might have been seen taking it."

"Well?" asked Vincie.

"On the other hand," I said, "a great many American firms put their names on the outside of their envelopes. If Musson recognised the name of the sender, and opened the letter—"

"You mean it may have been in reference to Musson?"

"Well, mayn't it?" I asked. "Lionel put up with Musson's bullying. He may have known he was in a cleft stick, and tried to keep the man sweet by every means at his disposal, while all the time he had written out to the United States for what they call the low-down on the man."

Vincie looked pleased. "That's quite an idea, now we know there was a letter, which is missing. If Musson read and destroyed the letter, en route to the wood, it must mean two things: first, the letter gave him a bad character, and, secondly, if Lionel read it, he would become a danger to Musson."

"So that Mr. Power may be right," I said.

"In that case, yes. But was Gerald Whick in league with Musson?"

"We have no evidence of it. He may have known something about Lionel which enabled him to levy a sort of blackmail, to get his satires subsidised, and overpaid at that. It would not help him if there was a murder trial, and that was brought out, but he can't have killed Lionel, considering where he was."

The rest of the party returned to luncheon, looking even more anxious and jaded than when they set out. Physical exercise does not really help to refresh you when your nerves are on edge.

Their tempers were also on edge, and when Power tried to create a diversion after luncheon by chipping Musson about his shooting most of them were glad to concentrate their fire on the breezy expert.

"You all know I am here to stand between Mr. Voce and his expected victim, Mr. Mercer," he said, with a grin. "Now, poor Fonders seems to have been well out of range of you all, but you're the sort of fellow who can shoot the eye out of a fly, Mr. Musson. You seem to fit the part of marksman best! Mercer was telling me some yarn about your having shot a pigeon like a speck in the sky."

Musson bellowed with laughter. "Shows what judges they are of distance, doesn't it? I admit a bird above you looks much farther away than it does when flying out at the side, but that pigeon was quite within range, forty yards, I should say."

Vincie admitted it. "Well, I call that a high shot, meaning, of course, for a twenty."

Power smiled. "I should like to have a pop with your gun, Mr. Musson, to try the range."

Musson nodded agreement. "Why not? I don't see why the police should hog all the facilities. Come outside, and you can try the range at a bottle; or a tree might be better, if you are not a crack shot."

"Or a barn-door?" Power laughed. "I think we might try all the guns, now that the police have done with them."

Somehow I felt that Power had side-slipped. He was just too clever in spots, and an excess of cleverness sometimes hampers the amateur detective, as it does the murderer. Privately, I hoped that the police would not hear the shots, and come up to interfere.

We all went out into the park near the house, after Musson had collected the available guns and handed them out, giving his own to Mr. Power, with a couple of cartridges, which Power stuffed into his pocket.

We found a fine oak with a broad bole to shoot at, and Musson pinned up a sheet of newspaper on it, then paced forty yards backwards.

He stood with us in a semi-circle behind the grinning Power, who loaded and fired the guns in turn, with great expedition, but no very accurate aim.

"Still, I did hit it," he said, as we advanced to the tree after the target practice, and found two pellets in the sheet, "and I hit it with Mr. Musson's twenty-bore."

"How can you say that?" Vanity asked scornfully. "Aren't all those cartridges loaded with the same size of shot?"

"They are," he replied amusedly. "But I saw the paper shiver when I fired Musson's gun."

Mr. Musson nodded. "That's right. I was watching closely. But I am afraid you would not shine as a gun expert, Mr. Power. I told you at lunch forty yards was within her range."

Power looked rather crestfallen, but had no time to reply, for Sergeant Bohm appeared in the distance, running and shouting.

"I hope he hasn't found another body," Vanity said nervously.

But it was not that at all. It was merely that the sergeant was furious when he heard the shots and realised that our lawyer was trying out the guns. He talked himself breathless, having saved very little during his run across the park, telling Power what he thought of him and his officious action.

Mr. Power protested. "My dear fellow, I have my client's interests to protect. How am I to work up a defence, unless I know something about the gun used on the day of the tragedy?"

"You're obstructing the police, Mr. Power," Bohm said sternly. "How do we know what you are doing with those guns?—tampering with evidence for all we can say."

Power looked angry. "Steady now! Be careful what you are saying, sergeant. Are you charging me with tampering with the guns?"

"I am not, sir. I am only saying that you have no permission to touch them!"

Musson intervened. "Now, sergeant, there is no great harm done. Mr. Power really started an argument with me about my little gun, and I let him have a couple of shots."

"Your gun, sir, may also be an exhibit, if it is the one you used that day," Bohm replied irritably. "In this country private individuals are not allowed to butt into police investigation, whatever they may do in yours."

"This *is* my country, sergeant."

"Anyway, sir, we can have no more of it! Take those guns back to the gun-room at once, and put yours there too. I shall have them collected and taken to Theby Wood at half-past three."

"I'm sorry, sergeant," Power said, with a side glance at us. "I would not have done it if I had known you would object."

"Then you should have asked me first, sir," said Bohm, and turned away sourly.

"I think, perhaps, I have heard enough about it now, sergeant!" Power said sharply.

Bohm turned again. "Look here, sir, you started some sort of unauthorised reconstruction yesterday, I hear, and we don't want any more of it. My inspector's away, and I have to try to make a test myself, with the aid of you ladies and gentlemen. Now, if you'll turn up and take your part, sir, instead of trying to butt in, I shall be obliged. Mr. Whick can't be here. Perhaps you will take his place?"

Power turned to us. "I think I had better have a word with the sergeant about this. I have my rights as well as he. I'll see you all later at the house."

We trooped off, Musson smiling broadly, and Addie very anxious to know what the sergeant meant.

"There's one thing," she said, when I told her. "The wood wasn't 'blind' when we shot there. We might have seen some way through the trees, only for the evergreens and underbrush."

"That is true," I agreed, "but they say all that holly, birch, rhododendron and laurel was planted there for cover for the birds. Whatever the reason, they helped to mask one hide from another."

Benjy joined us. "I say, Penny," he remarked, "your friend Power isn't a pet with that policeman, is he?"

"They had a brush in another case some time ago," I replied, "but Mr. Power can take care of himself."

The guns were taken back to the gun-room, and we were assembled in the drawing-room round a bright fire, when Mr. Power joined us, shrugging and smiling.

"I've managed to mollify the 'Kitten'," he said, "and he has told me what he wants done. It is a reconstruction of the scene of the accident, and anyone who does not wish to help is at liberty to refuse."

"I vote we all help," Musson said.

We agreed, and Power went on. "Right. But he says the idea is to check and cross-check each other's movements, so we shall have to reshuffle the stands. Bohm himself is to be Fonders, I am to take Mr. Musson's hide, Mr. Musson is to take Whick's place on the island covert, Mr. and Mrs. Mercer are to take the other stand on Little Covert, and Mr. and Miss Doe are to go to the Mercer's stand, No. 6. Mr. Varek and Miss Stole will change places: Miss Stole, No. 4: and Mr. Varek, No. 5."

"It's certainly a better cross-check than staying where we originally were," Musson remarked. "I can see if anyone crossed the grass slope towards Big Covert, so can Mr. and Mrs. Mercer from their angle."

"According to Bohm's instructions, we start off for the hides at three-twenty-five. A plain-clothes man will make a note of the times we arrive at each, and we must make an attempt to do what you all did on the afternoon of the shoot. My own 'unauthorised' attempt"—Power paused to grin—"is now wiped out. Also, I hope, my offence in attempting it. When Sergeant Bohm blows three blasts on his whistle, that means the recall."

"You mean we turn it up?" asked Benjy.

"Yes, we converge on the house and call it a day, Mr. Doe. Bohm now says we need not carry guns. Times and movements are all he wants recorded."

"What about my dog?" said Bob Varek.

"I should leave him here." Power smiled. "His movements aren't exactly relevant to the matter in hand."

He sat down and lit a cigarette, and Mr. Musson spoke up.

"I think Bohm is right. There are times when the Continental idea about reconstructing a scene does the trick. Not that I think it is always necessary."

Vanity Doe raised her eyebrows. "I suppose there are other views than yours to be considered, Mr. Musson? But as you took charge of everything and everybody on the day, there is no need for us to express ours."

Mr. Musson bowed. "Without flattering myself, Miss Doe, I may say that I was the only gun with some ideas about shooting. Even poor Fonders was a novice."

"He had a trained gamekeeper," she snapped.

Musson bowed again. "Quite. But it just happened that he asked my advice as to the arrangements."

"And I am sure you gave it most willingly," said Vanity, and left the room.

"Heaven help the authors she reviews!" said Musson. "She will always have the last word."

"Which is the way with reviewers, I believe," said Mr. Power, winking at us. "*A propos de bottes*, ladies and gentlemen, coats and mufflers are permitted this afternoon."

CHAPTER XXIII

WE ASSEMBLED in the vicinity of Theby Wood in good time; actually at 3.15. We were met by Sergeant Bohm and a plain-clothes man with a note-book and pencil.

Our party on the way down had been headed by Musson and Bob Varek, talking earnestly; then came Addie Stole, Vanity, and Benjy Doe. Mr. Power walked with us, a few paces behind.

"I am afraid you put up rather a dud show with Musson's gun," Vincie said softly as we started. "It really wasn't any test of the gun, you know."

I noticed a rather impish gleam in Power's eyes as he replied: "Why not?"

"Well, you got nothing from it," I said.

He put his hand in his pocket and just gave us a fleeting glimpse of a cartridge-case, then dropped it into his pocket once more.

"Well, I did—in a way, Mrs. Mercer. You see, Bohm came up very opportunely, and shooed you all away."

Vincie stared. "Was that all you wanted?"

"And very nice too," said Mr. Power. "A man isn't always wise to ask directly for what he wants. People want to know then why he wants it. Autolycus is my man—the picker-up of unconsidered trifles."

He wouldn't say any more, but I understood that he had picked up the ejected cases when we and Bohm had gone.

"Now," said Sergeant Bohm, when zero hour had come, and we had got into motion. "I think the party dropped Mr. and Miss Doe at their stand on Little Covert. We go there first. Time, three-twenty-six, Smith."

So we all set out for the stand the Does had occupied, and Vincie and I were left there to represent the brother and sister.

"If you see anyone in the open, make a note of it," Bohm said. "Now, Mr. Musson, we go with you to the other little wood."

They disappeared, and Vincie looked out through the trees to the front.

"I can see if anyone crosses the grass," he told me, "but, of course, I can't see Lionel's stand at all. There are oaks pretty thick in between, and what looks like a bank of laurel, high and straggling."

I was watching the grass slope to the west-nor'-west, and presently saw Bohm and his assistant, Addie, Bob Varek, and the Does cross to Great Covert and disappear in the trees. Addie was right. The wood might be generally bare of leaves, though some brown oak leaves still hung on, but the undergrowth, and particularly the unruly plantings of evergreens, made the wood pretty thick in places, to the height of six or seven feet.

"They have dumped Musson, vice Whick, who has done the Little Pig act and stayed at home," I said. "Vincie, you don't think Mr. Voce went to town to arrest Gerald, do you?"

"Unlikely," he said. "He may have cold feet, and I don't think the police could force him to turn up and take part in this. Their powers are limited."

"Well, what about that cartridge?" I asked. "It looks as if Power had bluffed Musson into letting him have a spent one."

"That is what he did, darling," said Vincie, "but what he wants with it is beyond me. Musson has done everything he could to help. We mustn't expect miracles from Power, you know. He admitted fallibility."

"But he had a funny look in his eye when he showed that case," I said. "Another thing, old boy! Bohm *did* come up opportunely. I suppose Power couldn't have arranged that with him, to get us all away, and enable him to collect the spent cartridge-case?"

"The blighter is quite capable of putting up a stunt like that, if the sergeant would agree to it," he said, "but let's keep our eyes open."

The party, as we heard afterwards, made the round of the stands, dropping a gun here and a gun there, till, finally, Power was sent on by himself to Musson's former place at the edge of the wood. The Does settled into our old hide last, and Bohm, representing Lionel, went on to his. From first to last we did not see anyone emerge in the open after that. Our evidence as to the movements of the others was obviously nil.

"So Vanity and Doe are definitely out," Vincie remarked, as we heard three loud blasts on a whistle, and started for home, "but no one could suspect them."

Musson joined us now and, turning to look, we saw Addie and Bob Varek coming into the open from Great Covert, with Mr. Power hurrying after them from the farthest stand of all.

"I could really do with a spot of hot tea now," Musson said, beaming at us. "It's darned cold. By the way, did you pipe anyone?"

"Not a soul," I said. "Did you?"

"No, but perhaps some of the others had better luck. Shall we wait for them?"

We waited, but no one appeared to have seen another gun either leaving his stand or moving about in the wood.

"I just see one snag in this method of reconstruction," Musson remarked as we moved off again. "If anyone failed to do what his predecessor in the hide did, it musses it up."

"I don't care two hoots if it does or not," Benjy said. "I'm perished. Race anyone back for tea?"

"I will," Addie said very sportingly, and set off running, with Benjy about ten yards in the rear.

"Well," asked Bob Varek, "did Bohm get any valuable clues from this silly stunt of his, Mr. Power?"

"You forget," Power said tartly, "that I was farthest away, and Bohm has not shown up yet. In any case, is he likely to confide in me?" Varek grinned. "Can't say he is. He sent you away with a flea in your ear this morning, anyway."

Power's disgruntled manner did not suggest that he had made any great discoveries as a result of our cold vigil, and Vincie and I rather sympathised with him. After all, a lawyer is not a trained detective, and optimists like our friend have a habit of counting their chickens not only before they are hatched, but even before the eggs are laid.

"The trouble is," I said, "that Mr. Power is trying to snatch a brand from the police burning, and they don't like it."

We were then at the house, and thankfully went in to the luxurious tea the butler had laid out for us.

After tea the Does went home. They were taken by one of the house cars to a main-line station ten miles away, having declared that they did not care what the combined forces of Voce and Bohm said to it. The rest of us had decided to leave by the first train next morning—Bohm permitting.

Addie, Mr. Musson and Bob Varek went to play life-pool when the Does had cleared out. Power and ourselves sat down before a nice fire in the library, and rather to my surprise Sergeant Bohm, smiling and utterly unfeline, knocked at the door, came in, shut it gently behind him, and was induced to take a chair and a cigarette.

Naturally our suspicions of some sort of collusion between our bland lawyer and the big, now purring "Kitten" were reawakened.

"Mr. Bohm," said Power, discarding the man's formal title in view of the informality of our conference, "has come in as *advocatus diaboli*. I think I had better tell you that."

"You're not telling me anything, sir," said the thawing officer. "I never heard you speak of that."

"The *advocatus diaboli*," I suggested, "was a person put up in certain trials, before the Inquisition, I fancy, to represent the prisoner, who might be said to be on the other side of the angels. But I may be wrong."

"The meaning here, Bohm," Power smiled, "is that you are here to put in anything you can against what I say—be a heckler, if that suits you better."

"I see, sir," said Bohm. "Carry on."

Power gave him a delicate grin. "You saw an apparition this afternoon, didn't you?"

"Yes, that's right. I did."

"At the hour of 3.55 p.m. or thereabouts?"

"That's right."

"A spirit—you saw a spirit," Power murmured, "or more accurately a substitute. I merely said it was a spirit you saw because no one else in the wood appears to have seen it."

Mr. Bohm was vastly different from Sergeant Bohm. With a cigarette going, and his toes to the fire, he smiled and nodded. His official namesake would have sternly rebuked this seeming irresponsibility.

"I admit you puzzled me, Mr. Power. Not for the first time," he added reminiscently.

"Meantime, you needn't puzzle us, Power," Vincie protested. "What, or whom, did Mr. Bohm see?"

"He saw *me*."

I began to feel rather excited. "In the hide, you mean?"

"Yes, ma'am," said Bohm. "I was taking the part of Mr. Fonders, as you know, and I went to my place last, and sat down for a smoke. I was just having my second cigarette when I heard a step near me, and in walked Mr. Power here. What I was going to say about that, as the advocate or whatever you call it, was that Mr. Fonders would have heard him too."

"Question!" Power remarked. "It is not suggested that the previous visitor got as near to the hide in the first place as I did."

"That's true, sir."

"You mean that you were able to sneak round to No. 3 without being seen by any of us?" Vincie asked.

"Looks like it, doesn't it? Yes, I could not be sure that I was unseen, of course, but I followed my prototype in trying not to be—successfully, as it turns out."

"Did you fix it up with Mr. Bohm that you were to be Musson?" I asked bluntly, "and that he was to be exiled on the island covert?"

He grinned. "Well, I have tried to be kind to Voce and Bohm, but I found both of them—Bohm especially—hard to convince that Musson could have done the deed."

"I am not convinced yet, sir," Bohm observed. "Only that he could have got round."

Vincie pulled out the sketch map, which he had been carrying round with him. "I studied this thing for a long time, but it did not give me any hint that Musson was the likeliest."

"You forgot," said Power, "that, on your own account, Mr. Musson seemed to be regarded as the sporting authority that day, deciding whether he would or would not join the earlier drives, and generally taking charge for his unpractised host, Mr. Fonders. It occurred to me that if anyone was to be killed during a shoot, a pigeon-shoot, where the guns were out of sight of each other, would be ideal."

"But that could not show you that Mr. Musson was in the best position, sir," Bohm remarked.

"Well, it did, Mr. Diaboli," Power replied. "It made me wonder if Mr. Musson had suggested, or arranged, the second affair, in which he joined. I got on the right side of our grim friend, Macpherson, and realised that I was right. Mr. Fonders had more or less given him to believe that Musson had had the brain-wave about the pigeons. Mr. Macpherson himself knew that Musson had gone round with him the previous afternoon to fix the sites for the shelters, which Macpherson and his assistant built up. I myself, from that, concluded that Musson might have arranged the list of occupants as were."

"Did Macpherson say that he had?" Vincie asked.

"No, but he said that Mr. Musson told him Stand No. 7 would give the most difficult shots, with which he agreed. Now Musson was apparently the best shot out that day."

"By miles!" said Vincie. "We just fired off guns; he *shot*."

"Just a moment, sir," said Bohm, "if you'll let Diaboli—"

"*Diabolus*," I said. "*Diaboli* is the genitive."

"Anyway," said Bohm, "it beats me why Mr. Musson, if he faked the whole thing, should choose the farthest hide, with other guns in between."

"It struck me that he chose the one least likely to hold a suspect," Power informed him. "It was the next best thing to a perfect alibi."

"Then you merely guessed it?" said Vincie.

"Guesses supported by guesses and confirmed by results, my dear Mercer, are called prevision—a word to suit Miss Doe, who calls a spade an instrument for excavation. Haven't I proved opportunity, Bohm?"

"Yes, sir, you have. No more than that, so far."

"The second guess, to be modest," Power told us, "was connected with the manner in which your party was shepherded from one spot to another, losing a gun here and a gun there, till finally you left Mr. Fonders to get to his place alone."

"You're like our younger poets," I said, "they know what they mean, so they leave out the links. Their readers don't know what they mean and, lacking the necessary links, never will."

"Let me supply them, Mrs. Mercer. You drop the Does. We pass them out. You drop Mr. Whick, we pass him out. You drop Miss Addie Stole at No. 5. You drop Mr. Varek at No. 4. There remain—your host, Mr. Fonders, you two, and Mr. Musson. Got that?"

Bohm was making notes now. We assented, and Power went on. "Studying the map till my eyes bulged, I saw the point. Mr. Fonders starting back with you from near Varek's hide, No. 4, proceeded with you to your hide, No. 6. What does 'A' do?"

"Who is 'A'?" Bohm asked.

"'A' is No. 7, otherwise Mr. Musson. I saw at once that, while Mr. and Mrs. Mercer were with their host, strolling through the 'tulgy wood' to their place of abiding, it would be quite possible for Mr. Musson to cut through the trees to the north of the wood, and take a more or less parallel course eastward on its outskirts. He might be a little behind you, but would arrive somewhere near Hide No. 3 a short time after Mr. Fonders reached it. If he was making any noise, and it would be as little as possible, you and Mr. Fonders would also be making a noise as you walked through the wood, perhaps talking on the way."

"Well, he could, of course, sir," said Bohm, studying the map which Vincie had handed to him, "but the same thing might apply to Mr. Varek, Miss Stole, or Mr. and Mrs. Mercer."

"It might have applied to Miss Stole, though we have evidence that she had never met Fonders before she visited this house. It could have been done by Mr. Varek, only that his dog would have been a nuisance, for I heard from Macpherson that it was ill-trained and wild."

"Yes, you can't easily control a wild dog in the open, sir, and it would be likely to run in and bark if it came near someone hidden."

"Apart from some other objections to Varek as the criminal," Power observed, "which I haven't cleared up to my own satisfaction yet, but which, I am sure, Inspector Voce will, I do not see Varek in this. As for Mr. and Mrs. Mercer you have only to look at them to see that their air of innocence is superb. And naturally I did not propose to try to convict my clients."

Bohm gave us an amused look. "They don't look or talk a bit more innocent than Mr. Musson."

"Ah, but he's a marvel, or I'm an ass. He's taken it all with such beautiful aplomb that one could almost imagine he had had practice at the game of getting away with it. The fact remains that I took the part of Musson, and got up to Fonders's stand, without being detected by any of the party. Isn't that so?"

"Why," I said, remembering something, "you joined us to-day when the whistle had blown, coming *from* Mr. Musson's place at the end of the wood."

"So he did!" cried Vincie.

Mr. Power raised his eyebrows. "Not much good proving Musson could have got there, and not got back. You forget that he had some pigeons to show for his shooting. What would you all have said if you had found him so far out of his place when Fonders was found dead?"

"That's one to you, sir," Bohm agreed. "You showed he could have got back too."

"Thank you, Bohm. I won't call you Diabolus any more. But when the case was presented to me in the first place, I was struck by the fact that there was a lady who had a sixteen-bore placed between Musson's twenty and Mr. Fonders. It struck me that that might be to confuse anyone who listened to the shots: say the two unarmed spectators, Mrs. Mercer and Miss Doe. A large bore near at hand sounds loud; the smaller a long way away may sound like a larger one dimmed by distance; and the smallest of all, if brought near, may sound like a bigger gun, if you have previously heard it, or expected to hear it fired in the distance. I took it that Mr. Musson, on business bent, would not like anyone to notice that he had not fired a shot during the time he was away from his stand."

"Mr. Fonders might think, or we might think, that the report of Miss Stole's gun was his?" I said.

Power nodded. "At any rate, I had a talk with Macpherson again. He was pretty sure that Miss Stole had been originally listed in Hide No. 2, and Whick in the place she actually occupied."

"Why, sir?" asked Bohm, who was scribbling in his book like mad.

"Because Mr. Musson never knew Miss Stole had a sixteen-bore till she came down here, my dear man. He was already staying with Fonders."

CHAPTER XXIV

"You've made a lot of bricks without straw, sir," said Sergeant Bohm, looking at Power admiringly when the latter paused. "The only question is: Are they bricks—I mean bricks you can build a case on?"

"With Voce's help and yours, I think so. Mr. Voce is bound to get on to one important point, and I may be able to supply the others."

"Just a moment, Mr. Power," I said. "May we know if Mr. Bohm butted into your target practice this afternoon by chance or arrangement?"

"Mr. Power asked me if I would come at a certain time, ma'am," Bohm told me. "We are always ready to listen to any outside hint, if we think it may be valuable."

Vincie laughed. "You took us all in. We really thought that you were going to eat our friend here."

"Best of all, he seems to have taken in Mr. Musson," Power remarked cheerfully, "for he went off with your crowd and enabled me to collect a sample twenty-bore cartridge when he was out of sight. Or rather two, for Mr. Bohm's police chauffeur rushed the other off to town for Mr. Voce."

"You haven't told me about that, sir?" Bohm reproached him.

"I have hardly had time, what with the preparations for this stunt, and other things. It was Musson 'forcing' his gun that made me ask myself what the conjuror wanted."

We had heard of a conjuror "forcing" a card, that is bringing a particular card to the notice of a member of the audience, though the latter is unaware that the performer has done so. But Bohm, more alert in these matters than we, at once nodded.

"I see. No guns were asked for. He brings his down here. He is anxious for you to see it, examine it, all fair and above board, and so on, sir. So there is, to your mind, some point about his bringing it."

"Exactly. But I concluded that the point he wants us to notice and the point I wanted to get at are not the same, Bohm. He as good as says: 'Here's my gun. Look at it, shoot with it. It's the same I had down before. So what more can I do?'"

"He would hardly risk that if it was not the same gun," I said.

Vincie suddenly interposed. "I see! It's one of a pair, like the late Lionel's."

"Pairs usually go in double cases," Bohm said. "I know that much. Wasn't this in a single case, Mr. Power?"

"Quite right. It isn't one of a pair, Mercer," Power grinned, and Vincie subsided. "To get on: I asked for a shot, and collected two cases." He took the cartridge-case from his pocket and put it on Bohm's large palm.

"See that?" he said. "Now, I want you to understand that the chamber is a recessed part of the barrel, necessarily larger than the barrel, to allow for the thickness of the cartridge wall. Now we have it that Mr. Musson was using a two-and-three-quarter-inch case that day, while the one I shot off, which Bohm has in his hand, is a two-and-a-half-inch only."

"You're pretty smart, Power," Vincie said. "Isn't that a good point, Mr. Bohm?"

"It may be, sir"—he looked at the cartridge again—"but he could also fire this in the longer chamber?"

"Obviously two-and-a-half into two-and-three-quarters will go," said Power ironically.

"And you say this is the same gun? Well then?"

"Only one thing to be said about that, Bohm. I did my best to measure the chamber, and I make it two-and-a-half-inch."

"Then you are out somewhere," Vincie cried. "You can't prove the impossible, smart as you are."

"Quite." Power looked at him whimsically. "I said to myself that a two-and-a-half-inch chamber could not fire a longer cartridge. But apparently it had, and if it had, it did it with the same gun. When you come up against the impossible, look about for a hint of the probable. There my study of Caesar at school helped me."

"I beg your pardon, sir?" said Bohm, prepared to treat this as a joke if it were one.

"*De Bello Gallico*, you know," Power murmured. "There Caesar discovered that Gaul was divided into three parts. I discovered, or remembered, that a gun is divided into three parts. The stock, with action and trigger; the barrels; and the forehand, which supports the barrels, and also acts as a pivot when you open the gun."

"Great Scott, sir, you've got it!" Bohm cried. "He had a spare pair of barrels."

"Is that right?" I almost shouted, and Bohm raised his hand warningly.

Power shrugged his shoulders. "I can't say. But I do know that it is the only explanation of the gun he brought here this time having the shorter chamber."

We were delighted at this discovery, but Bohm was not so highly impressed. Scotland Yard trains a man to see snags in what the layman considers a smooth path. "As he could have fired both cartridges in the first pair of barrels, sir—that is, your hypothetical ones—you must mean that there is something about them which can explain the shooting here," he said. "If not, all the duplicates in the world do not make sense."

"I saw that, too, Bohm. The conclusion I come to is that you are right. Now, what can be the difference between the two?"

Bohm frowned to himself, and flicked back some pages of his note-book. "Since you have got that point, sir, I may as well say that Mr. Voce conducted some experiments with a twenty-bore. He did what you did, got a tracer cartridge and cut the top off. That showed that the tracer pellet was fitted snugly into the centre of a thick felt wad. He assumed that the pellet was ignited by the flash from the powder, for the wad below had a small hole through it."

"I think so, too," Power said. "Carry on."

Bohm consulted his notes. "Here we are: 'Assume that the gun was fired with a tracer cartridge from which the shot charge had been removed. The upper half of the case is then empty, and the pellet in the wad is free to move forward into the barrel proper, and emerge from it at speed.' You see that, sir?"

Power replied promptly: "Yes. As the wad with the embedded pellet was shot out at great speed, the wad, being lighter, with a bigger friction surface, would fall down, leaving the pellet to fly on, and perhaps hit Mr. Fonders in the eye. That would also explain why there were no signs of lead shot in or near the dead man." Bohm read from his notes once more: "'Consulted gun-expert. He informed us that accurate aim was only possible because the bullet, or charge of shot, fitted or filled the bore closely as it was fired out. He believed that the pellet, which only occupied a diameter about one-third that of the breech, would have no great velocity, and would bang from side to side of the barrel as it went. Finally, the wad would not fly very straight, being a disk, and would deflect the pellet from a straight line."

"In other words," I remarked, "it was N.G."

"As it proved, ma'am," he replied politely, "but we daren't take things on trust, and Mr. Voce fired a series of eighteen cartridges loaded as he wished. Even at close ranges, the pellet would not fire very straight, and at longer ranges accuracy was out of the question. It might have killed a man by chance, but the best shot in the world could not count on hitting a mark with it once in fifty times."

I am sure we both felt depressed again. Power was clever and observant, and a great man for theory, but after all he had only proved that, even if Musson had a second pair of gun-barrels, it did not demonstrate how Lionel had been shot.

"Mr. Bohm is a destructive person," Vincie said. "I am afraid, Power, there is no reply to Mr. Voce's experiments."

But though Bohm was critical, he was also fair and judicial. "Just a moment, sir. Mr. Power has hit on something there, though I can't say what it is. Why should Mr. Musson bring down the second pair of barrels? Why leave the pair he used here at home—the pair he had on the day of the shoot? Obviously because there is something about them that he does not want known."

"I am glad you think so," I said. "I know several people saw, and may have handled, his gun that day, but no one seems to have seen anything special about it. And we know it fired full-size cartridges."

"Did anyone look inside?" said Power. "I think not. At most, it was a cursory examination. But run along to the gun-room, Bohm, and examine that breech-chamber now, before the party give up their game. If it is as I think, then the duplicate barrels will be found, and when found 'made a note on'."

Bohm got up and hurriedly left the room. I went to see if the pool players were still busy. They were paying up what they owed on the last game, and proposing to have another.

"Come and play too," Addie said to me. "It's the only joy in this mouldy house. We're rooking Mr. Musson. He may be a shot, but he can't pot for nuts."

I refused the kind invitation, beamed falsely at the victim, and went back to the library.

Vincie turned a very surprised face on me when I came in, a contrast to Power's amused countenance. "Do you know what this ruffian has been up to?" he said, as I sat down.

"Do tell me," I urged.

"He rang up Chief Inspector Voce earlier in the day, and persuaded him to make an immediate and pressing application for a search-warrant."

"For whom?" I asked, flabbergasted.

"Musson's room in the Sigma Hotel," Vincie told me. "Voce may be there now."

I began to see light. "Splendid! You want him to find the duplicate barrels, don't you?"

"I expect him to find them."

"But suppose there is nothing to be learned from them?" Vincie asked.

"That will be bad luck," Power smiled, "but may happen when any search is conducted on the authority of a warrant. You must search if you wish to find. And when Musson is down here, and out of the way, it's the best time."

Before we had a chance to reply, Bohm came back. "I did what you wished, sir," he said. "I am going to ring up the Yard now, to try to get in touch with Mr. Voce. If you stand by for a few minutes, you may hear something. After that I am getting back to town as quick as I can."

He vanished again, and we exchanged excited ideas. Personally, I hoped that the whole thing would not prove a wash-out. We could feel sure now that Vincie was not suspected of having shot Lionel, even by accident, but both of us were anxious to have the matter cleared up, so that we could go back to work.

Fortunately, Bohm had come back to us, and gone again, before the pool players gave up and came in search of us.

The sergeant's face was lit up when he entered the room. He even came over to pat Power on the back and beam in a paternal way at us.

"Duplicate barrels all right, sir," he said. "It's an old-fashioned hotel, and he had got them up the chimney, behind a gas-stove the hotel people had put in."

"Twenty-bore?" Power asked.

"That's right, sir, just the same as what he has here, except for the chamber, which is longer. Mr. Voce is sending them to the expert for micro-photometric examination. You'll hear about that later."

"Micro-photometric!" I said. "I wish Vanity was here now. Isn't it a lovely word?"

Mr. Bohm held out his hand to me. "Goodbye, ma'am. Goodbye, Mr. Mercer. I must get away at once."

Power was doing a fantastic toe-dance when the sergeant left the room. Then he stopped, grinned at us both, and subsided into a chair with a great sigh of relief.

"And now," he said, "if either of you gives a sign to Musson, by word, deed, or changing countenance, that he isn't your own white-haired boy, I'll go all homicidal, as he did!"

CHAPTER XXV

I AM sure only Musson's exuberance saved us from giving something away that evening. He dragged us all into the conversation in turn, and seemed specially amused when Power took to writing in a note-book after dinner.

We considered that this was either hysteria, or a firm belief that he had laid his cards so openly on the table that no one would find fault with them. What you show is not so closely examined as what you try to conceal.

Power's manner was perfect. He laughed as heartily as anyone at Musson's suggestion that he was doing his "homework," and remarked that the pursuit of criminals in the country must not make him neglect the routine work of his law office.

"Especially now, when I have practically solved the case," he added.

"If you settle Voce as well, it may help," said Varek. "He and his pal are jealous of your brains, Mr. Power."

"And not without excuse," said Power, "but do let me get on with the draft of this conveyance. Play cards or something. This is our last night in the old homestead."

We were glad to settle down to something.

As might be expected from the type of book she wrote, Addie was a great one for psychic bids. That is to say, when anything went wrong she said the bid had been psychic. She played some convention none of us had heard of, and Addie, I am sure, for the first time that evening. Still, she had cards. Vincie, who was her partner, said enthusiastically afterwards that he preferred to play with people who did everything wrong except fail to win. He had one-pound-five at the end of the evening, which he generously shared with me.

We were just going to get ready for bed, when someone slipped an envelope under the door. Vincie dashed for it, and we had it open in a twinkling. It was from Power.

> "I flit by car early to-morrow, so here are the speculative doings evolved from my home-work last night. Come to my office 3.30 to-morrow. Tea provided. P."

He had enclosed some sheets from his note-book scribbled over in his big, bold hand, and we sat down to read them.

"Reflections on a Country Sportsman.

"(1) The Thorp gun was made for another client about five years ago. Presumably it was bought second-hand by Musson.

"(2) He had a second pair of barrels made for it. Not by Thorps. If so, with their records, they would have told me.

"(3) Many gun dealers are not gunsmiths. They do not make, but sell. To fit a second pair of barrels to a fine gun requires skill. That narrows inquiries—*which will be made*.

"(4) U.S.A. sport is not the same thing. You do not learn covert and pheasant-shooting there. Musson was a shooting man before he left England. Where? Under what name?

"(5) Why did not the sender of the letter to Fonders cable here if he had information against Musson? It may be that news of Fonders's death only appeared in U.S. papers as an accident. Alternatively the name of a firm and that of its principal are not always the same. 'Scripto Ltd.' might be Mr. Musson.

"(6) Pellet was not fired by a rifle, revolver, or automatic pistol of small calibre. No marks of rifling. Air-pistol? Air-gun? Both smooth-bores? Air-gun hard to conceal.

"(7) Seeing Voce at once. Script of novel the subject. Interview Mr. Whick. He knows something. Birds of a feather. Fonders may have asked his advice.

"(8) How nice to work with the police for once!"

"An air-pistol, that's it!" I cried, when we had read the remarks.

"There is an interrogation mark after it," Vincie said thoughtfully. "In my mind there is also one. If he used an air-pistol, he would not require a second pair of barrels. If he did not require them, why hide 'em up the chimney?"

I smiled. "You must read more detective stories, darling," I told him. "That is called laying a false clue. They find the barrels, attach great importance to them, and micro-photometricise them! Oh, Vanity, why aren't you here!"

"And then?" asked Vincie doubtfully. "Then the police would find they were just ordinary barrels, and acquit friend Musson."

"As simple as that?" Vincie remarked scornfully.

The following morning the butler took leave of us without regret, but not without profit. We travelled to town together, and bade farewell at the station.

"Keep your eye on the evening editions of the papers," Musson said to us as we shook hands. "'Satirist arrested on Suspicion'! I felt there was something up, when Voce went to town and Mr. Whick did not arrive. A nasty bit of work, Mr. Whick."

But we had our own suspicions that Power and not Voce would be biting our friend Gerald. Vincie invited me to lunch at his club, which admits women, and after that we floated round to the Tate Gallery to see a picture by a friend of ours which had lately been bought for the nation. Having decided that the nation had been right for once, we had a look at a work by Buxton Knight, and set off for Power's office.

As the junior partner he had the smallest private office, but it was far too smart and clean and modem to be a respectable lawyer's. He had three small easy chairs set out and two boxes of cigarettes. I also, with a woman's eye, noticed a tray with four cups on it.

"Don't tell me Mr. Whick is coming?" I said, as we greeted him.

"Yes, but he's late," said Power. "I saw him this morning. His nerves are bad. I'm hoping to remove the incubus and release the pressure, you know."

Whick came in five minutes later, full of apologies and unusually friendly towards us.

"Now," said Power, squaring his elbows on his fine table-desk, "are you giving us the inside dope on the script, or do I shoot you over to Mr. Voce?"

Gerald dropped his cigarette on the carpet and I picked it up. "I am," he stammered, "but I swear I don't see what it has to do with Lionel conking out. I don't really."

"Immaterial," Power said. "You've seen that manuscript before, haven't you?"

"Yes, I admit that. But it was a good while ago. Before Musson—"

"Never mind Musson. How did you come to see it?"

Whick bit his lip. "I was in with Lionel at that time. I mean to say—"

"You mean to say you had touched him for some money to get one of your satires published. You were more or less friendly?"

"Yes. That's right. I was staying with him for a week-end, and a parcel came for him. It was from America, a novel, the—er—*Jumping Jane*. Some rough-necked fan of Lionel's had sent it to him. He showed me the note. I remember he went into fits over it. The author was, she said, a cripple, had to keep her bed."

"He had a nice notion of humour apparently," Power said in disgust.

Gerald reddened. "It wasn't the cripple part, you know. It was the gauche way it was put, and because she said he might get a thousand dollars for it if he made one of his publishers do it. She was mad about his books and so on."

"I see. What else?"

"Well, Lionel laughed so much that I asked him to let me read the script. It promised to be damn' funny, if it was anything like that letter. And I thought I might get a hint or two for a satire on literary aspirants. You can't believe they're as naïve as they are."

"And?"

"Well, I did. It was muck; it was clumsy, girlish stuff, not nice girl's stuff, but the sort that might be written by a repressed female who read too many novelettes. Crude was not the word for it, but, as I said to Lionel after, there was a smart idea behind it. I have amateur manuscripts sent to me sometimes. I send 'em back, of course, but I can tell you that if some professionals had the ideas some amateurs have, there would be more novels published."

"It was a very marketable idea, hopelessly written?"

"Exactly. Lionel said he would read it. A year after that I had a job from a rotten little weekly to review his novel, *The Girl from Gehenna*. That was Lionel, that was!"

We stared at him, but Power frowned. "I take it that, after that, you made a bit between the cost of printing your nice long poems, and what Mr. Fonders gave you by way of a subsidy?"

"Well, that hadn't anything to do with his death," Whick murmured, with his eyes down.

"Perhaps not, but it made you very anxious not to have the police inquiring into your spot of blackmail, Mr. Whick. That's what it was, you know; and you wouldn't have got any more reviewing, or other jobs, even for rotten little weeklies, if it had come out. So you were quite anxious that Mr. Fonders's death should prove an accident?"

"I don't know that it wasn't. Mr. Musson is the only one you can suspect, if the book manuscript has anything to do with it, and he was too far away."

Tea was brought in then by a junior clerk and I poured out, while Mr. Power resumed his examination.

"Mr. Fonders seems to have been a delightful creature," he said, "but surely, even to himself, he must have found some excuse for pinching the plot of a novel written by a poor crippled girl?"

Whick moved uncomfortably, and took a sip of tea before he replied: "I did say it looked a dirty bit of work."

"Ah, no doubt. That was your paying line at the time. But what did Fonders say?"

"He said what sounded good sense. The girl had sent the MS. uninvited. As it stood, no publisher would print it, for it was so badly done. If he sent it back, she would waste her time trying it out again; and altogether the thing was a wash-out. He also said something about 'unconscious cerebration'."

"Ah, he forgot that someone else had given him the idea. At any rate, Mr. Whick, you both decided that an ignorant girl, living in the wilds, would think her book had been lost in the post, and let it go at that?"

"That's right."

"Then why didn't Fonders tell you to go to the devil?"

"Well—er—" said Whick, redder than ever, "he'd shown me the letter, and I saw the name and address."

"And noted it?" said Power, looking as if he had half a mind to throw his cup in the man's face. "How well you and Mr. Fonders should have got on together!"

If Whick hadn't proved such a foul hound, I think we should have felt sorry for him then. But Power went on.

"Then Mr. Musson came along? What about that?"

Whick choked over a gulp of tea, and reached for a cigarette, which he lit with the trembling bravado of the man who makes a last attempt to keep his end up.

"That wasn't really my pigeon. Lionel asked me to come to see him. He was all of a dither because this man had written over from America. Musson had started as a literary agent, calling himself 'Booksol Inc.,' and he had a manuscript sent him from the wilds of Montana, or somewhere. He had to read it, not being burdened with assistants. A covering letter with it said the girl had sent a copy to Fonders, but it must have been lost en route. Well, Musson saw the point, as I had done, and he wrote to Lionel, and hinted gently that the story of a famous author, and bestseller, who had pinched a crippled American girl's plot and used it, would go over big from shore to shore."

"It would," said Power. "Apart from damages to be extracted from a sentimental American jury, when the sob-sisters of the Press wrote it up. But what did Lionel Fonders want with you?"

Mr. Whick hesitated; then he caught Power's eye, and resumed. "You see, I was a witness, a potential one. He wanted me to say that I had never seen the yarn."

"You could be very valuable to yourself, and to him," said Power. "Of course you refused. You knew you had only squeezed the rind of the lemon."

"Anyway," Whick hurried on angrily, "Lionel shilly-shallied, and we had a row. Then he heard Musson was coming over. Musson hinted that he could square the matter. All Lionel had to do was to make him his agent for all future work over there. That meant kudos and profit for the agency."

"Who has got those letters of Musson's?"

"He insisted on Lionel giving them back."

"In your several ways, you seem to have been masters of the art," Power said slowly. "You refused to give up what seemed a future source of income. What then?"

I am sure Whick would have shot him with pleasure, if he could have got away with it, but he merely choked, scowled, and remarked that Lionel had asked him what he ought to do. "I hadn't an idea," he said. "I knew that he couldn't afford to let the story loose in America, even if he won in the courts. His name would have been mud."

Power nodded. "Obvious. Did he at any time suggest making inquiries about Musson? You may be aware, having dabbled in such matters, that the man who holds you up to ransom may have a character which will not bear investigation."

"He said something about writing to a firm of private detectives, but I said some of 'em over there might be glad to use the story themselves to get on his back."

"Did he take that as right?"

"He dropped the subject, after saying that there were one or two big firms. That was some time ago."

Power looked at him very hard. "Now, Mr. Whick, all this is not very nice hearing, and it would make uglier talking aloud. I do not propose to tell the police what a cheap little blackguard you are. So, if I can manage without using your name and—er—fame, I shall do so. This simply because you have been rather helpful. If Voce heard that you had withheld all this, there would be trouble. And you don't want that. Now you can go!"

Gerald went out without a word. He did not even look at us. He knew that he had got off lightly, and went.

"Now what is behind the actions of a toad like that?" Power asked, as the door closed. "Pure criminality, greed, or what?"

"I think," Vincie said slowly, "that you're using a hammer for our draggled butterfly. Personally, I think he started by being anxious to get his satirical epics into print. He's full of conceit, and he knew, in spite of his 'consciousness of genius,' that to approach a publisher with a hundred pages of rhymed satire and ask him to publish them is like trying to climb Everest on skates. Once he got the stuff published at his own—or Fonders's—expense, it happened to catch on. But he'll never grow rich on poesy. What do you think, Penny?"

I agreed. He had shown up rottenly, but I believed, and still believe, that the genesis of it was his determination not to allow the world to let one of its major poets go to his grave unpublished.

Power nodded, rang, and had the tea things taken away. We lit cigarettes, and the lawyer began again.

"Voce, as you know, does not tell me anything, unless it arises out of what I have told him, and can't be investigated without my help. I don't blame him. He is not supposed to blab about his doings. But I told him my suspicions about that letter, and I hear he has cabled to the New York police. There may be hundreds of detective agencies. The police there will know them all. They will try to discover which of them, if any, was asked for information about Musson."

"You think Fonders did write?" I said.

"I do. He mentioned the idea to Whick, and may have seen that Whick would crab the idea, in his own interests."

"Then Voce may hear soon?" Vincie asked.

"Any time now. The police there, with a telephone, could go through a lot of agencies in a few hours. All they would have to ask is: 'Have you ever received a commission from Mr. Lionel Fonders, of Chustable Manor, England?' If so, what was the inquiry he made, and what was your answer? As they would try the big agents first, knowing that an Englishman would not be conversant with the names of the smaller fry, it should be easy."

"And, of course, they would cable a reply," I said. "Well, Mr. Power, I think you are wonderful."

He grinned. "You had better wait before you pile on the encomiums, Mrs. Mercer. Voce agrees that I have a sort of case. He has only one objection, and keeps that to himself—the blighter! I shan't reach for the laurels till I see what the police laboratory turns in. Even then the motive may have nothing to do with the book. Fonders once visited America, and he may have hurt somebody's husbandly feelings there, the result being revenge. I am sure Musson shot him, but I am not sure why."

"I still cannot see how he shot him?" I said.

"Think of one Englishman who deserves well of his country." Power smiled. "Lord Nuffield. That may help to put you where I stand at present."

As he chose to be cryptic, and as a clerk came in at that moment to say that a gentleman wished urgently to see him, we said good-bye and went.

"And Mannesmann is another good name to remember in that connection!" he called after us, as we were going.

"Keep your crosswords to yourself!" said Vincie.

We went home pondering. And arguing. We even considered Power's crossword clues, but came to no conclusion about them. The one thing we did agree on was the brutal castigation the lawyer had bestowed on Gerald Whick. The poet's moral skin must have prickled at every pore—what there was left of it after Power had flayed him.

"Mr. Musson," I told Vincie later, "must have been a fool to kill Lionel, if he himself had a bad record out in the United States. Did that never occur to him? I mean to say, if Voce's inquiries are made as easy as Mr. Power alleges."

Vincie shook his head. "Power made it clear to us all along that the man who shot Lionel did it so ingeniously that he felt sure he would never be found out. The perfect crime, and the perfect alibi, have one defect from the criminal's point of view—he feels safe."

CHAPTER XXVI

FOUR days passed, and we had not heard from Mr. Power. Mr. Voce had not visited us or communicated with us. We met Addie Stole and the Does, but they said the police had left them alone.

"Reculer pour mieux sauter," said Vanity.

"Can you tell me the French colloquialism for 'micro-photo-metric'?" I asked sweetly.

But, of course, she never saw the joke, and wanted to explain the origin of the word, from the Greek *mikro*, *phos* (light) and *metron* (measure). She was quite annoyed when I said I had no interest in philology. I think she wanted to tell me something about Metropolis, which comes from *meter* (mother) and *polis* (a city). She is always dreadfully informative.

On the Friday evening, when we were playing piquet, Mr. Power came in. He beamed, sat down, began to smoke, and begged us not to break up our game.

"What I have to say will keep," he said.

"But of course not!" I said. "We are all ears. Don't be secretive."

His face suddenly became grave. "Very well. I saw Voce this afternoon, and I think we have fixed it on Musson."

We felt very excited now. "Was it the letter?" Vincie asked.

"Yes. On my suggestion, Voce made inquiries at the post offices near Chustable—radius of ten miles. Fonders sent a registered letter some time ago to Messrs. Finkerton, the detective agency."

"Didn't the New York police get that too?" I asked.

"Yes, they interviewed Finkerton's. Finkerton's had to communicate with their agent in the far south-west."

"So Fonders did ask who Musson was?" Vincie said.

"No. I told you I was fallible, Mercer. What Fonders did ask them to discover was the actual existence of a crippled girl, in a small settlement in Nevada."

"Not Montana?" I cried. "Did he think he could square her more cheaply than Musson?"

Power shrugged his shoulders. "I have no idea. Perhaps so. But the agency made the inquiry, and I have the gist of their reply from Voce. There was a crippled girl at the place and she had been trying to write something, though the neighbours thought that a joke. She lived with her step-father, a commercial traveller. He was absent in San Francisco when a man, thought to be a drummer or pedlar, or something like that, was noticed near the house. When the stepfather came back next day, he found the girl shot."

"The crippled girl shot?" I exclaimed in horror.

"With what looked like a pea-rifle, or small-arm of narrow calibre," Power said.

"And that was Musson?" Vincie said incredulously.

"I can't say. No one can. The drummer was not seen again. Nothing in the house was touched. I merely say that Musson, to whom she had sent her manuscript, could have introduced himself, and got in."

"What is a pea-rifle?" I asked.

"An old term for a rifle of very small bore. I think in America they used them for shooting squirrels. But it may not have been a rifle."

"How dreadful," I observed, for this butchery of a crippled girl seemed a thousand times worse, warped of mind as she was, than the murder of Lionel Fonders. "But tell us if Mr. Voce is any further on than he was with the inquiry about the gun?"

"Yes," he told us. "Inquiries have been made all over the country, and in Northumberland they came on a gunsmith in a small country town, who was famous for his gun repairs. It turned out that he had been a highly-paid workman for one of the best London gun-makers, and had retired on account of his health to his native village."

Vincie leaned forward. "So he made the second pair of barrels?"

"Yes. Some years ago, a man answering to Musson's description came in and ordered a duplicate pair, with a longer chamber—two-and-three-quarter inches, to be exact. The customer said he wanted to use them for wild-fowling. They were made and paid for. The gunsmith is an old man, but has wonderful eyesight, and is sure he recognises Musson from a photograph Voce managed to take. At all events he is ready to give evidence."

"Splendid," I said, "but you still have the same bore, Mr. Power."

He smiled now. "Fancy you thinking of that. But surely you and Mercer have been busy working out my crossword clues?"

"Failing to work them out," Vincie remarked. "I know the Morris car. But my acquaintance with Mannesmann is to seek."

"Then you were never apprenticed to an engineer," Power said. "I'm not mechanical myself, but the name does remind me of Tubes."

"Why, of course," I said, rather crest-fallen. "I have seen the name several times."

"Translate and combine," said Power. "But that is what occurred to me some days ago. To use that pellet you had not only to have a smooth-bore gun: you had to have a very small-bore gun. But Musson did not turn up at the shoot with two guns."

"Then how did he do it?" I cried.

"One into one goes—just," he replied. "In my midnight researches I came on the Morris Tube; rifled, it is true, but a small barrel which can be fitted inside another, so that you can do target practice in a very small space. You could also use it for shooting pigeons sitting in trees, or young rooks on their nests. I have an idea that that is what Musson first had it made for. On the other hand, his could not have been rifled."

"Why, hasn't Voce got it?" Vincie asked quickly.

"No, he hasn't—yet. But it can be postulated, and it was on that account that I wanted the other barrels examined. I did not believe that the Morris gadget could be fixed without making some scratches or marks on the breech. Well, the—"

"The people who use Vanity Doe's favourite word?" I suggested.

"Yes. They bear me out. They are of opinion that something of the nature of a Morris Tube was used in Musson's gun. When they find it, they have Mr. Musson!"

There was a pause while Power lit a fresh cigarette. Vincie stared at him admiringly.

"I suppose Musson, when he opened that letter, saw that Lionel would link up things and conclude that he had found it cheaper to buy the girl off with a bit of lead than with some gold dollars?"

"I think so. Finkerton's say their name was on the envelope, and Musson would know at once who they were. It would have paid Musson better to cough up some money and buy out the girl's copyright."

"Then that wasn't really a tracer-pellet?" I asked. "Or have the police not given their verdict on it yet?"

"Voce says they have. He says it is a pellet taken from a tracer cartridge. It hadn't ignited, either because it was a dud or because it was fired from a shell loaded with a wad which was not pierced so as to allow the flame from the powder charge to pass through. Voce agrees that it is probable Fonders sat down and, for some reason or other, removed his artificial eye. Musson crept round within range, and let him have it. Then he hurried back to his hide, shot some pigeons, and joined the rest of the party after the shooting was over."

"Have they arrested him yet?" I asked.

"No. They want the Morris Tube variant before they do that; and they are going to dig up the wood, if need be. If they can't find it, they will have to rely on scientific evidence, and the scratches on the gun. But they'll find that heavy going."

"I don't wonder," Vincie observed slowly, "that the beast thought he would get away with it. I wonder where he came from?"

"So far," Power said, "they have an idea that he is the ne'er-do-weel son of a north country squire, who made a remittance man of him at the age of twenty. He went to Australia, came back when his father died, expecting to inherit, and found a cousin had been put in his place. He went from that to Canada, and then the United States. At least, he seems to correspond to the description of such a person."

Vincie nodded. "That accounts for his understanding shooting. People like that grow up with guns in their hands. But what puzzles me still is the kit he took with him to Chustable Manor. The gun, the spare barrels, for which there is no room in the gun-case, and the species of Morris Tube. Or did he leave the spare barrels at home?"

"I think not, Mercer. I take it that he did not go there expecting to shoot Fonders, though he may have found him a bit sticky lately. Take it that he had no idea of it then. That twenty-bore of his was one of the newer type, with twenty-five-inch barrels. I assume that the tube arrangement would go in the right barrel, which is not choked. The spare pair would fit quite easily into his suit-case."

"Isn't he aware yet that his hotel room was searched?" I asked.

"I think not. Voce had a warrant and, no doubt, showed it, but he would be anxious not to scare the bird. As I was saying, I think he travelled with his armoury partly in the case, partly in the suit-case. You remember that there were no footmen at the manor, who would have valeted the guests. Presumably he unpacked his own stuff, as you others did. So the servants may not have had a chance to notice."

We saw that he was proceeding logically enough, but the tracer cartridge Vincie had shown me remained unaccounted for. I asked Power about it.

He smiled gently. "Of course, when Voce knew about the fingerprints he was on to it like a bird. In his thorough way he had already made the minutest inventory of the contents of the gun-room, and in one drawer he found five cartridges of a pattern none of you had used. They were, in fact, old stock, and deteriorated. It did not take him long to find the truth. Macpherson said the last owner had left those cartridges, and also a partly-filled carton of tracers, he believed."

"But I never saw that lot," Vincie protested.

"Possibly not. Voce thinks that Musson did. He considers that the man must have seen them before your party came down."

"Do you mean that Vin—my husband was carrying one of them in his pocket?" I asked.

"Well, I leave it to you." He laughed.

"Didn't we make rather a point of the fact that there should have been *more* of your husband's fingerprints on it, if he first pinched it from the shooting-school, then put it in his pocket, then took it out to show you?"

"Of course we did," Vincie agreed.

"Which hints that someone put it there, my dear fellow. And we may also assume that Musson dissected another hastily when he saw that the American blokes had given him away to Fonders, and used the pellet in his Morris Tube arrangement."

"But could he load it?" I asked.

"I got advice about that. He could have loaded it. It would not give accurate shooting at long range but, close up, it would have done the job all right."

"Is it a cardboard case?" Vincie asked.

"It may have been one of those tiny cardboard cases they use in a .22 for small birds or rats, or a metal case. In the first, he would only have to remove the top wad and shot, insert the pellet, and turn the top of the case in. If brass, it would be thin metal, and he could pinch the top in round the pellet, after removing the bullet."

"But if he had such a small bullet," I said, "why not use that?"

"Because no one was using bullets, and it could not be mistaken for an accident." Vincie grinned at me. "That sticks out a yard."

Mr. Power told me not to mind Vincie. "Husbands are always superior," he said, "but how does the theory strike you?"

"I can see how he got all the armoury to the house," Vincie replied, "but you remember that Macpherson was given the gun-case to take down to the shoot. He took it, and as far as we know did not open it, since the gun was not required till later in the day. Where was the tube gadget then?"

Power wrinkled up his brows comically. "I see. Quite a good point. It might have been actually in the right barrel of the gun. Against that is the fact that Musson did not intend—but wait a moment. You can shoot pigeons sitting, I hear, without outraging the rules of sport. Perhaps he did leave it in the gun, intending to do some fancy shooting with single bullets at pigeons pitching in the trees over his head."

"Ah, that does seem likely," Vincie admitted.

"He liked showing off. But what has happened to that gadget since? The police did not find it in the hotel. Would he risk chucking it away somewhere, hoping it would never be found?"

"That is the only way I can account for it being missing," Power admitted.

I was pretty well aware by now that Voce would not move without having very safe grounds for doing so. You hear of people being wrongly convicted, but what I had seen of our detectives suggested that the greatest criminal was given a fair deal, and no action was taken without minute investigation. Vague evidence and airy statements from ignorant or biased witnesses were not accepted as a basis for prosecution.

"I suppose," I asked, "that Voce may have to arrest him, even if the gadget is not found?"

"He may, Mrs. Mercer, but he will not if he can help it. You might convince a jury on the rest of the evidence, asking them to postulate a gadget of the kind. But some juries are as stubborn as pigs when you want them to use their imagination."

"In fact," said Vincie, "the Morris Tube is a clincher, if found; and a sad miss, if not?"

"Exactly. The gadget and the spent shell from it. But the gadget itself would be enough. Voce is concentrating on finding that. He has men working all along Musson's route to his hotel from the manor. Railway compartments are not always carefully cleaned, and there is room for a small object stuffed between the seats and the woodwork. I wish the poor blighters luck of the job. But they never know when they are beaten." He got up, smiled at us, and said he must go. "So you can get on with your game," he added. "By the way, if Voce tells me any more you shall hear of it in good time."

"Look here, Mr. Power," I said, as we shook hands, "if you have any other interesting cases, do come and tell me about them. As Mr. Whick said in his lampoon on me, I like telling other people's stories."

He laughed. "I'll remember that, Mrs. Mercer. But you mustn't think I spend my time investigating crime. No such luck!"

"Won't the crooks be glad to hear that," said Vincie. "They'd hate you to take up investigation as a full-time occupation."

There was not a word about the case during the next two days. Voce's assistants were, I am sure, in danger of getting silicosis from the dust of countless railway carriages. Search for that Morris Tube seemed as hopeless as trying to count the sands of the sea.

As Vincie said once, you could stick it into the earth, or down a drain-pipe, or man-trap. "Stick it *anywhere!*" he added.

Call it association of ideas, or sheer luck, or memory suddenly waking up and jogging me, the fact remains that I howled out "Eureka," and made Vincie jump.

"*Darling!* His long, heavy, *hollow* shooting-stick!"

At my cry, Vincie gaped, kissed me violently and dashed from the room. I heard him the next moment ringing up *Whitehall* 1212 on the telephone in the hall. I ran out after him, and begged next turn to tell Mr. Power of my brainwave. He nodded violently and went on talking.

I gathered that Voce was out and he was speaking to Sergeant Bohm.

He rang off and mopped his brow. "Bohm's delighted," he said. "He thinks it is all useful confirmation."

"Confirmation of what?" I asked.

He grinned. "Well, my dear, it seems that you and Voce made a dead heat of it. He sprang the idea on the sergeant about a quarter of an hour ago, and was whizzed away in a flying-squad car to get the implement."

"Think of the man's nerve," I said, rather disappointed at not being sole discoverer of the vital clue. "He joked about leaving it behind when he came down to Chustable Manor last time."

I rang up Mr. Power, who congratulated me warmly; then I got on to the Does, Addie Stole and Bob Varek, and told them I thought we were all cleared.

Finally, I rang up Gerald Whick.

"Mr. Whick," I said, "I don't owe you anything, but, if it relieves your mind, I may say that there may be no necessity for anyone to tell the court what—well, *what you are!*"

The inspector found the criminal gadget that day, just where I had suspected it would be. And finding it, he arrested his man on a charge of murder. Incidentally, he received two cuts over the eye in the struggle which followed.

And now Mr. Power says that the jury is certain to convict.

THE END

CPSIA information can be obtained
at www.ICGtesting.com
Printed in the USA
LVHW032030230420
654333LV00004B/1012